Also by J. Penner

Adenashire
A Fellowship of Bakers & Magic
A Fellowship of Librarians & Dragons

A FELLOWSHIP OF GAMES & FABLES

J. PENNER

Poisoned Pen
PRESS

Published by Poisoned Pen Press, an imprint of Sourcebooks
1935 Brookdale RD, Naperville, IL 60563-2773
(630) 961-3900
sourcebooks.com

Originally self-published in 2024 by J. Penner.

Cataloging-in-Publication Data is on file with the Library of Congress.

The authorized representative in the EEA is Dorling Kindersley
Verlag GmbH. Arnulfstr. 124, 80636 Munich, Germany

Manufactured in the UK and distributed by
Dorling Kindersley Limited, London
001-352700-Sep/25
CPI 10 9 8 7 6 5 4 3 2 1

To all those who've buried emotions to keep themselves safe.
(Me included.)

THE NORTHERN LANDS

RIDGELANDS

THE PRESMAR GULF

THE SOUTHEAST SHORES

DRYWARD

THE SOUTHERN DESERT

N

THE LOWER OCEAN

D amn sssnow," Jez grumbled to herself through chattering teeth as she passed the florist on Adenashire's main street. She picked up the pace and burst into A Little Dash of Magic Bake Shop, flinging open the door so hard it slammed against the wall. The attached customer bell rang with a vengeance.

She ran her hand over her pointed, furry ears as a heady concoction of sweet and musky lavender, bright piney rosemary, and dried cherries mixed with sugar, flour, and vanilla hit her nose. The scent was completely different from the acrid woodsmoke from Adenashire chimneys she'd taken in on her trudge from the lake nearby, which harbored silvery rainbow-colored fish under its blanket of winter ice.

The aromas coming at her from all directions

overwhelmed her brain. Baked goods, smoke, lingering evidence of the morning customers…not to mention the scent of Taenya Carralei, a woodland elf and part bakery owner who was also one of her best friends. She was nowhere to be seen but had to be working there somewhere…probably in the back. The elf usually smelled of icing sugar and relief.

And that day was no different.

Being a fennex meant that Jez had an extraordinary sense of smell, but she had an extra magical edge to hers. She could smell people's emotions, their intentions.

And some days, she wished she hadn't been born that way. A regular sniffer would have been fine. Easier.

The gift mostly caused engulfment and exhaustion. So over the years, Jez had learned to control and repress the magic, but doing so made her tired…and cranky some of the time.

Most of the time if she was honest with herself. But the occasional shot of rum helped with that. And so had moving to Adenashire, where she didn't have to be reminded that she'd never lived up to her potential back in the Southern Desert.

Her fox-like ears twitched and her nose burned as she chafed her hands over her arms, shivering despite the coat she wore. A light sprinkling of snow fell to the floor and looked like scattered salt. Another of her best friends, Doli Butterbuckle, had hand made the woolen coat for her before the season's first snowstorm. For that, at least, Jez was grateful.

But for the snow? Not at all.

The snow and cold made the hair on her uncovered tail stand on end. And she hated that.

On her back perched a pack of winter fishing equipment, including an ax, a pole she'd bought from the local outdoor market, and a handful of other odds and ends. Two good-sized trout were nestled inside a double-lined cotton bag clipped to her brown leather belt.

Jez already had lunch plans for the fish—sautéed with butter, dried herbs, and a sprinkling of preserved lemon. Her mind sparked at the thought.

And although the lunch would be nice, she never went fishing for the fish. It was chiefly to get a break for a few hours. She loved Adenashire and her friends, but at least once a week she needed time to herself at the quiet lake to think. Snow or no snow.

Almost three quarters of a year ago she'd moved to Adenashire, right after the Langheim Baking Battle. She'd decided on a whim to apply for the competition after a disagreement with her father. Jez had always been a good baker, and the hobby had offered her solace in a noisy, bustling household.

But even after she received her invitation and snuck away to the Battle, she'd never honestly intended to win (and she didn't, but that's a story for a different day)—doing so would have brought her more attention than she could afford. Competing was only a diversion.

Then, to avoid returning to the Southern Desert, she'd followed her new friend Doli, a dwarf (who had also been running from a challenging family, and that too is another interesting story), to live in Adenashire.

Overall, the village was a peaceful home with minimal responsibility, unlike the place she'd come from. Always churning in the depths of her brain was the question of whether her family missed her. But she hoped they thought life was easier without her and would let her absence be.

She had left a note. Not a detailed one, but a note, nonetheless, which told them where she'd gone and that she needed space.

That said, all the snow in Adenashire had recently been making her regret her decision. Sand and sun were far more to her liking than the cold. But the discomfort wasn't enough to make her return to her former life.

And the friends she'd made had given her purpose. At least a purpose she actually enjoyed.

Jez gazed around the otherwise empty bakery and closed her eyes for a second. She breathed in deeply to calm her nerves, then mentally blocked the scent magic and persistent thoughts overwhelming her mind.

Thankfully, the buzzing at the rear of her sinuses settled after the third breath out.

Taenya, wiping her hands on a white cotton towel, pushed through the swinging door leading out of the kitchen. Her butter-yellow apron with strawberries embroidered at the top was speckled with flour. Jez suspected the needlework was Doli's.

The elf, whose nature magic gave her an incredible talent for baking and decorating cakes, had won the Baking

Battle for the third time in a row. She, too, had moved to Adenashire after the competition to start over.

Funny how that competition had brought the group of unlikely friends together. As if the stars had aligned.

"Oh," the woodland elf said, her green eyes brightening. "Jez. I thought I heard someone come in." A grin quirked up the corners of her bow-shaped lips, and she dragged her hand over her bobbed auburn hair, which had been pulled into two short bunches on each side of her head and tied off with cotton twine. The arrangement looked a little like she had wings sprouting beneath her pointed ears, but Jez didn't mind the style. She wasn't one who cared much about fashion. That was Doli's thing.

The action, however, left flour from her pale fingertips in her hair, making a powdery mess.

"Uh, hi," Jez said, her brown eyes trained on the flour specks. She lifted her clawed hand and pointed. "You got a little something…"

Taenya reached up reflexively as if to pat her hair again but caught herself just in time, instead holding her hand out to examine the mess the towel had failed to remove. "Oh, stars!" she exclaimed, her eyes widening nearly as big as the swirly cinnamon buns that lay piled on display. "I'm a mess."

The fennex shrugged, her dark sand-colored tail flicking behind her. "Yeah. You are."

Taenya rolled her eyes at Jez before tossing the dishcloth on the counter and grabbing a fresh one from underneath. "You could *try* being a little less blunt sometimes."

Jez bit her lip, one fang pinching at the skin. She turned

toward the nearest table and dropped into a wooden chair but kept her body angled to make room for her pack.

"Arleta's not here?" The fennex knew she wasn't since her scent of "human" (they had a particular *non*-magical smell she'd grown used to since moving to Adenashire) peppered with a rotation of herbs from her constant baking experiments was too faint. Arleta Starstone, whom Jez had also met at the Baking Battle, was the other part owner of the bake shop.

Taenya pinched her lips together and shook her head. "She's practicing sledding with Theo for the Yule Games next week."

Jez scoffed and rolled her eyes. "Yule Games," she said with a heaping of disgust. She released her pack from her shoulders, lowered it to the floor, then unclipped the bag of fish. It landed with a dull thump. "You won't find me getting involved with that nonsense. Other than fishing, I'll be inside for the season with something warm to drink."

Thankfully for Jez, Adenashire was mostly a sleepy village, fueled by gossip she tried to stay out of.

"It's going to take over the whole town. I'm not sure you can avoid it." Taenya eyed the cotton bag and crossed her arms over her chest. "You understand that fish smell doesn't really go with…bakery."

"Why not?" Jez said. "Fish is delicious. Patrons will come in, think of lunch, then the dessert they might have when they're done." She threw her hands in the air as if in celebration. "More sales."

The elf gave a low chuckle and made her way to Jez's

table. She pulled out the second wooden chair, its legs scraping the floor, and sat. Then she planted her elbows on the tabletop and rested her slightly pointed chin on her hands, leaning closer to the fennex. "It doesn't work that way, Jez."

Jez blinked three times, then said in a dry tone without moving, "Do you want me to leave?"

Taenya leaned back in her chair. "What pastries would you like today?"

For a moment Taenya's icing sugar fragrance intensified. But Jez quickly clamped it down and looked at the counter, where frosting-slathered cinnamon buns sat next to a pile of brown butter chocolate chip cookies, one of Jez's favorites. She twitched her nose as the caramelly notes of the cookies broke through her barrier and made her mouth water.

"I've already got those ready for you," Taenya said. "In the back. I bagged them before I arranged the rest for sale."

"You knew I'd be in?" Jez flicked her attention to her friend, who sat with a slightly smug look on her face.

"You always come in after fishing. And you always fish midweek."

Jez tipped her head in interest and brushed her mop of white hair off her forehead. "Really?"

"Really." The elf's normally pale cheeks for some reason turned a light shade of pink, and she pushed her chair back from the table and stood. "Now, what else can I get you?"

Jez sat for a moment in thought before she said, "How about those bergamot cherry scones?"

Taenya turned to eye the array of goodies on the counter. "They're not even out yet. How'd you know?"

"I smelled them when I came in." Jez fiddled with the twine on her fishing pole. "It's okay if you haven't frosted them. I enjoy them both ways."

The corners of Taenya's mouth pushed upward. "Me too."

Voices wafted in through the shop window, and Jez looked toward the sound. It was Arleta, warmly bundled in a heavy wool coat trimmed with sheepskin, and her Fated, Theodmon Brylar, a woodland elf like Taenya. His towhead was mostly hidden under a multicolored knitted cap, and he wore a coat similar to Arleta's. The pair had also met due to the Baking Battle and were disgustingly inseparable, except when Arleta worked in the bakery. Jez still didn't know exactly what Theo did with his time other than clean the home they shared, make dinner, and act as a servant to their forest lynx "house cat," Faylin. Jez couldn't fathom being around another person so much without considerable breaks, Fated or not.

Theo pulled a red sled behind him with one hand and held Arleta's gloved one with the other. As they reached the bakery door, he parked the sled and gave Arleta a twirl, making her loose chestnut hair take flight from the spin.

"Are they coming in or not?" Jez asked, watching the display with raised brows.

The human giggled and nearly tumbled into his chest. He pulled her close and began kissing her with abandon.

Taenya chuckled. "Guess not."

Jez averted her gaze, suddenly feeling flushed.

"They're so cute," Taenya said with a sigh.

After what seemed like an age, Jez glanced up to her

friend, who must have gone to the kitchen to retrieve the scones and cookies *and* come back, as she held the bag out to Jez without looking at her. The elf's stare was trained on the couple making out on the bakery's stoop, a goofy grin on her lips.

"Shit," Jez said, her eyes briefly landing on Arleta and Theo again before she quickly averted them, but not before noticing the green and gold magic radiating off Theo's pale skin. That tended to happen around Arleta…a lot. "I'd think *that* behavior would scare off customers considerably more than a few fish."

Taenya chuckled and returned her attention to Jez. "Could be. But don't you agree their story is romantic?" Taenya gently placed the bag on the table, sliding it over in front of the fennex.

The scent of chocolate and browned butter nearly made Jez forget about her friends' absurd behavior outside the window. "You'd think they didn't care if anyone was watching." She reached inside her coat and into a small pocket sewn into the lining. Jez tended to keep important things in that pocket. And one of those things was a silver flask.

The elf seemed to pay no attention to Jez's grumblings. "I mean, he'd seen her in his dreams hundreds of times, but he didn't know who she was when he showed up on her doorstep with a Langheim Baking Battle invitation. Can you imagine?" Her voice was lost in a daydream.

Jez took a swig from the flask and allowed the rum to pour into her throat. "No. I could *not* imagine," she said dryly as she returned the flask and opened the sack. She plucked out a cookie and took a bite. The sweet, buttery flavor with a slight bitterness from the chocolate made her melt a little bit. "But I *could* spend a lifetime with this." Jez held out and admired the large, golden, bumpy treat. "We might even be fated."

Taenya smacked the fennex on the shoulder. "Are you truly that cynical, fox?" The elf's brows furrowed, and her lips pinched. "Theo and Arleta developed a close friendship before it"—she looked through the window at the still-kissing couple—"developed."

Jez took another bite of her cookie and spoke with her mouth full. "Now why would I spoil a perfectly good friendship for something as ridiculous as romance?"

"Because friendship is the greatest basis for romance," Taenya insisted, twisting to Jez. "Sometimes, when life gets difficult, you want reassurance that you actually like the person you love the most."

Jez dropped the half-eaten cookie back in the crinkly bag and looked up at her friend. "And I don't need romance for any of that. I like *and* love all my friends here. I'll do most anything for the lot of you. But romance messes things up—"

"It doesn't have to. Not for Arleta…or Doli and her gargoyle, Sarson." Taenya crossed her arms over her chest, then gestured out the window where Theo and Arleta were no longer visible.

Jez raised one brow. "I think they left. Probably to…you know."

"Or possibly to practice sledding some more," Taenya scoffed, obviously flustered.

"Is *that* what they're calling it these days?" Jez stood and reached for her fishing gear.

The elf didn't answer.

While arranging her pack on her shoulders, Jez said, "Look, friendship is easier. Romance always complicates life." She quickly reclipped her bag of fish to her belt, grabbed her pastries, and then rested a hand on Taenya's shoulder. "And my life has been complicated enough. Having lots of friends but staying single is best for me. If *you* need something more, then go out and find someone. I'm perfectly fine watching from the side."

Taenya patted her friend's clawed hand. "It is a risk. I'll give you that."

"A risk I'm not willing to take," Jez said as she headed out into the snow toward the apartment she shared with Doli to prepare her fish.

2

Jez sat on her usual stool in the bar at the Tricky Goat Inn and Pub, nursing her third glass of rum.

Alone. Exactly how she liked it after a long shift at the It's About Tome bookshop, which was owned by her orc friend Verdreth.

The sourness of stale food and spilled alcohol hung at the back of the fennex's nose like an old friend. The bartender, a smallish pink-skinned ogre named Guzor who sported a dark unibrow and a single blunt horn in the middle of his forehead, wiped down the butcher-block counter with a nubby cotton rag, minding his own business and humming a jaunty tune.

Shortly after Jez's arrival in the village, she'd tried each of the barstools for the best fit. One had given a little squeak when she'd first sat on it. Another wobbled a bit too much since one leg was shorter than the rest. Each of the other ten had bothersome quirks Jez barely remembered. But the third stool on the right had suited her fine and seemed to be consistently available if Jez arrived early enough to plant her ass onto it. In a pinch, she'd use the fourth from the left.

Behind the bar, shelves lining the wall were arrayed with short and tall bottles, each filled with various types and amounts of alcohol. Some bottles were clear, showing off the liquid inside, while others would have been a mystery if it weren't for the scrawlish labels on the outside. Since she'd moved to Adenashire, Jez had tried most of them in at least small quantities. But she always returned to the rum.

It suited her.

It was comfortable.

That night she was in her seat earlier than usual. She was to meet the rest of her friends for a meal and wanted a few extra minutes to herself before they arrived.

But it was not to be. Instead of peace and quiet, boisterous tourists filled the space. Every seat at the bar was full, and from the chatter it seemed everyone was getting ready for the start of the Yule Games. Most annoyingly, a woman with two other humans cackled behind Jez as they played a disordered round of Fortress, a dice and card game. The noise was making her skin vibrate as if she'd stepped on an anthill but not realized it until it was too late. That was how the third rum of the night had come to be, and Jez's head had started to buzz. As more raucous laughter burst out behind her, the fennex's tail twitched erratically.

"I'm about to take all yer silver," the woman taunted her competitors as they groaned. None of the group was familiar, so they were likely tourists in town for the Games. Perhaps even from the temporary winter camp set up outside town to house the overflow, since the Goat only had so many rooms. Some of them had taken over her fishing lake for ice skating. Plus the southern end of town had been closed off for the week to prepare for the event.

Ears flat, Jez gritted her teeth at the annoyance of it all.

The people crowding the spaces she usually enjoyed were another reason she hadn't looked forward to the Games, which her friends, including Taenya, had been talking about since late fall.

"Damn snow, damn Games," Jez hissed under her breath and then took a tiny sip of her rum. She considered downing the glass and heading home to the apartment she shared with Doli over the bookstore. The warm, cozy bed called to her like a down-stuffed pillow siren…but the kitchen pantry was too bare to make a complete dinner, which she'd need after her belly full of rum. And she really did want to meet her friends, since they hadn't all gotten together for several days.

"Business'll be good for the next week," Guzor said, interrupting her conflicted thoughts.

"Huh?" Jez had heard the statement, but other than asking if she wanted another drink, the ogre usually left her alone, so she didn't know if he'd actually been talking to her. In all honesty the fennex opposed more business, but saying that was ruder than even she liked to be, so she pinched her lips and kept quiet.

One of the two bar servers, a willowy human named Pyke, came up and plunked down a small piece of paper. "Order in," he said. He wore a tight pair of cotton pants and a white shirt with the buttons halfway unfastened, probably for better tips. Jez eyed his hairy, slightly muscular chest with relative disinterest. He quickly scurried off to a table where the patrons waved their raccoon paws in the air to get his attention.

The ogre plucked the paper up in his meaty hand and read it. Then he reached for an opaque bottle on the top shelf labeled Sapphire, a viscous elvish liqueur. With his other hand he pinched two glasses onto the counter and poured a bright blue glittery liquid.

Jez wrinkled her nose. She knew by experience that it was sickly sweet and not to her liking. She took another sip of her rum, savoring the woody aroma and familiar burn in her throat, then checked the time on the old wall clock with a crooked second hand. Everyone was set to arrive in about fifteen minutes.

Guzor pushed the drinks aside for Pyke to retrieve when he circled back and then turned his yellow eyes on Jez. "You ready for the bill, fennex?"

Jez shot down the remains of her rum and plunked the glass on the bar. "One more."

The ogre eyed her for a moment with his bright golden irises but eventually turned to snatch the bottle of rum off the shelf. "After that, you need to go eat."

"That's the plan," Jez said as the bartender poured the drink. She picked up the glass and downed it in a gulp.

"I win!" the woman playing the game cheered, nearly causing Jez's drink to come back up. "I win!"

But the celebration was short-lived. One of the other players growled, "You cheated!"

Jez whipped her head around as the burly man with a mop of golden curls thwacked his hand down on the table, making the Fortress cards fly into the air like a kaleidoscope of flutterbees.

Several yips and gasps came from the other patrons.

"Oh, shit," Jez said under her breath. The last thing she wanted was a bar fight, and she was ninety-nine percent sure the woman, braggart as she was, wasn't cheating.

"No, I didn't," the lady declared. "Now pay up."

The fennex could generally smell that sort of treachery. It wasn't the easiest to pinpoint, but cheaters tended to put off a distinctive aroma to one with a nose as sensitive as Jez's. But to be certain, she inhaled deeply, allowing her magic to thrum in her sinuses. At the same time, the bar seemed to slow to a quiet crawl from the accusation.

And the olfactory evidence wasn't there.

"I will not," the man growled. "I don't pay cheaters."

"Do we have a problem?" the ogre bartender asked.

Jez pushed from her seat and stood, but her brain spun with the effects of the alcohol, and she realized she'd made a mistake asking for that last pour. But she steadied herself by grasping the back of her chair and letting the buzz settle. She pulled down her brown leather vest to straighten it and turned toward the bristling group.

"The lady didn't cheat," Jez declared to the burly man,

who was at least a head taller than the fennex, who was quite tall herself.

The accused older woman and the other player had taken a step back from the table, where several empty ale mugs sat at the human man's spot.

The accuser whipped around and narrowed his stare at Jez. "You in this hustle too?" He angled his head and ran a contemptuous gaze over her, landing on her tail. "What are you, anyway?"

Jez raised her hands chest high with her palms out, ignoring the inane question. "Look. I hate cheating as much as the next person." She hiccupped. "I also hate losing sssilver." She pointed to her nose. "But I can usually smell it if someone's taking advantage. And this lady… She's just happy to win. That's it." It was ridiculous to involve herself, and she knew it. But she couldn't have her bar destroyed. Where would she have gone in the evenings while it was being repaired?

But the reality was, too much alcohol often made the fennex do things she wouldn't have otherwise.

The man bared his teeth and growled.

Her middle roiled as she felt eyes on her from all around the room, but Jez maintained her composed stance. "Ask the barkeep about me." She tipped her head to Guzor. "I live here and never saw the woman before. There's no reason to defend her"—Jez's knees wobbled a bit—"to defend her if I didn't think she was honest."

"She's right," the ogre confirmed. "Now why don't you pay up and then go sleep it off?"

The human man wavered his attention between Jez, the game winner, and Guzor. Then he seemed to realize that everyone in the bar was staring at him. As quickly as everything had escalated, his anger subsided.

"Fine." He shoved the pile of silver from the middle of the table to the woman and several coins spilled onto the floor. Then he spun and stormed out of the bar into the inn's foyer, practically running into Maven, the owner.

"Stars," the middle-aged human said, nearly dropping the large stack of linens in her arms.

Paying Maven no mind, the man pushed past her and through the exit in a huff.

Jez turned to the woman and let out a long breath while most of the patrons resumed eating, drinking, and whatever else they'd been doing before the incident.

"Thank you," the woman said while gathering her winnings, which were scattered across the table. The third player was gone. "I'm Cali."

The fennex tipped her chin to the woman, but her head was spinning from the rum and from the scent magic she'd allowed to surface. Her own name didn't come to mind immediately. "Jezzz. I think. And…and don't mention it."

Her speech was slowed, and she dragged her attention to the bar. A halfling with a bright head of red hair had already climbed into Jez's barstool and ordered an ale. Jez pinched her lips and considered her bed at home again. Saying nothing more to the woman, she stumbled to the bar and threw down coins enough for payment and tip.

"I need some air," she managed.

Guzor nodded. "Good choice."

On her way out of the bar, Cali held her hand up. "Hope we see each other at the Games."

But the mention of the Yule Games only caused the alcohol in Jez's middle to whirlwind again, and she'd need to get outside sooner rather than later. She snatched her coat off a hook in the inn's foyer, threaded her arms clumsily through the sleeves, and stumbled out into the snowy night.

She nearly retched into a bush beside the Goat's patio seating but by some miracle held it in.

"Get ahold of yourself," Jez growled as a headache started to grow behind her eyes. She managed to lean against a square wooden column holding up the overhang at the inn's entrance.

The street lanterns were lit, and more people than usual were still out for the evening. Overhead, the night was clear, with the moon large and sprays of stars decorating the sky. Most of the snowfall from the day had been swept from the road. But to Jez's eyes the view was mildly blurry. She blinked several times to clear her vision.

There was a rowdy group of humans sitting at the patio tables in front of the firepit. They'd probably lit it themselves since outdoor seating wasn't open at night during the winter months.

Jez shook her head at them and pushed away from the column, ready to go home, but just then, her friends rounded the street corner. Arleta and Theo were, of course, nearly attached, and no one would miss Sarson's enormous light blue frame with the horns curling over his hair. Even with his wings tucked behind his back it was easy to see he had a massive wingspan. The gargoyle could look a bit threatening to anyone who didn't know him, but he was a big softy for Doli, who walked beside him. Since Doli was a dwarf, the height difference might have been eyebrow raising if they weren't such a perfect match.

Not that Jez cared about perfect matches. But she did like seeing her friends happy, even if she was sometimes reluctant to admit it.

Doli let go of Sarson's hand and jogged to Jez, who suddenly felt guilty for deciding to leave before the others arrived.

"Jez!" the dwarf exclaimed as if the two of them hadn't seen each other just a few hours earlier in the apartment they shared.

The fennex forced a crooked smile and mentally worked against her upset stomach as her friend nearly plowed into her and gave her a massive hug. The scent of vanilla and sunshine wafted up to Jez's nose, and she looked down at Doli's spiral curls before the dwarf turned up her umber face with a huge grin on her lips.

"You're *really* excited for the Yule Games, aren't you?" Jez moaned as she returned the embrace.

Doli's brown eyes twinkled under the streetlamps. "Sarson and I can't wait."

The other three came up behind Doli as she separated from Jez.

"Were you waiting for us?" Theo asked, not letting go of Arleta's hand.

Jez glanced toward her apartment and sighed. "Something like that." She had no desire to talk about why she had truly been outside. "Where'sss Taenya?"

Arleta glanced back at the street. "Tae's right behind us. We left her to finish up some icing work at the bakery."

"Should we wait for her or go inside for a table?" Sarson fluttered his still tucked-in blue wings slightly as he took Doli's small hand and leaned down to kiss it.

Doli let out an over-the-top sigh.

Doing her best to ignore all that, Jez eyed the door with its carved image of a winking goat on it and weighed the condition of both her head and stomach. "It's pretty crowded. How about I wait for her and you all go inside for a table? The less I have to hear about the Yule Games, the better. I'm only here for the shepherd's pie."

"Well, I hope you'll come out to at least one event to cheer our teams on," Doli chirped.

Jez groaned, finding it difficult to disappoint her smiling dwarf friend. "We'll see."

Doli grinned from ear to ear, and Arleta patted Jez on the shoulder before the four of them made their way inside, leaving the fennex once more to herself.

Not counting the loud, annoying group on the patio.

In an attempt to ignore them and fend off the alcohol still working against her, she stepped back to the porch, leaned against the column, and closed her eyes. She may have even dozed off just for a moment.

"I'm meeting friends inside." Taenya's voice in the distance woke Jez.

She blinked open her eyes to a blurry scene that quickly cleared. Two humans from the group of strangers had gone from the patio to the street and seemed to be blocking someone.

"You should join us," a human said. "Landon over there lost his partner. You'd be perfect."

"No." Taenya's voice came from behind them. "Thank you. I don't need a Yule Games partner." She didn't sound worried, and she had the skills to fend off any human if necessary, even one larger than herself. But the elf's scent hit Jez's nose with a twinge of annoyance, and the fennex's feet moved on their own with barely a wobble.

In seconds, Jez had trudged across the snow and rounded the group of humans. A scowl dragged at her lips.

"Oh, Jez," Taenya said, surprise in her tone.

Jez grabbed for the elf's hand and pulled her protectively close. "You all need to go back to whatever you were doing."

The shortest of the two, with a head of curly blond hair and bundled in a winter coat, looked Jez up and down. "You her girlfriend or something?"

Jez snarled, baring her fangs, and the men each receded. The fennex should have left it at that, but her alcohol-loosened tongue had other ideas. "Yeah. I am. So why don't you mind yourself?"

"We…uh…should get inside, Jez," Taenya stuttered. She tugged on her friend's hand and leaned closer. "Are you drunk?" she whispered.

Jez, her face heating as she realized what she'd said, fully appreciated that she was indeed plastered. But so were the humans.

The tallest one, a big burly man with ginger hair and beard, chuckled. "*Well*...if you two are any indication of our competition, we'll be taking first prize for sure." He elbowed the guy next to him. "Right, Brady?"

"Yeah, Ronan." The smaller guy, presumably Brady, chuckled.

Taenya huffed. "I thought you wanted me to team up with Landon over there." She pointed to the man still at the table.

"Maybe we don't want Landon to win," Brady said with a hearty laugh.

Landon threw a few curses their way.

The fennex lunged slightly at Brady, making him flinch. "We could kick your asses twice over."

"Should we make a wager?" Ronan egged Jez on.

"Twenty sssilver!" Jez blurted, not even knowing why the words were spilling from her mouth. Clouds had started to roll in, and a fresh sprinkling of snow floated through the air.

"We need to go inside!" Taenya's voice became more insistent as she hooked her hand into the crook of Jez's elbow and looked directly at the men. "Please excuse us." With that, she yanked on Jez. The fennex nearly lost her footing, but Taenya kept her upright.

"Done," Ronan called.

Jez turned, grasped his hand, and shook it vigorously. "May the best team win."

Ronan gripped her hand hard before letting go. "We'll see you at the starting line."

"Yes, you will," the fennex said before Taenya pulled her away for good.

"What in the stars are you doing?" the elf whispered into her ear.

Jez had no answer.

3

Jez sobered up a bit as she and Taenya walked back into the Tricky Goat and hung their coats. All the way through the foyer, which suddenly looked like a giant black tunnel instead of one of her favorite hangouts, she groaned at the memory of her drunken actions.

Not only had she roped herself into the Yule Games with a ridiculous bet, but had she actually said that she and Taenya were dating? That couldn't have happened. Could it?

Taenya hadn't uttered a word since they'd left the humans, but her icing sugar aroma had doubled in strength. She must have been mortified by Jez's actions and words.

The aroma of shepherd's pie wafting out of the kitchen was a relief. Even so, she instinctively pulled back her scent magic to block anything coming from Taenya.

Verdreth and Ervash waved from a corner table where they sat by themselves, but Jez didn't respond.

She and Taenya finally found the rest of their friends at a large table with bench seating. The place seemed even louder than it had before Jez had left, and she rubbed her temples in a failed attempt to banish her now-pounding headache.

"Tea!" she practically yelled at Doli.

The dwarf scooted over to make room but looked at the fennex in utter confusion. "Tea. You want tea? Don't you mean rum?"

"You have tea magic," Jez growled at the dwarf, looking her up and down but not sitting. "Why in the stars are you asking so many questions?"

"I only asked two…" Doli raised her brows at the others while she reached down to unclip a teacup from its holster.

"And don't speak of rum. I never want rum again." The vow rolled around in Jez's mind after it escaped her lips. She felt like she meant it. "Or anything like it."

Sliding in next to Theo, Taenya said, "I think Jez has a few regrets."

Tightness clamped down on Jez's chest and her head went light at Taenya's words.

"Damn right I have regrets." The fennex finally sat and buried her forehead in her hands to keep the room from spinning like a top.

"Regrets?" Sarson leaned forward in interest. "We only just left you. How much could have happened in that amount of time?"

A lot. Jez kept the thought to herself and avoided looking at Taenya. What was the elf thinking? Maybe she hadn't actually heard Jez call her "girlfriend." She hadn't said anything about it, and if she did hear, she *must* have known Jez had only said it to get her friend away from those bastards.

Doli placed her hand over the cup and a little sparkling magic fizzed in the air. "There you go, love. It's chamomile. That seemed like a good choice." She pushed it over to Jez, who immediately downed the tea, which, in her opinion, had the flavor of brewed hay.

Not the best. But she didn't care.

"Another," she demanded, shoving the cup and saucer back to Doli. "A double this time."

Everyone but Taenya stared at her, obviously unsure what in the stars was going on.

But Doli did as she was told and made a second tea. "What happened?"

"Can I get something started for you?" Pyke was suddenly at the end of the table with his order book. His hair was mussed on the top.

Everyone gazed around at each other, silent.

Jez downed her tea, looked up at the server, and bared her teeth. "We *just* sat down." The statement came out as a growl.

Pyke held his hands in the air as if in surrender.

"We haven't had a moment to look at the menu," Theo said politely. "There's been a small…emergency."

Pyke studied Jez again, who still had her lips curled and fangs exposed. "Take all the time you need." With that, he scurried away.

"Well," Arleta said from the other side of Theo. Her olive skin was still rosy from the cold outside. "He'll probably spit in our food now."

Jez eyed her friend. "You're *not* helping. And that doesn't happen."

"How do you know?" The human let a grin play at her lips. "We'd help if you told us what was going on." She looked expectantly at Taenya, then back to Jez.

Across the tavern, the three raccoons who'd ordered the Sapphire drinks before the cheating incident had started a dance on top of their table, even though the music stage was empty that evening. They looked like little gyrating road bandits with their furry, masked faces.

Wishing she could disappear, the fennex dropped her head into her hands once more. *Why didn't I just go home?* Then none of that disaster would have happened.

"It was some tourists out front," Taenya finally said. "They were…in my way."

"In your way?" Sarson's already deep voice dropped, and out of the corner of her eye, Jez saw the skin on his neck and jaw hardening. Since he was a gargoyle, that tended to happen in dangerous situations or from high emotions. "What do you mean? Were they bothering you?" He gripped the edge of the table as if ready to spring into action.

The elf reached across and touched his forearm. "They were a little drunk and looking for a Yule Games partner for one of their friends. Perhaps a mite too insistent. But Jez helped."

Sarson's shoulders relaxed.

"Helped," Jez scoffed. "Not sure I *helped*."

"What's *that* mean?" Doli asked, then gestured at the teacup as if to ask if Jez wanted another.

With the brewed hay taste still lingering, the fennex demurred. "I think I'm at my limit."

Everyone stared as if waiting for the answer to the question Doli had voiced.

Jez's breath shortened. "I might have made a bet that we'd beat them in the Yule Games."

"You agreed to compete?" Arleta said, surprised. "Jez. You've been complaining about the Games for months. Even swore you'd lock yourself in your room until they were over."

She wished she *had* locked herself in her room earlier that day.

"I don't know why I agreed," the fennex moaned. "It all made sense at the time." But *it* was the rum. She knew that. "I wanted to get Taenya away from them…so I said she was my grlfrnd"—the word came out quickly in hopes that no one would hear it—"and somehow I wound up betting them twenty silver that our team would beat theirs."

"Twenty silver?" Sarson said.

"Did you say *girlfriend*?" Doli had *not* missed Jez's barely audible admittance.

Taenya jumped in. "It was just to get them to back off."

Jez's neck warmed, and her tail, even fluffier than normal, twitched with irritation behind the bench, half dragging on the floor. "Yes. Exactly."

"It wasn't a big deal," Taenya insisted a little too quickly.

Doli sat up on her knees on her seat and squinted as if in thought. "Let me get this straight. Some group out front was bothering Taenya and"—she pointed her finger at Jez—"then you stepped in and told them you and Taenya were a thing. But then, instead of leaving, you made a bet that if you competed, you'd win?" She smirked. "Sounds like a great story plot." Doli forever had her nose in a book. It was no surprise that the gargoyle she'd ended up with was an actual librarian.

"She said we'd kick their asses," Taenya said, grinning slightly.

"He insulted us," Jez muttered, knowing all of it sounded ridiculous as the words came out. "I should have just kicked his ass right then and there."

Arleta chimed in, "But you didn't?"

"Of course I didn't," Jez muttered.

Doli dried out the teacup with a napkin and returned it and the saucer to her holster. "It *does* seem like something you might do."

The fennex scoffed. "You've never known me to *actually* kick anyone's ass."

"Doesn't mean you haven't," Doli said.

"Come to think of it…" Arleta leaned forward to see past Theo. "We don't know that much about you before your life with us."

Why were they getting so off topic? Jez nearly froze but choked out, "There…there's not a lot you need to know. I'm from the Southern Desert, have a huge annoying family, and that's it!" The last part came out all squeaky, and Jez shoved her suddenly clammy hands under the table as everyone stared at her.

"So? Are we ready yet?" Pyke's tenor voice asked again as he seemed to appear out of nowhere.

The entire group whipped their attention to him. "No!" they shouted in unison.

Eyes wide, he slowly backed away and then hurried toward a party of towheaded elves.

"We need to leave him a *really* big tip," Sarson said, his forehead scrunched.

Doli nodded. "But I still don't understand what made you say you'd compete in the Games."

"It was the damn fourth rum!" Jez finally admitted.

The dwarf pinched her lips and patted her teacup. "That explains the demand for tea, then."

"I'm swearing off rum from now on," Jez said with resolve, then sat up straight. "Too much trouble."

"Admirable, but what about our immediate problem?" Taenya said softly.

Jez glanced at the elf, wondering if she was referring to how she'd called Taenya her girlfriend outside and wanted an apology for stepping in where she wasn't needed. "You mean about the Yule Games?"

"Yeah," she said. "Do you suppose you can get out of it?"

Jez hazily remembered shaking the man's hand. A fennex's word paired with a willing handshake was their bond. She sighed, hung her head, and said, "No. I think I'm stuck. I gave my word."

"You could just pay the bet," Arleta offered. "Maybe that would work."

Jez considered the option for a second but then shook

her head. "It would clear out any savings I have. There aren't *that* many events, right?"

"Well," Theo said, "there's a scavenger hunt, ice sculpting…an ice maze—"

"Ice maze?" Jez's chest constricted at the thought of freezing to death in an ice maze. It sounded as bad as heights. Jez hated heights.

Doli leaned her head on Sarson's muscular arm. "It'll be fun, Jez. You'll see. You and Taenya are going to have the best time. It'll be just like the Baking Battle again…all of us together!" She clapped her hands with joy.

"Well…I didn't win *that* competition," Jez groaned, still thinking about being trapped in the ice maze.

"But I did," Taenya said.

Jez eyed the elf.

Taenya's lips quirked up a little. "I did want to compete but didn't have a partner."

"Then the stars have turned a bad situation to good," Theo remarked.

Doli sat up straight as if she suddenly got a thought. "But if you go through with competing, you two will need to act like you're together."

"What?" Jez and Taenya said in unison.

"Well," the dwarf said, "that's what you said to those humans, right? So they're expecting it. You'll just be faking the relationship, though. No big deal." She grinned slyly.

Jez fidgeted with a bit of her hair at her neck as she looked at Taenya. "It won't come to that, right?"

The elf paused and bit her bottom lip before she said, "I

don't think so. It's none of Ronan's business anyway. We're teammates and that's it." She stuck out her hand to Jez.

Jez stared at her waiting hand, the fingertips slightly stained with blue cake frosting dye. But then she clasped Taenya's hand and shook it. "Teammates…for the Yule Games."

Just as they released, Arleta said, "Pyke is heading back. Do you all know what you want?"

"I'm going last," Jez said, even though she already knew she'd order the shepherd's pie. Like she always did.

"Oh…and then there's the sledding competition," Theo said as if suddenly remembering.

"Oh, stars. Sledding." Jez eyed Taenya, who snickered while the fennex brought her hand to her head.

"What?" Theo looked at Arleta. "What's wrong with sledding?"

Arleta shrugged. "I don't know. I enjoy sledding."

Jez groaned. "*Enough* about sledding."

4

With the alcohol effects mostly worn off, Jez took the last bite of her shepherd's pie (ordered with extra peas), tossed her fork onto the plate, and dug coins from her pocket to pay her bill—along with a hefty tip for Pyke, of course.

To avoid learning what Taenya thought about their situation, Jez had completely locked down her scent magic after ordering. It had made her dinner taste of little more than salt, which had been an utter disappointment since it was her favorite meal. But the proper goal was to fill her belly, and that had been accomplished.

And she'd avoided any of her friend's scents giving away their private thoughts about her actions.

Still, she wondered. Did Taenya really want her as a

competition partner, or did she feel pressured into it due to Jez's foolishness? She'd probably rather have someone else on her team. Jez wasn't sure she'd be a very effective team-mate. On a full night's sleep every night…possibly, but that was unlikely. And afternoon naps were probably out with all the festivities. Not to mention all the people…ugh. The *people*. But the fennex's mind was too tired, and the thoughts quickly jumbled.

After plunking the coins on the table, she announced, "I'm going home." The call of her bed had gotten too strong. Her arms were like two logs pulling her shoulders down, and her eyelids drooped.

"Me too," Doli said with an overly honeyed tone. She maneuvered out of the bench's middle seat without even waiting for Jez to get up.

"I thought you were going home with Sarson?" Jez said, looking at the blue gargoyle, still eating his vegetarian casserole of roasted beets, rutabaga, and parsnips covered in a caramelized white cheese sauce.

Since the two of them had gotten together a couple of months before, Doli basically split her time between his cottage on the outskirts of Adenashire and the apartment she and Jez shared above Verdreth's bookshop. Sometimes Jez missed the dwarf's company, but the fennex had been counting on being alone that night. The place was always much quieter when Doli was absent, and there would be no one to wake her up in the morning.

"You don't need to come if you weren't planning on it," Jez continued, avoiding any snark in her tone. She even threw in a forced smile as she turned, swung her legs over the bench, and stood. "I won't get into any more trouble on the way home."

But Doli shook her head. "I should hope not because I'm coming too."

A barely audible growl tickled the back of her throat, but Jez didn't have it in her that night to argue. Crawling into bed was hours overdue. So she glanced at Taenya, who had spoken little since the food arrived. "We'll figure all this out tomorrow."

"Of course," the elf said.

Doli kissed Sarson goodnight, and Jez tipped her chin to Arleta and Theo.

"Stop by the bakery in the morning," Arleta said. "We're selling a limited run of Doli's Jam Spice Cookies before the start of the Yule Games."

"My grammie's recipe?" Doli asked, a tiny lilt in her voice.

"Mm-hmm," the human said. "They'll be perfect."

Unable to wait any longer, Jez waved one clawed hand. "I'm going. If you're coming, dwarf, now's the time." She eyed Taenya to say goodbye, but the elf seemed to be concentrating on her food. Or ignoring Jez. She wouldn't have blamed her if it was the latter.

"Coming." Doli quickly gave Sarson another peck and handed him her part of the bill, which he waved off, then she hurried after Jez, leaving their other four friends to finish their meals.

The entrance had a roaring fire going in the enormous fireplace, crackling and popping from freshly added logs, and there were also several comfortable seating areas for guests to congregate, all of which were full.

After making her way past all that, Jez grabbed her coat from the rack, as well as Doli's, which of course was the frilliest of all the coats hanging there, purple with a lace collar. Jez turned and tossed it to her friend, who caught it in her plump hands.

Tired as Jez was, she had her own woolly coat on in a few seconds.

"Is it working out for you?" Doli asked while donning hers over her pink dress.

Jez buttoned her coat all the way to the top and pushed open the door. "Is what working out?"

"Thank you for coming in!" Maven shouted from behind the inn's check-in station, interrupting their conversation.

Doli turned toward the innkeeper and waved. "Thank *you* for all the hard work you do around here. We always enjoy our meals."

The fennex rolled her eyes. Her friend's compliments were a part of her nature. The meal probably *had* been good, if she could have tasted it, but in her current state of mind the delay grated on her nerves. She wanted to get home. Even so, she stuck her hand up and waved. After all, Maven *was* nice and always overworked. Before anything else could be said, Jez hurried through the door, hoping the humans who'd gotten her in all that trouble were gone.

They were. Thank the stars. And in the time she'd eaten dinner the streets had mostly cleared. The temperature had dropped even more, and snow descended in a steady stream.

As the icy air hit her face, Jez immediately wished she'd brought a cap to cover her head.

"Is your *coat* working out?" Doli's rapid steps trailed behind Jez's long stride. "That's what I was asking before Maven spoke to us."

Despite the icy tips of her furry ears, Jez considered her warm chest and arms. "Yes, Doli. I love the coat."

"I'm so glad," she said. "You really did need it."

The mounting snow crunched under their boots, and the street lanterns sparkled like miniature stars. For the moment Adenashire felt normal, but at dawn crowds would line the main street to watch or take part in the Yule Games.

All the way home Doli kept up her chatter, but Jez barely heard any of it and only managed a few grunts in reply.

She navigated the streets to the darkened bookshop by rote and soon found herself inside, up the staircase, and safe in the apartment living area. She struggled slightly with her buttons, fingertips still frozen, but managed to unhook them all and let the coat slip off her shoulders.

"I think this Yule Games experience might help you come out of your shell," Doli said as she hung her own coat on the lower hook beside their front door.

Jez's back stiffened. "I like my shell, thank you very much. It's warm and cozy."

Doli took a step back, nearly running into a large box behind her that had not been there earlier. She raised her hands chest high with palms out. "I know you don't mind competition and getting yourself out there a little. For stars' sake, we met you at the Baking Battle."

"That was different." Jez eyed her bedroom and wished she could magic herself inside with the door closed.

"How?" the dwarf asked, placing her hands on her ample hips. "I think you would be particularly good at ice sculpting…then with Taenya on your team? She's a detail genius."

Jez gulped. The Baking Battle had been on a whim…and an escape. But she couldn't tell Doli that. Then the dwarf would have more questions. Questions Jez didn't want to answer. Not *ever* if she could avoid it…but particularly that night when her bed was so close.

And apparently so far away.

"It's too cold." Jez managed a partial lie. "It wasn't cold at all in Langheim for the Battle. And I could grab a nap anytime I needed between competitions."

Doli pinched her lips together as if aware the fennex wasn't telling the entire truth, and then said, "Then you should back out of it. You're not even signed up yet. It's not as if Taenya is going to hold it against you, and that human doesn't really care. You said they were all drunk. They may not even remember the bet."

Jez considered the idea but then cast it aside, gritting her teeth. "I shook on it."

Doli squinted with suspicion. "You shook on it with Taenya at dinner too. Does *that* mean anything special?" She walked around to the other side of the box, which came up to the dwarf's chin, and lifted the top.

The fennex's mind spun with confusion and the desire to sleep. "Shit, I…I don't know. It's just how fennex do things. We don't try to slip out of messes that we get ourselves into.

And I got myself into this. I chose to drink too much, and then instead of walking away from that guy, I popped off to protect Taenya when she didn't need protection. It was ridiculous, and now I'm paying the consequences."

"It does sound a little ridiculous." Doli reached in and pulled out a snowflake-shaped dust catcher made out of a carved blue gem. "But I respect your willingness to follow through." She set the snowflake aside and reached in for something else as Jez watched. Out came a matching dust catcher in the shape of a pine tree.

"Thank you." Jez turned and took one step toward her room but then twisted back to her friend. "What are those things for?"

"Yule decorations," Doli said, holding the tree up to her eye level as if she could peer through the green gem. "I had my parents send down a box from Dundes Heights. They arrived just before dinner, and I didn't have a chance to look through everything." She lowered the knickknack and caught Jez's gaze. "You don't mind, do you? I can put them in my room if they're a bother."

Jez wasn't much for fancy things, but Doli was. Beyond that, she didn't have the strength to care. "They're fine. It's your home too." She paused for a second. "Now I'm going to bed. Try to be quiet."

The dwarf nodded and hoisted her whole body to the waist over the side of the box. "Good night!" The sound of her voice had a slight echo since her head was buried. "The festivities start tomorrow."

Jez thought about retrieving the step stool from their

kitchen but only sighed, turned and let her feet drag to her bedroom door. "Don't remind me." The dwarf probably didn't hear her since she was digging enthusiastically through the decorations.

Safe inside her room, Jez could see the snow falling more heavily outside her window. She lit the lantern beside her bed and drew the dark navy linen curtains, which blocked most of the light save for a small crack at the top. Jez unlaced and pulled off her heavy boots, allowing them to clunk on the floor, and she left them where they lay.

For a blink she considered sleeping in the clothes she'd worn all day, but she'd get better rest in something fresh. So off came her simple cotton sweater and pants in exchange for a billowy but plain cream nightshirt that flowed to her knees and allowed her tail to stick out the back. The fabric was expensive…silk or some other fabric from her past that she didn't remember or even care much about. But it was comfortable. One of the few things from her old life that still was. And that was why she hadn't gotten rid of it.

With her boots, pants, and shirt lying in a heap on the floor, the fennex threw back her warm blanket, blew out the lantern light, and fell into bed. She curled up with the covers pulled up to her neck. Her fluffy tail relaxed and curved to match the contours of her body, and she drifted off.

5

Jez woke with a start.

And a headache.

A big one, zipping its way from the right temple to the left.

And it wasn't just a side effect from the rum. Repressing her scent magic was exhausting. It always had been, but sometimes it was necessary to maintain her state of mind.

She quickly shut her light brown eyes and tried to will her body and mind back into slumber. But it was no use.

The memory of what had transpired the night before floated like a thick fog coating the fennex's brain, and a part of her was nearly convinced—for a second—that it hadn't actually happened.

That her poor choices had been a mere dream. She had

not truly interfered with Taenya's dealings with the humans, and she would barely need to admit the existence of the Yule Games. Or remember the fact that she'd called Taenya her girlfriend.

But no. She'd had to take her drunk ass over to Ronan and Brady, get all offended by their drunken boasts, and promise to beat them in the Games. With her supposed girlfriend.

Yes. That part of her was the ridiculous part.

If Jez felt compelled to do something, why hadn't she only waved from the front stoop of the Tricky Goat when she'd seen Taenya stopped by that group and said something like, "Hurry up! We're all waiting for you!" Surely that would have produced a better outcome.

Perhaps she needed to take a few lessons from Doli instead of saying or doing whatever came to mind at the moment.

Or start drinking more tea than rum.

She cracked her eyelids open again, which of course caused the headache to pound like a blacksmith hammer beating down on an anvil.

Light streaming through the crack in the curtains stung her barely open eyes, letting her know it was at least the next day. Perhaps she'd slept past the deadline to sign up for the Yule Games.

If she had, then that was the stars telling her that she didn't actually *need* to compete, despite her innate compulsion to keep her word.

She groaned. There was the ridiculous part of herself rearing its head again.

Then came a clatter from outside her bedroom door. Probably Doli making breakfast, but it seemed ten times louder than usual. Jez stuck her fingers in her ears for a blink to block the sound, but after this failed to make a noticeable difference, she decided to muddle through the day.

Or at least the next few minutes.

She sniffed, allowing her sense of smell to return, but there was no familiar scent of bacon and eggs or cinnamon oatmeal. The fragrance was something new…dust and pine.

The fennex dragged her head up from her pillow and sat. The room spun, and she quickly closed her eyes again to make the world still. As soon as the twirling stopped in her brain, she took in a deep breath, let it out, opened her lids again and resolved to stand. After that, she threw off the blanket, swung her legs over the edge of the bed…so far, so good…then placed her hands down beside her on the mattress and pushed off.

The entire drawn-out process was a lot of work, and Jez nearly considered reversing the process to go back to sleep.

Amazingly, she found herself still upright. Goal one accomplished.

Not moving, she peered around at her sparse, dim room. Unlike Doli, who'd dragged trunkloads of her possessions from Dundes Heights—linens, teacups and saucers, perfumes, clothing—Jez had brought next to nothing from the Southern Desert. Reminders of the past would only make her dwell on it, and Jez's goal was forward motion. And since moving to Adenashire, she'd only bought the necessities, which wasn't much. Who needed more than a few changes of clothes and a comb?

Some people…but not her.

Verdreth, who owned the apartment, had provided the furnishings when she and Doli had moved in, so all the coins she made from working in his bookshop below could be used for food or whatever else came up.

The thought of the bookshop caused Jez's headache to spike. "Oh, shit."

She'd told Verdreth she wasn't competing in the Games, so he'd planned on her staffing the bookstore at least limited hours to accommodate all the tourists.

Doli, who also worked in the store, had concocted a fancy display of books on the history of Yule and accounts of past Games. Even some fiction.

"Ugh." The complaint slipped from her mouth. If she was going to go through with the competition, she would have to tell him she wasn't available. But that was the least of her problems, and one to be dealt with later. Her eyes wandered to the silver flask on her dresser that she knew was at least half full of rum. That would need to wait…no more mistakes until the Games were over.

The fennex picked up her leaden feet and walked to the door, opening it.

To a winter wonderland?

Maybe she'd grab the flask after all.

The room was completely decked out with pine garland, fairy lights that Doli likely bought from a fairy's stall at the outdoor market, and what must have been a hundred dust catcher figurines arranged on the table, the fireplace, and next to the rocking chairs in the living room. Even the kitchen was lavishly decorated.

Doli stood with her back to Jez securing the last—Jez hoped it was the last—of the pine garland to the top of one wall.

The dwarf was already dressed for the Yule Games, decked out in brown leather boots, pink woolen pants, and a chunky sweater with a purple and pink flower design knitted into the garment below her neck. The colors matched the pink stone necklace she always wore, which had the magical ability to call on her dragon friend, Evvy, whom she'd helped raise. And she must have been wearing a new perfume since instead of vanilla, she smelled of cranberry and cinnamon.

"Ummm," Jez managed, her head spinning with visual and olfactory overwhelm. A roaring fire crackled in the fireplace.

"Oh!" Doli turned, grinning from ear to ear, a lock of her dark hair flopping in her face. She brushed it aside and said, "You're up! I didn't expect you for at least another hour."

The clock on the wall read five minutes until eight.

But then her brown eyes scanned over Jez, and the fennex realized she still wore her silken nightshirt—something she never wore outside her bedroom, even in all the months she'd lived with Doli. Her hands immediately couldn't find a place, and the best she could do was clasp them behind her back.

"What's all this?" Jez said, looking around, before Doli could say anything about her fancy sleeping shirt.

Doli bit her lip. "Yule decorations?" She eyed the room, then ended up back on Jez. "I *might* have gone the tiniest bit overboard."

"Did you stay up all night?" Jez asked, trying to hold back her near horror.

"Well," Doli said, sounding a mite regretful, "I was excited and couldn't wait."

It wasn't a complete admission, but Jez had no idea how the dwarf would have gotten it done all on her own otherwise. Jez marveled at how much *junk* had been inside the box from Dundes Heights. Looking at it again where it now sat next to a full-ass pine tree loaded with ornaments, strung popcorn and berries, and more fairy lights, she thought there must have been a *lot* in the crate.

"There's a tree in our apartment, Doli." The words came out flat.

The dwarf hopped from the step stool with its peeling white paint to the floor with a thump and jogged over to the out-of-place plant life. "I know! Isn't it incredible?" She ran her hand lightly over the branches. "I know it's not common for Yule around here, but a Yule tree is one of my family's traditions I really loved growing up." She bent and picked up the sparkly green skirt at the trunk, exposing a pot. "The tree is still alive too. So we can plant it again when Yule is over." She spun back toward Jez. "You're not mad, are you?"

In all honesty, Jez wasn't mad. Slightly annoyed? Confused? Wanting to know how the tree got into their apartment overnight? Yes, yes, and yes. But mad? Mad was what she was at herself. Doli decking out the apartment for Yule was…well…something Doli would do.

She gazed around the room, and it did look attractive, *if* you liked that sort of thing. Doli had a knack for pulling design and fashion together. "Does Sarson's look like this too?"

The dwarf flopped down onto the rocking chair by the fireplace. "Not yet, but he has decorations. We were planning to put them up tonight after the opening round of competition."

Jez groaned. "Of course he has decorations."

"Right?" Doli said, her tone light and cheery. "The more we get to know each other, the better everything becomes. You were wrong when you said the stuff in my romance books would never come true." She patted a stack of books beside her with words on the spines like Court, Lover, and Shadows.

The fennex *was* happy for Doli. She was. But she couldn't help but wonder how the future might change for them. "Are you considering moving in with him…permanently?"

"Oh." Doli tipped her head in interest. "Are you trying to rid yourself of me?" Immediately after the question left her mouth a smile stretched over her lips as if she were jesting.

Even so, Jez's chest tightened. She knew it was a tease on Doli's part, but somehow it hit the wrong way. "No."

While standing and holding up her hand to indicate the room, Doli said, "You wouldn't have to wake up to a surprise like this."

"Only Sarson would," Jez joked, trying to relieve the churning in her belly at the thought of being alone.

"But he loves it." The dwarf made her way into the kitchen and brought out two teacups from a low cupboard. "Did you decide what you're going to do about the Games?"

"Unless they canceled the whole damn thing, it's the same as last night," Jez said in a low tone.

Doli placed her hand over the first cup and a sprinkling of light magic shimmered over her fingers. When she removed it, steam curled into the air, and she moved onto the next. "Why don't you take a peek outside to check if it's canceled?" She didn't even look up from her tea conjuring.

Already regretting it, Jez walked to the window and pulled back the curtain, flooding the room with light. Sure enough, the streets were absolutely packed with people who had come in from all over the Northern Lands.

Yule must be pretty boring everywhere else for Adenashire to draw that sort of crowd. Just how she liked things. Boring and the same. She quickly threw the curtain closed, blocking out the morning rays. "It's still on."

"Then how about you go back to your room and change?" Doli said. "I'll make us some breakfast."

⁂

Dressed in warm clothes, with a belly full of blackberry custard toast and a side of eggs, Jez headed out.

Clacking and thumping hinted that Verdreth was downstairs already, and sure enough she found the large, muscular orc restocking a bookshelf. He didn't seem to have heard Jez, though, since he said nothing and continued arranging books.

The bookstore always smelled of burnt candles mixed with the must of old books, due to the antique tomes Verdreth kept in a special section in the back. In the front window was Doli's elaborate display.

"Ahem." The fennex cleared her throat and her tail thrashed behind her, a telltale sign of her nervousness.

Still holding an enormous book titled *The Secret Lives of Elves* (apparently there were a lot of secrets), the orc spun on his boot heel toward Jez. "Oh, good morning." He pushed his spectacles farther up on his green nose. "Just doing some last-minute preparation before we open. You ready to start your shift?"

Jez bit her lip. "About that."

"About what?" The orc quickly tucked the book away on the shelf and crossed his arms over his massive chest. He wore a thin cotton shirt buttoned almost to the top, unlike Jez's warm sweater with a leather vest over it and her coat in hand. But orcs tended to run hot, so warmer clothing wasn't as necessary for them. His partner, Ervash, would often be found with no shirt at all, even in cooler weather. But Verdreth was too well mannered for that sort of thing most of the time and kept his clothes on…in public, at least.

"Last night I may have gotten myself into"—she had trouble making the admission—"committing to the Games."

Verdreth raised one dark brow, and Jez cringed, remembering a slow day several weeks before in which she'd babbled on for an age about how she would *never* compete in the Games.

"How did that happen?" His tone was kind.

"It's kind of a lengthy story I'm not sure I want to retell," Jez said. "But in the end, as long as there are still openings, Taenya and I are a team. That means I may not be able to work after all."

The orc pursed his lips for a moment as if disappointed but then said, "Well, I guess there's one more team Ervash and I have to beat." There was a sudden mischievous glint in his eyes behind his glasses.

Relief at his reaction settled into Jez's shoulders, and her tail dropped. The orcs had been taking part in the Games for years and had actually won ten years before. What she really wanted to say was "Yes, please beat us," so after losing she could go on with her quiet plans. But if her team was taken out early, then they might also lose to Ronan's team. And that thought made her hair stand on end. Jez couldn't let them outplay her and Taenya.

"You don't mind?" Jez asked.

Verdreth shrugged. "In the past, I've always closed the shop for the festivities. I was only staying open for your sake so you'd have something to do. But no one should have to work *all* the time."

Jez's chest tingled. She couldn't get over how much each of her friends and even her boss cared about her. "Thanks."

The orc pulled out a pocket watch and looked at the face. "You should be on your way if you're planning to sign up."

"I guess so." Jez gritted her teeth and reluctantly headed out the door.

6

Snow had piled up overnight, but the horde of tourists traipsing around had packed most of it to a thin layer on the main street. Shop owners were out shoveling their walks. The pavement out front of the bookshop was already clear since Verdreth was one of those near-mythical, in Jez's opinion, early risers.

Before joining the throng, Jez remained in the doorway watching the chaos. The whole thing made her want to turn right back around.

"Damn people. Damn snow," she muttered. A small part of her had hoped they'd all disappeared in the time it had taken her to walk downstairs. With a deep breath, she stepped out.

Jez slipped into her usual crowd-walking mode and

simply pretended they weren't there. Keeping her attention fixed on anything but the people, they virtually faded away in her mind while her fennex instincts kept her from bumping into anyone.

It was a skill she'd perfected when she was very young after her magic had become too much for her to handle.

Signs hanging on lampposts pointed the way to the Yule Games registration or touted the competition schedule. Most of the information immediately slipped from Jez's mind but one thing caught her attention—that evening there was to be a banquet celebrating the official start of the Games the next morning.

A growl resonated at the back of her throat. She wouldn't be attending any banquets.

There would be one event each day for four days: scavenger hunt, ice sculpting, a winter maze, sledding... She couldn't even look at the last one, but she'd just have to cope with each one as it came. Then there were balls and a Yule Market scheduled each night, which of course she would also be skipping. But then she froze as she read the words at the bottom:

Contestants are obligated to attend evening events or face disqualification.

She looked around at the crowd behind her as her teeth clenched, then turned back to stare at the sign once more. She zoned out while biting at the inside of her mouth with her right fang until she tasted the tang of iron. The unpleasant flavor brought her back to reality, and she realized with a start that a young faun child, with little goatlike legs and hooves, had materialized next to her, a massive grin on their round face.

"Look, look, Rhegea!" They turned and waved as another faun, probably a sibling, came running up with a small stack of cards clasped in their little hands.

"Do you think she's competing?" Rhegea asked, voice giddy. "We can get her autograph this time too."

The first pointed at something on the sign. "We don't even know if she's here."

But then Rhegea flipped over the top card on the stack and Jez's eyes widened. It was a sketch of Arleta holding a bowl in one hand and spoon in the other, complete with a scrolly frame surrounding her head. The top of the card read "One Hundredth Anniversary of the Langheim Baking Battle. Arleta Starstone. Second Place."

The Baking Battle has collector cards? Jez chuckled to herself.

"She's gotta be here." Rhegea looked around behind them and flipped the card over to the back to look at it. "She lives here, Ronorae. Says right here. Arleta Starstone, from *Adenashire*, was the first magicless to progress to the final round of the Langheim Baking Battle."

"Some of the others live here too!" Ronorae said, clapping her hands. "We've got to find them!"

Looking at the rest of the stack in Rhegea's hand, Jez was almost curious if she had a card in there. She hadn't won, of course, but she'd progressed pretty far in the rounds. Doli could be too. But before she could say a word, the two fauns ran off down the street giggling.

Even if they hadn't recognized Jez, which she didn't *really* want anyway, something about seeing the children's excitement made everything better for a tiny moment. It made her miss her own siblings…and the rest of her family.

Her lips quirked up at the edges. But then she remembered what she had to do.

Jez blew out a quick breath, and a white puff swirled in front of her. She glanced right, then left, but the thought of heading to registration sank a brick in her middle. Instead, her feet took her past the Spells and Sortilege shop, which was packed with tourists, toward the bakery to see if Taenya was there. It would probably be best if they signed up together. Besides, she could get some of the spice cookies Arleta had promised.

With A Little Dash of Magic Bake Shop in view, Jez picked up her pace, but when she arrived, the sign in the window was turned over to display the word CLOSED.

"Maybe she's already at the registration booth," Jez muttered to herself. But then she realized they hadn't even discussed meeting there—or whether to meet at all. Her breath picked up as unwanted thoughts crept around in her mind. What if Taenya was avoiding Jez, embarrassed at her behavior the night before? She should be, since the fennex was embarrassed of herself.

Her fists curled into a ball. Could she have ruined her friendship with Taenya over the whole thing? She'd been too pushy. Too drunk. Too much.

"Shit, shit, shit!" The words slipped out under her breath as a group of halflings passed, and she clamped her mouth shut. Suddenly, scents from all over that she'd been subconsciously blocking hit her nose. Soap and musky body order from the people passing, the bitter aroma of hot drinks like coffee and tea, woodsmoke, all amplified by her magic and wiping out any reason she might have thought she had.

Not this again. Not here. Not now. Her breath came in ragged pants.

Beside her, the door clicked and swished open, the customer bell jingling.

"Hi, Jez," came Taenya's friendly voice.

Startled, the fennex looked up and immediately did everything in her power to regain her composure, slow her breath…including clamping down her sense of smell again. She couldn't risk discovering the truth about Taenya's emotions. All she could hope would be to get through the next few minutes and then try to make it through the next four days. Then everything could go back to normal.

Taenya smiled—Jez could not imagine in what land the expression could be genuine—and pushed the door open wider to allow Jez to enter. "I figured you'd stop in. I'm finishing up in the back and we can head out."

Jez eyed her with sudden suspicion. The elf sure was good at hiding her true feelings about the situation. "You sure you want to?" She stood there on the cold street, not moving.

"What's wrong with you? Come inside already," Taenya said, looking directly at her. "It's cold."

It was cold. Jez had no argument there.

Jez uprooted her boots and forced herself past her friend

into the bakery. Taenya closed the door behind them and locked it.

"What do you mean, do I want to?" the elf asked as she walked toward the counter and retrieved a brown paper bag. "You're the one who doesn't want to compete. Not me. Stop projecting."

The fennex blinked three times. She wasn't projecting. Was she? Jez grumbled to herself and pushed away the possibility. "I shook on it with that guy."

Taenya turned and chuckled. "You made a hasty bet with a *drunk* person. It's not a magically binding contract."

"You sound like Doli." Jez rolled her eyes and planted her hands on her hips, but she was glad not to be discussing her emotional state.

"Doli is smart. You should listen to her," Taenya said and held out the package to Jez.

She took it and said, "What's this?"

"We already sold out this morning," Taenya said. "But Arleta held these back for you."

Jez unfolded the top of the bag to find half a dozen frosted spice cookies inside. She quickly popped one whole in her mouth to ease the stress, something she'd normally take care of with a swig of rum.

As Jez chewed the spicy molasses cookie, Taenya retrieved her coat from a hook on the wall.

"But if your fox pride won't allow you to back out," Taenya said, "I'm going to take advantage of the situation. Because I, for one, *want* to take part in the Yule Games."

It wasn't pride. Not exactly. Just the fennex way of doing

things, particularly in *her* family. If they'd made a promise or a bet, they were obligated to follow through, drunk or not. Jez had been unable to fulfill obligations once, and for damn sure she didn't want to go through that again.

Now if Taenya had said she didn't want to participate in the Games, that would be a different story. Jez would drop out in a heartbeat, even if it meant losing twenty silver over the bet.

But instead, Taenya hooked her hand onto Jez's arm and pulled her toward the exit. "You can always change your mind before we get there."

Jez ate another cookie.

✧

She could have sworn the temperature had dropped even further since she'd left the bookshop, which would normally make her more agitated. And in the back of her mind, she still doubted Taenya actually wanted to be there. But walking next to the elf made Jez feel calmer despite the ever-growing crowds.

Being around *all* her friends usually made her feel better about life…that is, if she didn't need a break from them too.

"After we sign up, we'll need to develop a strategy," the elf said. "We can go back to the bakery and hash it out."

"A strategy?" Jez asked, stopping in her tracks.

Taenya pulled her along. "Of course. As much as my brother back in Langheim pushed me too far, he always helped me anticipate the challenges the Baking Battle judges might throw out. I won all three years that I competed, and those sessions were a big part of why."

The fennex hadn't considered any sort of strategy. She should have if she actually wanted to come in ahead of Ronan's team, but she'd been too caught up in worrying about everything else. During the Baking Battle, she'd mostly taken the time to relax. It was the first time that no one had known who she was. In their eyes she was simply Jez, a random fennex from the Southern Desert. She'd barely even looked at the schedule between naps. Of course, meeting Doli and Arleta had caused some commotion, but no eyes had been on her, and it was good to do something she'd wanted to try without the stress of anyone caring.

"You okay with that?" Taenya asked, interrupting Jez's thoughts. "We can work on it over lunch."

Jez looked around and spotted the registration booth. "Sure, that works. But let's get signed up first."

"Of course," Taenya said. "One thing at a time."

But just then trouble approached—Ronan. Without her vision and judgment clouded by rum, the ginger-haired man looked bigger and stronger than he had the previous night. Brady walked a few paces behind him.

"Well, if it isn't our lovebirds," he said in a jovial tone, holding his registration paper. "On your way to sign up to lose that twenty silver? You two could always back out now and save yourselves the embarrassment."

Jez's stomach dropped. But she spotted the humans' names written at the top of their paper: Ronan and Brady O'Brien. In seeing it, something snapped her mind back into a different place. The person who pretended nothing could hurt her. The person who wasn't going to let fear hurt the ones she cared about. All the anxiety she'd experienced that morning vanished.

"I think it's you that might want to reconsider," she said, her neck burning with anger. She stepped toward the two men with her chest puffed out like a winter-ready bird.

"Okay, okay," Taenya said, putting her hand up between Jez and Ronan. "I think we're done here."

But Jez didn't back down, though she knew she should have. Even sober, she couldn't stand something about that man.

"Last chance to sign up for the Yule Games!" called a woman at the registration table, and Jez's head whipped toward her.

"You better get over there," Ronan goaded with a ridiculous grin on his lips, while Brady just stood nearby.

Taenya tugged on Jez's arm. "Let's go." As they walked away, she whispered into Jez's ear, "What's gotten into you? Are you sure you want to do this?"

It was the out she needed, but instead of taking it, Jez opened her big mouth and said, "Oh, we're doing it, all right." The words were a little too loud, and she glanced back at Ronan, who gave her a scowl.

Aware that Ronan's eyes were on them, Jez marched right up to the table. "Sign us up," she nearly shouted.

The woman smiled and handed them two pieces of paper and a quill. "Fill this out. The fee is two silver." She had a wooden name tag on that read "Naura."

Jez and Taenya simultaneously dug in their pockets, produced the coins, and held them out.

"This is because of me, so I'll pay," Jez said.

"I don't mind," the elf insisted.

Jez tucked her coins into the woman's hand while Taenya grabbed the papers.

The registrar looked back and forth between the women before she spoke. "The first page is basic information, rules, and waivers just in case you're injured in the events, though I assure you that we do have a wizard healer tent on-site. Just fill that one out now and sign it. The second needs to be turned in before noon. Most people weren't expecting it, so we're allowing extra time."

"What is it?" Taenya asked as she placed the first paper on the table and signed it.

"Oh, something new and fun," the woman said in a cheery tone. "This year we thought some contestant stories would add interest to the festivities."

Jez looked down at the paper in Taenya's hand, her bravado fizzling.

Naura continued, "So you'll tell us a little bit about yourselves and why you're teammates."

"Like what?" Taenya asked, her eyebrows scrunched.

A pit drilled its way into Jez's stomach at the elf's expression.

"Such as how you met. You two are girlfriends, right? I overheard that ginger-haired man talking to you."

Jez and Taenya looked at each other and said, "Yes?"

"Then it should be easy," Naura said. "How you met,

how long you've been together. Really whatever you want to share."

Nothing? Jez thought as she furrowed her brows in confusion. "But how will everyone know what we put down?" She glanced at the first paper with the rules. The first was that magic was explicitly forbidden in order to level the playing field. Not even looking at the rest, Jez signed the document and pushed it toward Naura.

"Oh," she said, waving her hand in the air like it was no big deal. "The ceremony host will introduce you all in front of the audience tonight. Everyone is loving the drama of it all."

Jez gulped. She didn't want anything to do with drama. She had enough drama in her own mind.

And there wasn't enough rum in the world to make that okay.

7

With the second paper in Taenya's hand, the two women made their way through the crowds back to the bakery.

Jez's heart was pounding. Everything about them was going to be announced to the whole town? She should have backed out after all.

"We have to come up with a story about *us*. We can deal with strategy later." The elf shut the door and locked it once they were both inside.

The clank of the mechanism latching sounded like thunder in Jez's ears. Her mouth was as dry as desert sand and her insides twisted into knots. Why had she called Taenya her girlfriend in the first place? It was complicating everything. "Maybe we broke up this morning," she blurted. "In the end, whatever our relationship is, it's nobody's business."

Taenya leaned against the counter. "Right. But we've already inadvertently told people we're dating. So if we've broken up, then we have to play that part. I'm not sure it would be any easier."

"It would be easier if we were still just friends," Jez said flatly as she hung her coat up by the door.

The elf pursed her lips as if in thought. "We are, of course, but what kind of story is that for the spectators? I say since we got ourselves into this…we should have a good time with it. People like an exciting drama at these kinds of things."

Jez's eyes widened in surprise. "What do you mean?"

"I think we should play with this whole debacle," Taenya said, removing her own coat and setting it aside. "What if we stop stressing out and just go with it?"

The fennex stared at the elf for a moment. What if she was making a big deal out of nothing? "So you're not mad at me for what I did last night?" Jez said, her tail drooping on the wood-planked floor.

The elf beamed, and the corners of her eyes crinkled. "You're one of my best friends, and you made a mistake." She looked the fennex up and down. "It's obvious that you're already making yourself pay for it, but there's no need. We can do this. And the competition will give us some time to get to know each other better." She took Jez's upper arm. "Look. You like baking, I like baking, and the bakery is closed. I have ingredients for some new muffins I've been wanting to try. Let's make them together and figure this whole thing out." A glint formed in her eye. "And playing to the crowd will be fun."

Jez didn't really want to play to the crowd, but the idea of baking instantly made her feel better. Back home that was often her escape. She hadn't done as much of it since moving to Adenashire since she could usually come to the bakery for free pastries. Fishing had kind of taken baking's place…but with the lake swarming with tourists and competitors, that was out. The fennex nodded and followed her friend to the kitchen.

If nothing else, it would get her mind off what she'd committed to.

"I've been wanting to make some cranberry orange muffins. It's a pretty standard recipe but not something we've offered yet." Taenya placed the backstory paper down on the counter and dug through the cupboard. She pulled out a jar of dried cranberries as well as some brightly colored orange peel, then gestured to the shelf holding stacked bowls. "Can you grab one of those?"

Doing as she was asked, Jez realized that the morning's stress was draining away. "You're really not bothered by all this?" The fennex set a large wooden bowl on the counter and grabbed a spoon from a nearby drawer.

"I love baking." Taenya eyed her friend. "Why would I be bothered by it?"

"You know what I mean," Jez groaned.

Taenya removed some orange extract and a few other ingredients from an upper shelf, then flipped up the lid on the nearby flour bin. "When I was a child, I had the biggest imagination. I could get lost in making up stories for hours about the adventures my imaginary friends and I would go on."

"Why were your friends imaginary?" Jez asked while taking the bowl and spoon over to the elf. Although they had known each other for more than nine months, she hadn't been privy to much about Taenya's past. She had an overbearing brother, but that was about all Jez knew.

And the elf definitely knew almost nothing about her past. No one did. Not the whole truth, anyway.

While Taenya prepared a muffin tin with butter she said, "My family, my parents, brother and me, are"—she thought for a second as if searching for the right word—"quite serious by nature, and there was always pressure to be the best at everything we did. So there wasn't a lot of time for friends." She lit the oven and closed the door to let it heat up. "Everything we did had to be perfect. We were required to look perfect, act perfect. Including our hobbies...even baking. Nothing was only about fun." She measured out the muffin ingredients while Jez watched, engrossed in her story.

Taenya continued, "So imagine when my parents discovered that my magic was an asset to baking and cake decorating. They assigned my older brother to make sure I'd win the Baking Battle one day, and he arranged lessons for me. Of course, the competition is well-known all over the Northern Lands, but in Langheim it eclipses everything else when it rolls around for the year."

"Assigned?" Jez asked as she leaned her hip on the counter's edge. "That sounds pretty formal."

"Because it was," she said as she dumped flour into the bowl. "My parents traveled a lot on ambassadorships for Langheim, so it often rested on me and Vesstan to represent the family name. Even when we became adults, he still acted like he was in charge of me. I could barely stand him at the Baking Battle. He was in my face every day telling me I needed to win."

"Your parents are ambassadors?" Jez's voice nearly hitched, then she cleared her throat.

"Mm-hmm." She added the sugar. "They missed the Battle every year I competed because of it. It was so import-ant for me to win for the family name, but not important for them to be there. Part of me wanted to walk out on the whole thing, but I knew if I won, I could take the prize and leave. And that's what I did. I couldn't stand the expecta-tions anymore." Taenya looked up at Jez. "Will you get the vanilla?" She gestured to a shelf with several clear bottles of baking extracts.

Jez retrieved it from the shelf and removed the cork stop-per. The nutty, sweet aroma hit her nose even though she was still repressing her scent magic. "How much?"

Taenya shrugged. "You're a baker. What do you think?"

The fennex inhaled the vanilla's scent again to determine how strong it might be, then eyed the mixed ingredients already in the bowl. After a quick assessment, she poured what would amount to one and a half spoonfuls. "I think that's right. I like a strong vanilla flavor."

The elf mixed in the vanilla, and the entire concoc-tion smelled delicious. The bright citrus of the orange, the tartness of the cranberry, and just the right amount of earthiness from the spices. Then there was a chaser of vanilla at the end that brought the fennex into a more relaxed state.

"But even with all that, you still like to bake?" Jez asked, not knowing how much she'd want to bake if it were practically forced on her.

Taenya kept stirring until everything was completely mixed. "I had expected to give it up. But when I came here and Arleta asked me to partner with her, something in me shifted. I'd forever loved baking…I just didn't enjoy being forced. Getting to bake like I want to is a complete relief."

Her last word caught Jez off guard, and she licked her lips. Relief was always one of Taenya's primary scents… when Jez was paying attention.

"What's interesting about that?" Taenya asked, glancing up from her mixing.

Jez gulped. "What do you mean?"

"I said something you found interesting," Taenya said, not looking away from the fennex.

Jez's neck flushed hot. She didn't like to remind her friends that she could smell their emotions on them. She did tease Doli about it occasionally, but they lived together and that was different. But the elf continued looking at her for an answer, so Jez finally admitted, "Relief has an unusual scent. I can't quite describe it."

Taenya returned to her mixing, then looked up again. "And I'm guessing that's how I smell?" She gave a quick smirk. "I hope it's not bad."

The fennex tipped her head. "It's not." She twisted her

lips for a moment. "It's like nothing I can describe exactly…except possibly like the scent right after the sun sets and the light is disappearing beyond the horizon."

The elf gaped at Jez. "You can smell the sunset?"

Jez blinked twice. "You can't?"

"No. No, I can't," Taenya said. "But its sounds amazing, and if I knew what relief smelled like, I'm sure 'sunset' might describe it."

Blood flushed in Jez's cheeks, and she shrugged. Sometimes she forgot that most people had nowhere near the sense of smell she did. "All right, let's get these muffins in the oven." Jez took the bowl and spoon over to the muffin tin and started filling the cups. "I think these might be good with a crumb topping," she said.

Taenya's green eyes lit up. "Ooh…then how about an orange drizzle over the top?" She gathered a smaller bowl from the shelf and began dumping in the ingredients for the topping. It came together quickly, and not long after Jez filled the baking cups, Taenya was sprinkling the topping on each one. "Perfect," she said, eying them. "I love a team effort."

"Well, get used to it, I guess," Jez said as she opened the heated oven and placed the muffins inside. "But you did most of the work." It had been fun though, as had hearing some of Taenya's story. A good distraction, at least.

The elf wiped her hands on a cotton cloth and then tossed it aside on the counter. "That should take around twenty-five minutes." She plucked the waiting paper and held it in the air. "Just enough time to fill this out."

Jez groaned.

"Come on." Taenya waved her to the table in the corner. "Let's weave something *juicy*."

"Juicy?" The space between Jez's brow wrinkled.

Paying her no mind, Taenya grabbed a pencil and plopped down in a chair. "Yeah, juicy. What if we had been dating in secret all this time since the Baking Battle and no one knew about it?" She leaned in across the table. "Something torrid."

Jez sat quietly and slumped back in her seat, crossing her arms. "If you must know, I kind of hated you in Langheim. I basically wanted to kick your ass."

Taenya kept her gaze on the paper and said with a jest in her tone, "Oh, everyone hated me. Me included."

"Arleta didn't."

"Arleta was not thinking clearly at the Baking Battle." Taenya tsked and then let out a little laugh. "Because she should have."

The fennex quirked her lip to one side. "You don't mean that."

"You're right. I don't. If it weren't for Arleta, this"— she waved her hand in the air—"wouldn't have happened. Aaaannd…how would we have ended up dating without her?" The elf smirked at Jez.

"You're having too much fun with this." Jez's tone was flat with faux annoyance.

"I can't have our friends have better love stories than we do!"

It was true. Arleta and Theo were Fated, the orcs had

been together for decades, and Doli had saved Sarson from a murderous wizard.

"You're right." Jez reached across the table and took the pencil from Taenya. "Let's do this."

So they spent the next hour in the bakery, inspired by their competitive natures (mostly Taenya's) and the fragrance of cranberry orange muffins—which were delicious, by the way—weaving their story, along with an agreement on their boundaries and comfort levels when it came to the actual fake relationship.

8

The planning session had not been nearly as bad as Jez thought...until it was.

Feeling jittery after her time spent with Taenya, Jez tucked the paper into her inside coat pocket and made her way from the kitchen to the front door.

She needed a drink. But that was out of the question, of course.

And Jez needed to get out of the shop. With her back turned, she held out her shaking hands. She couldn't have the elf noticing something was wrong and asking about it. The fact that Taenya had shared a private life story would probably mean that she'd expect Jez to reciprocate at some point, and the fennex needed to think about what she was willing to share. What was safe? It was easier when people didn't know about her. She was just Jez.

To tell something right then, Jez would have to lie, and she didn't enjoy doing that.

A fresh start was better than dwelling on the past. But people often didn't allow that sort of thing: Friendship didn't work that way, and Jez knew it.

"Are you sure you don't want me to go with you?" Taenya followed behind her carrying a small brown bag.

The fennex shook her head, trying hard to ignore the buzzing in her chest and hands. "No…no need. I'm going to drop this off"—she patted the tan woolen fabric over her pocket—"and then get back to my apartment for a nap before all the stars break loose tonight." A nervous laugh slipped out. She'd tried to make it sound like a joke, but nothing about it had come out right. Jez sounded nothing like herself.

"Just need a little time to myself," she managed while staring out the window where clusters of people and vendors waited, already making merriment. Jez shuddered at the sight of them.

While holding out the bag to Jez, Taenya looked up at the clock on the rear wall of the bakery. Her normally pale skin was flushed.

Was Taenya embarrassed? Or something else? Jez didn't know, but it was as if something deeper had changed between them while filling out the paperwork and agreeing on their "relationship" rules. And Jez didn't like it. She didn't like change. At all. So she'd made extra sure to block any scent Taenya might give off since she didn't really want to know what was going on with her.

It made her head hurt.

Jez took the bag, held it up, and nodded. "But thank you for this."

"You made them too," Taenya said. "It's only fair to split them. And there's plenty in the back for the orcs." She let out an awkward laugh.

The sack crinkled beneath Jez's clawed fingers. She allowed the aroma of the still slightly warm muffins inside the bag to enter her nostrils. She loved orange-flavored anything. Unable to help herself, she opened it up to see the two large muffins, speckled with a generous buttery crumb topping. Her stomach rumbled at the sight, but she quickly rolled the top down again. She had to leave.

"Make sure you get the paperwork in before noon."

"I heard what Naura said too," Jez said and reached for the door handle.

"Our registration isn't complete until the second half of the form is turned in. And they close at noon." Taenya clasped her hands behind her back. "I *could* go with you, and then you could go take your nap."

Jez eyed her. "You don't trust me, do you?"

"I trust you," Taenya said with a hint of indignation. "But you only have fifteen minutes. And you seem a little nervous."

"Then I should get going." Jez opened the bakery door, the bell ringing as cold air rushed in. The icy temperature hit her nose and forced the hair on her tail to stand up.

Everything in her wanted to close it again and stay in the warm shop, but she pushed herself through the opening.

Taenya's boot steps clunked on the wooden floor behind her. "And the banquet starts at 6:00 p.m. I'll meet you and the others outside the hall at 5:30 so we can get decent seats."

And listen to them announce everything we dreamed up in the last hour about what supposedly brought us together, Jez thought as she gulped. *How can Taenya act like this is no big thing?* The whole town of Adenashire, including hundreds of tourists, would look at them as a romantic couple. She'd have to put on a performance. And Jez hated performing. One of the main reasons she'd even moved from the Southern Desert was so she wouldn't have to do that anymore.

"I'll see you there," Jez said, keeping her voice as steady as possible without even looking back.

Once outside, still holding the paper bag, she wrapped her arms around herself and put her mind in the state that allowed her to get through the crowd as if in a tunnel of her own. But she couldn't seem to repress her sense of smell as much as usual. Likely due to the sheer number of people and the unfamiliar scents that came with each one of them.

The aromas of the individuals, as well as the street vendors with their carts full of spicy hot drinks, savory sausage, meat pies filled with potatoes and carrots, and smoky popped corn covered in caramelized sugar accosted her nose. And those were just a few of the smells. During the entire journey back to the Games registration, Jez's mind swirled like a dust tornado.

Her head pounded, and each step made her limbs feel heavier.

"Oh," Naura said, all bundled up in her coat, knitted hat, and warm-looking winter gloves. "You're back." The woman's cheeks were nearly as rosy as a pair of cherries. She seemed to be packing up the table and placing everything in a wooden crate behind her. "I was almost ready to go since no one has come in the past hour."

Jez was surprised to find herself there already; she barely remembered the walk apart from the ghost of all the scents still lingering at the back of her nose.

All she wanted to do was get back to her room, her plain room with limited stimulus. But then she remembered the explosion of Doli's Yule decorations she'd have to wade through before making it to her sanctuary. Jez groaned.

"Yes. I'm back." Focusing on what she was there to do, she fumbled around with her free hand and found the folded slip in her pocket. "Here's the rest of it."

The woman took the paper and searched for its mate in a stack she hadn't yet put away. Then she produced two blue tickets with the words "Yule Games Banquet" in scrolled letters and handed them to Jez. "These are for tonight's dinner. They'll get you into the seating area with the other teams."

Jez grasped them but almost immediately wanted to hand them back. "How…how many teams are there?"

"Twenty-four," Naura said and placed the rest of the papers and items on the table into the crate. "You'll find out your number tonight. Good luck!" Her voice was incredibly chipper. Considerably more chipper than Jez felt she could handle.

But she forced a grin anyway, showing off her fangs. "Um, thanks?"

Naura looked up and her eyes widened, probably alarmed by the strained, fangy expression. Jez just didn't have it in her to do any better.

"You have a good day, okay?" Naura said.

"Sure." Jez tucked the tickets in the same pocket the form had occupied.

But she wasn't having a good day already…and it would not get any better until the Games were over.

The walk back to the bookstore was like torture. Jez struggled to breathe as she made it through the people— halflings, ogres, a few elves, a scattering of other races from all over the Northern Lands, but mostly humans.

But no other fennex. And because of that, she was glad. Jez would have smelled them immediately if there were. Fennex were desert people, and traveling north into the colder regions did not appeal to the vast majority of them. Including herself. But some motives transcended climate.

Finally, the bookstore came into sight with the Closed sign in the window. Good. No one would be there, and she was pretty sure Doli would have gone to Sarson's by now.

Her stomach rumbled, and she clutched her bag of muffins more tightly as she rounded to the back alleyway to let herself in.

Once inside, she stepped past the open office door.

"Ready to lose, fennex?" came Verdreth's jolly voice.

Jez froze and turned her head to the orc. She said nothing while her tail drooped to the floor.

Her boss sat at his desk with a pile of receipts to his right and a steaming bowl of something on his left. The scent of savory chicken and noodles hit Jez's nose a second later.

As he took in her appearance, his mischievous grin sagged, and he stood. "Are you all right?" The large green orc came around the desk toward her.

"Do I look all right?" Jez asked, not even trying to be polite.

"No." At least the orc was honest. "What happened?" He pushed his spectacles up on his nose. "Did someone hurt you? Do I need to do something about it?"

If Jez had been in an even slightly better mood, she probably would have laughed, or at minimum cracked a smile. Verdreth and Ervash were some of the gentlest people in her life, honorary dads not only to Arleta, but to everyone in her friend group. But when they got protective…

"No, Verdreth. Thanks. I appreciate the sentiment," Jez said. "But what I really need is a nap."

The orc leaned in, eying her. "You sure?"

"Yes." It was a lie of course. But other than herself, there was no one Verdreth could "go after" to make it all better. And if he did, Jez wasn't sure he'd know what to do when he got there. The guy was a big softy. He'd probably just give them a talking-to.

Case in point, Verdreth got a sudden glint in his eye and said, "I have just what you need." He turned back into the office and plucked up the bowl of soup. "Ervash dropped this off so I could finish getting some work done before tonight. But my mind isn't into balancing the books, and

I'm heading out." He shoved the large bowl of soup at Jez, who struggled to take it with one hand already holding muffins.

"I…I…" Her first thought was that she didn't want the soup, but as the steam of the sloshing liquid reached her nose, the rosemary and thyme made her think differently.

All she'd had that day were muffins, eggs, and Doli's custard toast. So, could be the sugar was getting to her. The chicken soup caused her stomach to rumble again.

Noticing her difficulty, the orc gently pulled the bowl back out of her hands. "I'll carry it," he said. "You've had a hard day and it's barely past noon. Really, it's the least I can do."

Jez let out a long stream of breath and nodded.

Verdreth grinned and placed his massive free hand on her shoulder, then escorted her through the bookshop and up the stairs to the apartment…with only a little of the soup spilling along the way.

Once inside, Verdreth gasped behind her. Jez simply gritted her teeth as the decor accosted her eyes. The place was like a fairy exploded with sparkly Yule magic all over it.

"Doli" was all Jez said under her breath.

"Well," the orc said wryly, "I didn't think *you* did it."

Clutching her muffins, Jez made her way over to her bedroom door. If she could simply make it inside, she'd be safe.

"I don't know," Verdreth said from behind her. "I kind of like it."

"Traitor," Jez mumbled while reaching for the handle, not intending for Verdreth to hear her.

He chuckled. "But of course I could see one of your disposition not appreciating the festivity of it all."

The fennex gritted her teeth. "I need a nap. After that it won't be so bad anymore. And Doli likes it."

"Yes, yes." Verdreth pushed the door open, revealing Jez's neatly made bed. "Now that's better." He gestured for Jez to go in and took the muffin bag from her. "You have a seat, and I'll get this all settled for you."

Barely thinking, Jez pulled off her boots, letting them clunk to the floor. Then off came her coat, but not before she'd pulled the two blue tickets from her pocket and handed them to Verdreth.

"Give these to Taenya," Jez said. Then she dropped the coat next to the shoes.

"No problem." The orc arranged the soup and muffin bag on Jez's side table, then he pulled down her blanket. Eyelids heavy, the fennex crawled into bed. Verdreth drew the blanket up around her shoulders and patted her on the head.

"There you go," he whispered. "Your soup is right there."

"And my orange muffins?" Jez muttered, already half asleep.

"Is that what that is?" the orc asked.

"Don't eat them." Her eyelids shut, and sleep quickly began to take hold.

"Who do you take me for?" Verdreth chuckled. He likely knew *exactly* what she took him for. "Sleep tight."

And that was the last thing she heard.

9

Jez pulled the blanket up higher and rolled over in her warm, cozy bed. While asleep, she hadn't even dreamed—at least none she remembered—which was refreshing since she often dreamed about life back home. The thought of her former life made her shudder, and her eyes fluttered open to a dark room.

Verdreth must have shut the curtains before he left.

But as her mind came into focus, she realized the room was not just naptime dark…it was *dark* dark. Only faint light came through the top of the curtains onto the ceiling.

How long had she slept?

Panic welling in her chest, Jez tossed off the blanket and sat up. She reached for the matches and lantern that sat on her side table, but instead her hand plunged into something wet.

Cold chicken soup.

The briny scent hit her nose, and Jez jerked her hand back, knocking the crinkly muffin bag to the floor in the process.

"Shit," she groaned and flicked what was likely a noodle from her finger and away from her bed. Whatever it was produced a faint splat on the ground. Undeterred, Jez fumbled around on the table, her eyes adjusting to the dim room, and finally made out the form of the lantern and matches. She plucked the matchbox, pinched a match from it, and struck it on the side of the box, the small flame lighting up the room. In the next second, she lit the lantern.

Sure enough, on the floor sat a gloppy white noodle, along with two muffins rolled out of the bag next to it. But none of that mattered at the moment. She was late meeting Taenya. Or at least she might be. What if she'd missed the banquet entirely?

Eyes wide, the fennex jumped to her feet and ran to the window. She threw back the curtain to reveal the night sky and a steady stream of people walking toward the village center. The banquet hall was that way. Maybe it wasn't too late.

"I don't even want to do this damn thing," Jez muttered. But the thought of breaking her word to Taenya grated on her.

Heart racing, Jez snatched her boots and coat from the floor and ignored the noodle and muffins. Those were a problem for another time. On the way out the bedroom door she somehow pulled on the boots and threaded her arms into the coat, deliberately ignoring the Yule explosion in their living room. She grabbed a look at the clock. 5:35 p.m.

It was later than she'd wanted to sleep, but she could still get to the banquet hall on time. Her mind flashed with a vision of Taenya waiting for her on the snowy street, scowling and frustrated with her. Maybe even thinking Jez had backed out.

But Jez was a fennex of her word. No way would she let Taenya down if she could help it. But what if she couldn't help it? The thoughts flip-flopped, allowing self-doubt to creep in. She was going to be a terrible partner…teammate. And if she'd needed a four-hour nap after virtually zero physical effort this morning, she simply could not imagine having the stamina to push through the Games.

Jez froze for a blink with her hand on the door handle. She wasn't the easiest person to get along with. There was no arguing that fact. What if by the end of the competition none of her friends liked her anymore? It might happen. But she cast aside the thoughts and made her way out, down the stairs and out the back exit of the bookstore into the frosty, starlit evening.

The acrid scent of crackling flames coated the insides of her nostrils as she wove through the crowd toward the center of Adenashire. It wasn't long before she approached a group gathered next to a fire and playing some kind of dice game she'd never seen before.

"We'll start taking bets as soon as all the teams are announced," came a familiar deep voice, and Jez recognized the speaker. It was one of the drunken humans who'd been with Ronan and his brother the previous night. His name might have been Landon.

Gambling always made competitive events more interesting. She was sure the Baking Battle had its share of wagers, but she'd paid no attention to the matter. But something about hearing them talk about it caught her attention. Especially since it was coming from one of Ronan's friends.

But she didn't have time to eavesdrop on any more of the conversation; every second wasted made her later and twisted a sudden knot in her back tighter.

A shortcut opened up where the outdoor market was usually held. A few vendor stations were already set up for what would be a massive Yule Market throughout the entire Games.

"Get yer sausage!" One seller directly in front of her was hawking sausages on a stick, and the aroma of roasted pork, fennel, and a hint of spice tickling her nose reminded her she'd never actually eaten any of the chicken soup Verdreth had given her. And it had been most of the day since she'd eaten anything at all.

Forcing herself on, she hoped whatever was served at the banquet would be just as good.

In moments, her destination was in sight. She'd actually never been inside the tall building before but had seen it many times walking through town. Sometimes couples held weddings and parties there, and Taenya had delivered quite a few custom cakes to the location in the past few months.

Thinking about cakes, the aroma of icing sugar met her nose, and she slowed her pace. It tracked behind her and she twisted her head toward the smell.

Past young gnomes, Jez spotted a head of bobbed auburn hair and a pair of pointed ears.

"Taenya," she called, relieved to see her teammate and friend.

The elf turned. "I was headed to the bookstore to check where you were," she called and made her way to Jez. "I was worried."

"Worried?" The words took Jez by surprise.

"Yes, *worried*." The elf arrived at the fennex's side, and she took her by the elbow. "What happened? Did you get sick?" Her tone was stressed.

Jez didn't want to admit what happened. That she'd been completely overwhelmed and needed a nap to recover. "I lost track of time."

Taenya clicked her tongue. "Well, the others are saving us two seats, but some badgers kept eyeing them when I got up. So I have no idea if they've been able to fend them off while I came to look for you."

"The orcs couldn't handle the job?" Jez joked to lighten the mood.

Taenya wrinkled her forehead. "Badgers have pretty sharp teeth." She laughed and pulled Jez along. "I'm glad you're okay."

The knot in Jez's stomach loosened slightly, and her chest warmed despite the cold air. She knew her friends cared, but tolerance tended to wane if one's shortcomings came out too often. She could only hope agreeing to enter the Games wouldn't cost her more than twenty silver in the end.

"Tickets," a hairy minotaur said as they approached the entrance.

Taenya reached in her pocket and produced the pair of blue tickets.

The minotaur squinted to look at the paper, nodded, and gestured the two women into the hall.

The aromas of rich food immediately wafted into Jez's nose, making her mouth water and stomach growl. She gazed up at the high ceiling where large painted paper snow-flakes hung from the rafters, as well as the same magical fairy lights Doli had put up in the apartment, giving the room an enchanted ambiance.

If one liked that kind of look.

Decorations aside, the inside of the banquet hall reminded her a lot of the Tricky Goat: warm wooden floors, a bar in the corner, and lengthy family-style tables. Food and drink servers with white aprons flitted around the place with trays in hand.

Most of the tables were full, and the guests' chatter made it difficult for Jez to focus. There must have been at least a hundred and fifty people in the room. So with only twenty-four teams, tickets for the opening banquet had obviously been available for purchase.

Her head spun with the sight of all the people, not to mention the kaleidoscope of their individual scents. She clamped that portion of herself down with some regret because she knew the food wouldn't be nearly as tasty.

"Why would anyone willingly come to one of these parties?" Jez muttered. She considered heading to the bar for a drink until she spotted Ronan roaming at the back of the hall.

No. Rum was out until the Games were over.

Taenya acted like she didn't hear the question. "Over there is where I usually set up cakes," she said, pointing to the back left corner of the room. The space sat beside a large stage lit with fairy lanterns and multiple giant rolled-up parchments hanging lengthwise in the air. There had to be more than twenty, but she turned to the elf before counting them all.

"I'm sure that's nice," Jez managed before she caught sight of Arleta waving her hand high to catch their attention.

They'd been able to commandeer a long table positioned directly in front of the stage. Two seats were still open beside her and Theo, while Doli, Sarson, and the orcs sat across from her. Two tables over sat a pair of large badgers, who Jez surmised must have been the ones vying for their spots.

More servers appeared from several doors around the hall, each holding large trays piled with chicken, potatoes, meat pies, and, yes, sausages that at least *looked* as if they smelled delicious.

A frustrated growl rumbled at the back of Jez's throat.

"Come on." Taenya took her hand and pulled the fennex toward their friends.

"You made it," Verdreth said as he devoured a buttered roll from a basket in the middle of the table. "I told Taenya I didn't think you'd still be asleep, but that's where I'd left you."

"You weren't still asleep, were you?" Ervash asked. He wore a half-unbuttoned, flimsy white cotton shirt and no sweater in sight.

Jez gave the orcs a forced smile and pulled out the wooden chair next to Arleta. "I was just running late."

"I found her out in the snow," Taenya said as she took off her coat and hung it on the back of her chair.

Jez eyed the elf, who wore what appeared to be a freshly knitted sky blue sweater, since she hadn't seen it before. Not that she noticed that sort of thing. The fennex tipped her chin to Doli and Sarson and gave Theo a wave before removing her own coat and sat.

"Please, everyone, find your seats," Mr. Figlet said from the stage. A quokkan and the local outdoor market owner, the marsupial wore a smart woolen suit. A few tables over Jez spotted another quokkan who must have been his wife, since she not only was clapping for him exuberantly but also had four younglings seated around her.

Arleta leaned over to Jez. "Is he the master of ceremonies?"

In the past, Mr. Figlet had not always been the fairest to Arleta when renting her a market booth to sell her pastries, but over the months since the Baking Battle the two of them seemed to have made peace.

Jez shrugged and clasped her hands under the table. "You know more about the Yule Games than I do." Jez's palms were damp, and she didn't really care about Mr. Figlet's part. All she wanted was to get the night over with.

"We at the Yule Games committee decided on a few changes this year that I believe you'll all like," Mr. Figlet said. "While we all enjoy our excellent food, I'll be introducing the sponsors and each of the teams participating. But first we'll begin with a surprise."

Jez hated surprises.

"Pardon me." A woman with a tray of food brushed Jez's shoulder, and Jez leaned over to let her set a platter of mini golden roasted chickens on the table. They looked delicious with green herbs tucked under the skin, but she couldn't smell any of it.

In fact, her head was spinning again as the orcs plucked chickens with both hands and placed the roast birds on their plates.

"Save some for the rest of us, Dads," Arleta said with a grin, but her voice sounded muffled with Mr. Figlet still rambling in the background.

Doing everything possible to keep her breath steady, Jez looked to Taenya, whose eyes were on the stage as Mr. Figlet said, "And this year we'll begin by introducing the team that involves a local celebrity."

He turned and gestured behind him to the hanging scrolls. As soon as he did, one of them dropped down, unrolling to reveal what was inside—a massive portrait of Jez and Taenya.

And in the image Jez was, of all things…smiling.

10

Mr. Figlet flung his arm into the air toward the banner. "Team One, Taenya Carralei and Jez!"

Everyone in the hall applauded enthusiastically. Jez felt as if her arms were frozen to her sides. Her tail stiffened, and the hair stood on end.

The marsupial gestured to someone in the audience. "Our sincerest thanks to Ms. Oakstone for creating these lovely banners at the last minute."

Ms. Oakstone, a local artist and wizard, tossed her hands up and golden sparkles danced in the air above her head. She could create any type of portrait by simply using her magic.

Taenya turned to Jez, her brows knitted with concern. "I didn't know anything like this was going to happen," she whispered. She looked across the table at Doli, who shrugged, showing she hadn't been aware either.

When Naura told them their stories would be announced, Jez wasn't thrilled. But this? This was so much bigger than she could have imagined. Her and Taenya's smiling faces stared out from the hanging parchment for all to see.

"These two women met at the Langheim Baking Battle last year," the rotund quokkan said with a chuckle as he read from a parchment in his hands. "And apparently were *baking up* a little something of their own." He gave the audience an exaggerated wink.

Verdreth leaned in and whispered to Jez, "You two are dating?"

Arleta hushed him and said, "I'll fill you in later, Dad."

The orc bobbed his head as he cleaned a drumstick with his teeth.

People all around laughed. Many raised their glasses, some to the stage and others toward Jez and Taenya.

Heat rushed to Jez's neck, and the elf shot her a glance again, her cheeks pinker than they had been a minute before.

"When did Mr. Figlet become a comedian?" Theo asked.

Ervash, chewing on a chicken leg, said, "You give a person a willing audience…"

"And add in some wine." Verdreth held up his glass and took a swig.

Jez eyed the wine she'd only just realized was in front of her. Her dry mouth called for it, but she'd sworn off alcohol until the competition was over. Instead she grabbed the glass of water beside it and downed it.

"So these partners in real life decided at the last minute to join the Yule Games," the quokkan announced, "and plan to put up a fight to win! If you two would stand, please." He stared down at them with his brown eyes.

More thunderous applause came from the audience as Taenya eyed Jez and pushed back in her chair. Reluctantly Jez did the same and they stood together. The elf bowed her head slightly to different parts of the room. Jez did no such thing.

"Whoop!" someone hollered from the back, and Jez whipped her attention to the sound. It was Ronan and his brother.

He gave the fennex a chin tip and she twisted away, mortified. This much attention was the last thing she'd wanted. Now or ever. Jez held her breath and flopped back down in her seat.

"We'll be learning more about Team One over the course of the Games," Mr. Figlet announced, "but on to Team Two." With a flick of his wrist, the second parchment unrolled.

Jez stared at the smiling faces of two round-faced halflings while she wrung her hands together under the table. She didn't catch their names. In front of her was the giant platter of chickens, already one quarter gone due to the orcs' appetites. Another smaller platter held the sausages she'd wanted earlier, but they suddenly made her stomach turn.

"I have to go," she said under her breath and apparently caught Doli's attention.

"Now?" the dwarf asked as Sarson, looking a tad cramped with his wings tucked in tightly behind him, sat happily eating his plate of honey-roasted carrots and buttered bread and watching the show.

"Yeah, now," Jez said.

Taenya twisted to Jez. "What are you talking about?"

The fennex paused for a second as she looked at the elf. She almost wished she felt different, but the start of a headache was edging over her brow. "I don't feel well. If I'm going to do this tomorrow, I need to get out of here." Jez had made her appearance at the event and fulfilled her obligations to be there according to the rules.

"Oh, okay." Taenya looked confused but reached for Jez's coat and helped her put it on. "Then I'll see you in the morning?"

Jez nodded. "At the starting line."

"Do you want me to walk you home?" Doli asked, turning as if she planned to hop from her seat.

Arleta must have finally realized what was going on. "Everything okay?"

Jez looked back and forth between the two friends. "I just need to leave," she said, then addressed Doli. "I can make it home by myself this time." She turned to Taenya. "I'm sorry. Really."

"Don't be." The elf's voice was soft against Mr. Figlet's background chatter as he announced yet another team.

The fennex gave her another nod and made her way back down the aisle between tables.

"Is she leaving?" she heard Verdreth ask, but she took in a big lungful of air and breathed it out slowly and didn't look back.

She hated all this. She hated looking weak.

All the way through the hall Jez kept her eyes on the

wood-planked floor and kept up the deliberate breathing until she made it out the exit into the snowy night.

Somehow even the cold air felt better than being inside at that event. Not far out the door, she spotted Landon again, standing with a group around him.

Someone dressed as a server and breath puffing out like a cloud said, "The names of all the teams are being announced right now."

"Get me all of them. Plus any details," Landon said while handing the guy something.

"Yes, sir." The server turned and jogged toward the back of the building.

The fennex eyed the group, wondering how big that operation was, but she kept moving and ignored as much of her surroundings as possible.

"Jez!" Taenya's voice came from behind as the fennex trudged through the snow. "Slow down!"

Everything in her wanted to keep going. Jez wanted time to herself before life got even more complicated the next day. But the elf was her friend, and none of this was her fault.

"What?" Jez turned and snapped, even though that was not how she'd meant it to come out.

Taenya slowed and her face fell. "Never mind. Why'd I even come out here? You go home and I'll head back to the banquet to represent us." She shifted as if turning toward the hall.

"No, I'm sorry." Jez's eyes stung and tears welled up in the corners, something she hadn't allowed herself in a long time. She blinked them back. "Why did you come out here?"

"Because we're friends, Jez," she said with a slight edge to her tone. "At least I thought we were. But you're acting so strangely."

"We *are* friends," the fennex stated, ignoring the people walking past her as well as the cold biting her nose. "Look. I've had a tough day, and it's not right for me to take it out on you. I'm exhausted and haven't eaten anything since we made muffins."

The elf's expression softened. "Do you want me to make you something?"

"Make me something?"

Taenya eyed her for a shake or two. "Yes. You could come to my house, and I'll cook us dinner."

Jez could barely even process that Taenya hadn't called her silly and insisted that they go back to the banquet where the meal was already prepared.

"*That* was all a bit much." Taenya gestured with her thumb at the banquet hall. "Even for me."

The fennex had no idea if she was lying for her sake. "I have food at home."

"Yes, I'm sure you do. But I'm guessing that you'll get up there, march right past the kitchen, and crawl into bed. Then you'll end up not eating anything at all."

Jez remembered Doli's Yule decorations and let out a long breath. "You're probably right."

The elf threaded her arm through the crook of Jez's elbow. "Then that settles it. I need to take care of you."

Jez's cheeks flushed. "Why?"

A grin took over Taenya's lips. "So we can win, silly."

Taenya's cottage lay on the outskirts of town, and Jez had only been there a handful of times since moving to Adenashire. The elf had bought it with some of her winnings from the Baking Battle, those she hadn't used to buy Arleta the bakery.

Taenya pointed off into the distance as they approached. "I love this section of the walk."

Jez gazed toward the forest across the dark field.

"A couple months ago, all those trees were orange and yellow," the elf said. "When the sun was setting the entire scene glowed, almost like amber. There's a path to follow too."

Jez pulled her coat in tighter. Taenya's description sounded nice, but right then it was dark and freezing.

The cottage was nothing fancy, probably even less so than Arleta and Theo's and the orcs' modest twin homes. With the snow reflecting the moon and starlight, Jez admired the stone pathway leading to the lightly colored home trimmed with dark contrasting wood and complete with a thatched roof. Beside the door a lantern affixed to the wall cast a warm glow on the entrance.

"It's so quiet out here," Jez said, looking around at the shadowy trees and shrubs surrounding the home. And it was. In the warmer months she could imagine the buzz of insects or frogs. But in winter? The air was still. Peaceful. The atmosphere almost made Jez feel less cold. Almost.

"When I first saw this place after I arrived from Langheim, I immediately knew it was for me," Taenya said. "The prior owners were moving north and gave me a good price. There's even a firepit out back where I can sit and watch the stars at night…when it's a little warmer."

Jez was surprised to find that she actually liked the sound of that. "It had to be good to make it on your own."

The elf chuckled. "More than you know."

But Jez did know, though she said nothing.

They reached the door, and Taenya pushed it open to reveal a dark room. In moments she had several small lanterns lit and bathing the room in soft light. Magic sparked in her hand, and she tossed the enchantment toward a waiting stack of wood in the fireplace.

"That will only take a few minutes to get going," Taenya said as the small flame crackled.

"I wasn't aware you could do that." Jez watched the fire dance. She'd seen the elf work her magic on cakes, but nothing else.

Taenya clapped her hands together, and a few sparkles danced over her fingers. "In the past, I mostly used that part of me when I was angry. Did I tell you I gave Arleta a zap once?" She chuckled.

"No. When?" The heat from the fireplace had already reached Jez's face.

"At the Baking Battle, out on the castle grounds." The elf removed her coat and laid it over one of a pair of stuffed chairs. "Don't worry. I've apologized. And since I moved here, I've worked on controlling myself, so I mostly use that part of my magic for simple, useful things." She looked at the fire. "Like that."

Jez chuckled. "That's good. We have enough powerful magic in our circle since Doli's magic started to grow." She removed her own coat and hung it at the door.

At one time Doli had thought her magic was restricted to making tea, but inheriting a dragon egg and tangling with a nefarious wizard had proved that notion false. That said, Doli still mostly stuck to tea magic.

"Absolutely." Taenya walked from the small living area into a tiny kitchen and leaned her elbows on the counter. "Now, what would you like?"

Jez flopped into the chair next to the fireplace and took stock of her body. Hunger nudged her, but her energy was completely sapped. "Whatever you have is fine."

"A surprise it is, then. You stay over there until I'm ready." The elf looked around the space and then dug into the cold box. From her vantage point Jez couldn't see what she had pulled out, but as she chopped and sautéed, the aromas soon wafted throughout the house. Not wanting to eat another meal without her sense of smell, Jez dropped her guard and settled into the soft chair. She watched Taenya fly around in the kitchen for a good twenty minutes, humming.

She let her eyes travel around the space, landing on two paintings hung on opposite sides of the room. From the lush forest landscape she guessed they were Langheim. And the two chairs were covered in an expensive green fabric. Jez ran her pointer finger claw over the soft material on her chair's arm, leaving a mark that was easily removed if she swiped it the other way. But other than those items, the room was fairly sparse. Taenya had expensive but simple taste—different from Jez's, but she still liked it.

"Garlic, onion." Jez sniffed the air as the nutty, savory smells relaxed her even further. "Butter." She sniffed again. "Chicken."

"You missed one thing. Sautéed chicken thighs with parsnips and peas," Taenya said as she stood over the sizzling pan. "With butter sauce."

The elf always seemed to remember that Jez loved peas. Jez licked her lips and a little guilt nudged her to stand. "Can I help?"

Taenya nodded and gestured to a cabinet behind her. "The plates are in there if you'd like to set the table."

The fennex retrieved two plates as Taenya added another pat of butter to the pan. She swirled it around, then sprinkled salt, pepper, and dried thyme over the top and plated the meal.

Her cooking was a masterpiece, just like her cake decorating. Jez glanced up to the elf and was suddenly filled with gratitude that Taenya would make so much effort for her when she'd been so rude. But her words came out a little clumsy. "Um…looks good."

"Thank you," Taenya said and walked around to the two stools at the counter.

They sat and ate their meal in silence.

But not an awkward type of quiet…a comfortable one.

By the end Jez inhaled deeply and realized that her headache from earlier was gone. She hadn't blocked her sense of smell the entire time she was there. But nothing had overwhelmed her either.

It was the first time she'd done that in a long time.

"That was delicious," Jez managed as she finished her last bite and glanced down at the remaining butter sauce. What she really wanted to do was lick the plate…but that would be bad manners, of course.

"Thank you." Taenya rose and took their cleared plates into the kitchen. "Tea?"

Jez thought for a moment. A tiny part of her almost said she should go home, but instead she uttered, "Sure."

When it was brewed and poured, the two of them took their drinks to the living area and sat by the fire until all the tea had been drunk and Jez dozed off in her cozy chair.

Completely unbothered.

11

B ut the next morning she awoke with a crick in her
neck. And the realization that she was actually going
to be participating in the Games.

And that she'd spent the night at Taenya's cottage.

"Shit," she mumbled and looked around the room.
Taenya had gotten a new fire going before Jez had even
woken up.

The house had the buttery aroma of warm pastries and
steaming tea.

"Morning," Taenya said as Jez peeled herself from the
chair. The elf was freshly dressed in a warm-looking white
and black sweater and a pair of loose woolen pants. Her hair
was pulled back in a tiny low ponytail, except for a chunk on
the right side that didn't want to stay secure.

Jez stared at her a little too long, and something stirred in her chest. She realized that it was her heart speeding up. "You look"—she stopped and gulped the word *pretty* down—"well rested."

The elf tipped her head and squinted as if confused. "Yes. Well, I slept in a bed and not a chair."

"Um…yeah." A lock of her short, white hair flopped in Jez's face and she blew it off, but it just resettled on the opposite side. She felt uncomfortable in her own skin. Standing up, she realized that her feet were bare, so at some point she must have taken off her boots and socks. Heat prickled the back of her neck. It was silly since she and Taenya *were* friends, but Jez felt embarrassed that she'd made herself completely comfortable and fallen asleep in the elf's house all night without an actual invitation. Plus, in what land did she even *think* about calling a friend *pretty*? "Look. I'm sorry I didn't wake up and go home."

Taenya waved the apology away. "I could tell you needed a quiet evening. There's nothing wrong with that. Staying here was a good option since your house is out of sorts right now."

"Out of sorts?" *Jez* felt out of sorts.

The elf chuckled. "Doli told me about all her decorations."

"Yes. Those." Jez only shook her head. "It's a little much. But she's taking them down after the Games, I think."

"Still, after the banquet, you seemed like you needed a break." Taenya took a tray of sunny lemon-filled pastries from the counter and held it out to Jez. "Tea is keeping warm on the stove."

"Thanks." Jez chose a pastry and retrieved a plate from the cabinet, then poured herself a cup of tea. She sat on the stool closest to the fireplace and bit into her breakfast. Tart lemon burst in her mouth, and she must have made a face, because Taenya laughed.

"I think I went too heavy on the lemon," she said.

"Just a tad." Jez's mouth puckered and she drank her plain tea to wash the sourness down.

"Apparently the Games have got me off balance too, but looks like it's going to be a nice day," the elf said, then took a bite of her own pastry.

Jez watched her mouth as she chewed. Her lips had a natural pink tint that somehow perfectly complemented the yellow of the lemon filling. The fennex mindlessly munched on her own pastry, not finding it quite as tart anymore.

Oh, my stars. Jez caught herself in her thoughts. Only the morning before, she'd been upset that something had shifted between her and Taenya. But what if it wasn't the elf? Maybe Taenya was the same person she'd always been, and Jez had been reading her all wrong. *What if it's me who changed?*

The fennex gulped to swallow her bite and sniffed the room. But nothing had changed with Taenya. She still smelled like icing sugar…and perhaps a bit of anticipation for the Games? She quickly stuffed half of the pastry in her mouth and turned her attention to the large window in the living area, showing a clear view of the woods. There wasn't any more snow on the ground than there had been the night before, so it didn't look like it had stormed.

And Jez thanked the stars for that.

But not much else. She glanced at Taenya again and clamped down her sense of smell. But this problem of hers was unacceptable, and she took a deep breath to settle her mind.

Jez was only grateful to her friend, that was all. Thinking a friend was attractive wasn't a big deal. People did that all the time, right? Noticing anyone's looks didn't need to mean anything more than that. Once the silly Yule Games were over, everything would go back to normal. Like it was supposed to be.

She shoved the last of the pastry into her mouth, and without her sense of smell it was no longer sour. "Should… should we get going?" Jez managed to ask after she washed down the food with a swig of tea.

"I did want to arrive a little early to ensure we're settled," Taenya said, still munching on the rest of her breakfast.

"Okay, good…good idea." Jez's mind was a jumbled mess, and she suspected it would only get worse at the Games. But she stood and retrieved her coat from the hook by the door and threaded her arms into it. "Let's go." She turned back to Taenya.

The elf had a wry smirk on her lips and looked the fennex up and down as she gathered her own coat. "I think you're forgetting something."

"What?" Jez noticed that Taenya's eyes had dropped to the floor. Looking down, she saw her bare feet on the wooden floor. Instinctively she wiggled her toes. "Oh, yeah."

The walk into town was quiet and all too short-lived.

"Get yer sausages!" The sausage seller was out early in the market with a breakfast variety that once again looked delicious, but Jez didn't allow herself to smell them. She had a belly full of lemon pastry and tea anyway.

Spectators shuffled all around the square as the two women made their way toward the starting line, and Jez blew out a nervous breath.

"You okay?" Taenya asked.

"Why wouldn't I be?" Jez said a little too quickly as she jammed her hands in her pockets to ward off the cold nipping her fingers. In her hurry out to the banquet the night before, she hadn't put any gloves on.

Taenya dug through the sack she'd brought. "Here." She pulled out a set of black-and-white striped gloves. "You're going to need these."

Jez eyed them with longing since her fingertips already seemed like they might snap off from the cold. "No. You will too."

The elf shook her head. "I have another pair." She reached back into her bag and produced a pair of fuzzy red gloves.

Jez took the first pair and quickly put them on. "Look at you, all prepared."

"Oh, I'm nothing if not prepared." Taenya gave a quick chuckle and puffed up, looking a mite proud of herself, then donned her own gloves. "Speaking of preparedness, we never actually went over Game strategy." She kept her voice down as if to avoid being heard by anyone else.

Jez sighed, but she knew she needed to take her

participation seriously, at least to beat Ronan. All the two of them really needed to do was outplay him and his brother, and she'd get that twenty silver. She planned to give Taenya half, of course, for all the trouble. "Fine, what've you got?"

The elf's green eyes lit up. "I'm so glad you asked, because I stayed up pretty late last night thinking about it after you fell asleep."

New horror spun its way around Jez's chest at the mention of her falling asleep right in front of Taenya. She had vaguely pictured the two of them dozing off at the same time and Taenya waking up later to go to her bed…no harm done. But Jez knew for a fact that when she was exhausted, she snored.

"And yes," Taenya said. "You do snore."

With cheeks of fire, Jez whipped her attention to the elf, wanting to ask how she knew what she'd been thinking. But instead something else came out of her mouth. "All fennex snore."

It wasn't true.

Taenya laughed and waved off her response. "We all snore sometimes. Including me. I'm just glad you fell asleep first." Her eyes crinkled at the corners. "Sorry I brought it up. Now, back to strategy."

At that point, Jez was happy to talk about anything besides her snoring. "Yes, that."

Up ahead, Arleta, Theo, Doli, Sarson, and the orcs stood at the starting line. Behind it was a large field and a snow-covered hill. A small stage had been erected for announcements, and the team banners from the night before were affixed to tall poles. Jez pinched the bridge of her nose at the sight of them.

Taenya leaned in close again, and despite keeping her sense of smell at a minimum, Jez still caught a whiff of her icing sugar scent. Her stomach fluttered. *Damn lemon filling.* She firmly resisted the notion that anything else might have caused the feeling.

"Since we haven't had a chance to practice for the events themselves, I think we need to really play up the whole dating thing," Taenya said.

"What?" Jez nearly choked and stopped in her tracks. She coughed two more times to cover up what she'd said.

Taenya quickly patted her on the back. "You okay, there?"

"Uh…yeah," Jez got out. "I…I'm not sure what that was."

The elf beamed and said, "Did you notice the reaction to Figlet's silly baking puns about our"—she made air quotes with her fingers—"relationship? They ate it up."

"*Ate* it up?" Jez forced out a chuckle, not sure what else to do.

Taenya's eyes widened. "See! The puns are great. I know it's not really your thing to be so silly…but what if it's like our little inside joke? It might make the competition fun."

Jez pinched her lips together as Taenya slipped her hand through the crook of the fennex's elbow and started walking again.

"Plus, we have to have a hook," Taenya said.

"Why is that?" Jez managed.

"Didn't you read the paper with the rules?" Taenya asked.

"Um, sort of. No magic, right?"

"And this year the audience decides when contestants get extra points," Taenya said. "So even if we don't come in first, we can improve our score in other ways." She paused for a beat. "And because everyone else has cute love stories, we can compete on that basis. Arleta and Theo have the whole Fated thing, Verdreth and Ervash hated each other when they met—"

That got her attention. "They did?" Jez hadn't ever heard that story and found herself suddenly interested to know all about it.

"That's the rumor," Taenya said.

Jez made a mental note to get the full story someday.

"And Doli and Sarson...they're adorable." Taenya brought her left hand up to meet her right one at the crook of Jez's elbow.

The fennex's eyes darted to the elf's delicate hands, and words became difficult. "Not...not that I'm exactly the adorable type," Jez said flatly.

"I can take care of that part," Taenya said, fluttering her eyelashes. "Just play along."

The fennex was unsure what to do with herself. But she forced a grumble. "Do I have a choice?"

Yes. That sounded more like her.

"No." Taenya gave her a wink.

But Jez didn't have long to think about it as they crossed the perimeter of the Games area. Her eyes widened at the amount of tiered bench seating there was. She'd never had reason to venture this far south of Adenashire, so she'd had no idea the gathering area even existed. Gregarious laughter came from the crowd waiting for the start of the competition. As they approached, she spotted Ronan standing on a box in front of them, telling jokes.

She'd nearly forgotten about him.

"I was thinking the other day…why do we even bother making snowpeople?" the human said. "We spend hours gettin' 'em all gussied up for everyone to see…everything looks good…then the sun comes out. Before you know it, all that's left is a pile of sticks, some coal, and a carrot." He threw his hands in the air. "It's like winter's take on a horror story!"

Jez and Taenya groaned at the same time.

It was a terrible joke, but the crowd burst into more laughter anyway. Somehow Ronan had them eating out of his hand. Jez was even sure she saw that woman Cali from the cheating incident at the Tricky Goat having a good laugh.

Taenya shook her head. "No choice at all if you want to beat that guy."

"Piece of cake," Jez said as he started in on a new bad joke, making the group laugh even harder.

She knew it would be anything but.

12

As she stood under their banner, the wintry morning air bit at Jez's ears, and she clenched her teeth to keep them from chattering. Her tail's fur stood on end while it flicked back and forth, mostly without her permission, and she couldn't help but wonder if some kind of coat for it might be possible.

"Ugh," Jez muttered.

"You okay?" Taenya whispered, glancing back at the agitated tail.

Jez kept her gaze on the massive and ever-growing crowd and spotted the two faun youths who'd been searching for Arleta with their cards. They had an unobstructed view near the front, and each waved a small flag while cheering. A pair of adults, likely the parents, stood next to them.

"Never better," Jez managed without sounding too bitter about her current circumstances. She forced a smile, but the elf gave her a brow raise anyway.

The fennex wasn't fooling anyone.

"Welcome to the first Yule Games event," Mr. Figlet announced from the small stage decorated with a large banner declaring THE ADENASHIRE YULE GAMES overhead. The marsupial looked a bit like a trussed chicken bundled up in his winter clothes. The audience whooped and hollered with excitement. Up in the bleachers some held signs with team numbers on them or faces drawn on, looking vaguely like one of the contestants.

She didn't recognize her own nor Taenya's face on any of them.

How anyone could be excited about standing out in the cold with snow all over the ground instead of inside where it was warm was a complete mystery to Jez.

She took her eyes off the crowd and glanced back up at the ridiculous banner above them, then at the other twenty-three team banners. Down the row she saw team nine, Doli and Sarson; team twelve, Arleta and Theo; the orcs, team fourteen; and then way at the end, team twenty-four was Ronan and Brady, preening and pandering to the crowd. Jez was annoyed to see several number twenty-four signs.

The human didn't seem to let up with the jokes and laughter. He didn't even live in Adenashire, but everyone seemed to be loving it.

"Ridiculous," Jez muttered under her breath while Mr. Figlet kept blabbering on.

Not too far from Ronan stood Landon with a stack of paper and pencil, looking back and forth between the competitors, Mr. Figlet, and his notes.

Did they just catch eyes? Just for a second? What if they're into something together? Jez thought as she narrowed her gaze at the man. Something about the lot of them was definitely shifty. A growl rumbled at the back of her throat.

"You see that?" Taenya leaned in and pointed up to Mr. Figlet.

"See what?" Had she noticed Ronan and Landon too?

Taenya crossed her arms over her chest. "What Figlet said."

Jez hadn't heard a word of it. "Oh, sure. Got it all." She quickly drew her attention back to the announcer, knowing she needed to catch up.

"Today's event will be…" The quokkan paused and pinched his lips as if revealing the most important thing the Northern Lands had yet experienced…and as if the events weren't the same every year. "The scavenger hunt!"

She scoffed. *Great, we'll all run around town like ants who've discovered a honey jar.* The thought gave her a shiver, enhanced by a sudden gust of wind that kicked up some loose snow off the field behind them.

"And don't forget," Mr. Figlet said, raising his paw in the air, "today's event is sponsored by *me* and the Adenashire outdoor market." He leaned forward like he was telling the crowd a secret. "Which will transform into a Yule Market this evening after the sun goes down. There'll be plenty of food vendors, hot drinks, souvenirs, entertainment…and"—he gestured to the line of teams—"each of our competitors will be there to sign autographs and answer questions."

"We have to what?" Jez asked too loudly and the two halflings shushed her at the same time.

People in the audience were staring too.

"It's one of the things we have to attend," Taenya whispered and grabbed Jez by the waist, pulling her in close. A smile stretched over her lips as she gave the audience a little wave. "But like the banquet we don't have to stay the whole time."

Jez gulped and forced a happier expression onto her face.

Taenya's jaw softened, as did her tone. "Let's take this one step at a time. There's no need to worry about tonight before we even start the first event."

Jez could barely think with Taenya's arm around her waist, and she shook her head at herself.

"Each team will receive a sealed envelope," Mr. Figlet said. "Inside is a clue to the first destination on your scavenger hunt. When you figure out the clue and go to the correct location, you'll receive another clue. There are seven locations you must visit; gather all the clues and return to this spot to be declared the winner. But remember, the last six teams to arrive will be eliminated from the remaining events. So don't dillydally."

Jez scoffed at the ridiculous word, but elimination didn't sound so bad as long as Ronan's team came in behind them. She didn't need to win the Yule Games…just do better than *them*. And maybe the men would be really terrible at the whole thing.

As Mr. Figlet finished his announcement, five choreographed fairies dispatched from behind him in a sparkling sunburst, each carrying a stack of envelopes. Down the way Doli let out a whoop and clapped her hands at the display, leading the audience into applause, along with oohs and aahs.

Magic trailed after the group of fairies as they flew toward the contestants. Jez had no clue where they'd been hiding while the quokkan was speaking. She stood on her toes to see if there was a trapdoor or something. But just then, a fairy with curly, pink hair and tawny skin buzzed close to her face, wings buzzing like a dragonfly.

"Delivery," she said in a high-pitched tone. "Team number one." The fairy held out a cream-colored envelope larger than she was. She wore a sparkly purple sweater and matching pants. On her feet were the tiniest pair of purple lace-up boots the fennex had ever seen. Fairy magic often involved coloring ordinary things bright colors. Sometimes Doli had her nails colored with fairy magic. Jez had tried it once at the dwarf's urging but only chose black…with a *little* sparkle. "Please wait to open it until you are told to do so."

Jez stared at her for a second and then reached up to pinch the clue between her clawed index finger and thumb. Reluctantly, she flipped it to the other side where it read "Team One" in loopy handwriting.

"Thank you," Taenya said.

"Uh, yeah. Thanks," the fennex managed as the fairy buzzed off to deliver the halfling team's clue.

"My pleasure," she chirped without looking back.

"Each envelope holds a different clue," Mr. Figlet announced. "This way there can be no cheating or relying on anyone else to get ahead."

At the word "cheating," Jez glanced down the row at Ronan to make sure he hadn't opened his team's envelope yet. The bearded man only held it up while the audience near him clapped and hollered.

She narrowed her gaze at him and sniffed the air in his direction in case she might pick up anything suspicious. But all she got was a big whiff of popcorn from a nearby vendor cart.

"Let's hold hands or something," Taenya whispered into Jez's ear, interrupting her thoughts.

"What?" But Taenya had already taken her free hand.

"Our friends are looking all cute and in love." The elf gestured to their friends. The orcs, Ervash shirtless and looking snack-worthy while Verdreth gave off a friendly academic vibe. Sarson with that damn gargoyle wingspan that made passersby swoon and Doli bundled up like a toasted marshmallow and smiling from ear to ear. Then Theo and Arleta, wrapped around each other as if they were a candy twist.

And even the teams that weren't paired romantically seemed to have some kind of "hook" or other to please the crowd, like Ronan and his jokes.

Jez wrinkled her nose. There was no way she'd be able to keep up with all that. Or *think* if Taenya was trying to hold her hand all the time.

"No scowling," Taenya singsonged. "After the competition you can scowl all you want."

Jez looked down at her hand and then back at her friend. She was right. In four days this would all be over.

Mr. Figlet held out his paw and declared, "Now that everyone has their clues, I'll count to three. Then you can read them, and off you go! One…two…three!"

Jez stared at the envelope for what was apparently too long for Taenya, so the elf plucked it from her clawed fingers. She flicked open the seal and held open the paper for both of them to read. It was a riddle:

Blooms, sprigs and coiling twigs
Will tickle your fancy with a bunch so big.
Off to the village you will go
And find your next clue to keep in the know.

Jez zipped through the riddle and glanced down the row of teams again. Some were still reading, while others had already left the starting line.

"Well?" Taenya squeaked. "What is it? I'm terrible at these things. Why does it have to be a riddle?"

Jez didn't even look back at the paper. "It's the flower shop, Floral Fantasies, not too far from the bakery." She'd been pretty good with riddles ever since she was a kit.

"Ugh," the elf complained. "Of course." She grabbed Jez's hand and yanked her forward.

"Good luck," Doli yelled from behind them, but Taenya didn't slow down.

All the teams now appeared to be heading back to the center of town as the crowd cheered them on. Jez and Taenya weaved through the crowd, and Jez was grateful they were holding hands so they wouldn't get separated.

A few minutes later, the florist's shop was in sight, though in winter there weren't any flowers out front. Instead there were Yule trees...*just* like the one Doli had set up in the apartment.

It had to be where the tree in their apartment had come from.

A cloth sign hung from the storefront, with HAPPY YULE painted in bright red. The owner, a woman named Bonnie, stood out front as Jez and Taenya nearly slid into the tree display, both out of breath.

"Can I interest you in a tree?" Bonnie chirped, her cheerful demeanor pairing well with her rosy cheeks.

"No, no." Taenya held out the clue to the woman, showing her the riddle. "We're playing the Yule Games. We have this."

Bonnie stared at it for a second and started patting her coat. "Oh, yes. How lovely. Congratulations. Aren't you so excited about all the traffic the Games have brought to Adenashire this year?" She continued patting her coat and not giving them the next clue. "Sales have been wonderful."

"We're kind of in a hurry." Jez tried to keep her tone friendly but had already spotted the orcs coming out of the leather shop with their new envelope.

"No problem, no problem." Bonnie turned and looked back at the Floral Fantasies store. "It has to be around here somewhere." She looked back up at Taenya and Jez. "You're the two who met at the Baking Battle, right?"

"That's us," Taenya said, her brows knitting a sweater of concern. "Do you want us to help you?"

Jez's skin heated up, which she didn't exactly mind since it took her thoughts off the cold. For a second she gritted her fangs to hold back what she wanted to say and forced the edges of her lips upward. No scowling...like Taenya said.

Across the way, the halfling team, also with a new envelope in hand, raced away from a vendor cart selling dried meats. The fennex couldn't hold it back any longer. "Did you seriously lose our clue?"

Bonnie flicked her attention back to Jez. "Well, dear, you don't have to be quite so rude."

Jez growled and balled her fists, but Taenya hooked the crook of her elbow.

"We're in a bit of a hurry." The elf gave a nervous chuckle. "It *is* a race, you know." She coughed. "We have to *bake* good time."

The florist chuckled. "That's very cute, love."

Just then, Jez spotted the edge of a cream-colored envelope poking from the inside of Bonnie's coat. Without a thought, she reached out and grabbed it.

"Is this it?" Jez asked, holding the clue up. Now she could see the words "Team One" on it.

Bonnie giggled. "Oh yes! I think it is." She patted Taenya's shoulder. "Now, *bready*, set, go!"

"Yes!" the elf said. "No *loafing* around."

As the florist stood there cackling, the women made their getaway from the flower shop.

"Come again!" Bonnie called as Ronan and Brady jogged across the way. Ronan gave her a friendly wave.

"You think she did that on purpose?" Jez whispered as she watched the men disappear around a corner.

"The puns?" Taenya unfolded the next clue and read it aloud:

Mountains high, this beast can climb
But rather would he spend some time
With friends making merry toasts
As a generous, gracious host.

"It's the Tricky Goat," Jez said immediately. She didn't correct Taenya but still wondered if Bonnie had "lost" their clue deliberately, and if Ronan had something to do with it.

"How are you so good at this?" Taenya asked, and Jez grinned in spite of herself.

"It's easy," the fennex said as Taenya pulled her in the inn's direction.

All the riddles were just as easy for Jez. Before long they'd racked up a stack of clues, the last one from a candy vendor near the Yule Games main stage.

"I like your team. We're all calling you the Bakers," said the gnome as she handed Jez their envelope. "From what I can tell, you two are ahead."

"Really?" Taenya asked, excitement in her voice. She turned to Jez. "You hear that? We're ahead. And this is our last clue!"

The candy vendor chuckled and handed them each a

pink hard candy. "But don't tell anyone you heard it from me."

Jez popped the candy into her mouth. Maybe the Games would be easier than she'd thought.

13

The sweetness of the candy made Jez feel almost excited. At least that's what the buzzing in her chest told her. She and Taenya were making excellent time. They could win this round. "Open it!"

The elf tore off the seal and held the paper out so they could both read it.

Wander the way of a golden hue
To keep in these Games with much ado.
Into the gathering, meet in the middle.
There you will find what you seek from this riddle.

"Golden hue?" Jez glanced around at the snow-covered ground while panic rose in her throat. "There's nothing golden around here right now." Her mind was completely blank.

Taenya stood there with her mouth open, then said, "You don't know?"

"Damn it." Jez never should have gotten her hopes up so much. Nothing ever worked out that easily. All the energy she'd had now drained away as if a spell had been cast on her. "Are we really going to get taken out with the last clue?"

"Well," the candy-selling gnome called from behind them, "you should move along."

"Yes. One moment," Taenya said, her voice sounding strained as she looked at Jez. "Come on, think."

But the more Jez tried to think, the blanker her mind went.

"Wait, I think I have an idea." Taenya pursed her lips for a moment while she stared at the paper.

Jez swallowed. The elf hadn't solved any of the other six riddles.

"What if it's not golden *now* but is in the fall?" Taenya held out the paper, showing Jez the words again. "Remember I told you about those trees on the way to my house?"

"Uh. Yeah."

"There's a hiking path through there called the Gilded Trail," Taenya said. "Maybe the Games committee set something up…some kind of gathering along that trail."

Jez blew out a breath. She was already tired, and with all her energy gone, a hike in the snow sounded terrible. And why wouldn't it be in town like all the rest? She took the clue from the elf's hand and stared at it. But her riddle-solving skills had apparently petered out. It just looked like a jumble of words. "You realize how many trees there are out there?"

"I pass them every day when I go home," Taenya said. "So yes, I realize. But I'm right about this. The 'way of the golden hue' is the Gilded Trail."

"Then I'll have to trust you," Jez said.

Taenya's eyes twinkled. "That's all we've got," she said as she waved to the gnome. "Thank you!"

"*Bake* a leg!" the vendor shouted.

The two raced toward the trail, and Jez's heart sparked with hope. If nothing else, once they found the clue they could finally get back to someplace warm.

But nearly thirty minutes later, the snow and trees had all started to look the same…nothing but annoying white. Jez's feet ached inside of boots that suddenly felt too tight. Her back hurt, and all she could think about was getting warm in front of a fire.

"Damn all of this," Jez spat while wringing her frozen hands inside their gloves. "I knew I didn't want anything to do with these stupid Games." She plopped down in the snow and buried her face in her hands. "We're in completely the wrong place."

"I know this is right. We just haven't figured it out yet." Taenya lowered herself next to the fennex. "We should take a break." She pulled her bag off her shoulders and fumbled inside.

"But if we do that, we'll definitely lose," Jez said, defeated. "Everyone else has probably finished anyway."

The elf shook her head. "If there's one thing I learned in

my three years at the Baking Battle, it was never to assume your opponent is doing better than you unless you see it with your own eyes." She held up the clue again. "I'll bet other people are struggling with theirs too. I've heard that the last clue is always the most difficult."

Jez took the clue from her hand and stared at it again. It still made absolutely no sense to her.

Taenya could have been right about the others struggling, but Jez couldn't help herself. "I'm going to let you down."

"Let me down?" Taenya stopped digging in the bag. "What are you talking about?"

An ache gnawed through Jez's stomach…partially hunger, but not entirely. "I'm not the kind of person you want as a teammate."

"Why would you say that?" The elf twisted further toward Jez and the sun created a halo over her auburn hair. "If this is about resting…I need a few minutes too. We've been wandering around for hours. I'm hungry and my feet hurt." She rubbed at the front of her boot.

Jez wanted to spill everything whirling through her mind to Taenya… She was cold, miserable, tired, and her body wasn't made for this kind of thing. As a fennex, others looked at her like she was tougher than she was. Her kind didn't look helpless with the fangs and claws, but there was a small part of her that felt that way sometimes. As if everything was out of her control. Competing in the Baking Battle was the first time in her life she'd actually stepped out of her comfort zone. She'd pretended she was more confident than she really was. But no one could maintain that for a long period of time. No matter what Doli thought about Jez coming out of her shell, it *was* a comfortable place most of the time—when people prodded her to do something new or she got herself into trouble. Her problems were much greater than a silly scavenger hunt. And Taenya didn't need to know all that.

But she also truly didn't want to let the elf down. She didn't want to let any of her friends down. Jez had been a disappointment in the past, and she didn't want to repeat it.

"I...I..."

"Eat this." Taenya stuck a cookie in front of Jez's face, and the chocolatey, caramelly notes hit her frozen senses.

"Chocolate chip?" Jez asked as she took the massive cookie.

"Mm-hmm." The elf nibbled a second one she'd pulled from the bag. "I made a big batch yesterday."

Jez's mouth watered as she took her first bite of cookie, and something about the flavor made everything seem a bit better. She looked up toward the bright sun, and it even seemed a little warmer. "How'd you know?" Jez continued chewing and licked a smudge of chocolate from her index finger.

"You love chocolate chip cookies," Taenya said. "I figured I should bring a secret weapon."

Jez chuckled. "A secret weapon? What's that mean?"

"You get a little"—Taenya pinched her fingers together and squinted—"tired and cranky sometimes—"

"You noticed?" Jez tipped her head and took another bite. Of course everyone had noticed, and something in her hated that Taenya might be bothered by it.

"Oh, I've noticed." Taenya's eyes crinkled. "But we all do that sometimes." She held the cookie at eye height to take a look at it. "Our favorite treats tend to make us feel better, and they also make things clearer."

The hair on Jez's arms stood on end, and to avoid looking at the elf she gazed toward a small clump of evergreen trees near the path. Although the growth was natural, it almost appeared as if all the smaller trees had assembled around one larger one. A *gathering*. She grabbed the clue from Taenya's pocket.

"'Into the gathering, meet in the middle,'" she mumbled. "'There you will find what you seek from this riddle.'" Jez pointed to the still green trees flanking the ones that had lost their leaves over a month ago. "What if it's not a gathering of people, but a gathering of trees?" She finished the cookie.

"Oh stars, you're right!" Taenya exclaimed. She jumped up, put her cookie away, and held her hand out to Jez.

The small of the fennex's back hurt, but she took Taenya's grasp and stood. The two raced across the way and stopped in the center of the trees.

"Now what?" the elf asked.

Jez craned her neck to study the largest tree in the center. "It has to be in this one." She moved a step to the left and saw it—the last envelope was stuffed inside a small squirrel hole higher than either of them could reach.

"Right there." Taenya pointed at the envelope. "We did it!" She threw her arms around Jez's neck and squeezed.

"Not yet," Jez barely got out. "We have to actually reach it."

The elf quickly released Jez. "Okay, how about I give you a boost? You think you could reach it then?"

Jez had no desire to be the one up in the air. She hated heights…and the only other people who knew that were Sarson and Doli. Jez didn't want to go into that with Taenya just then. She'd exposed enough of her vulnerabilities that day.

"I'll do the boosting," she blurted. "You're a woodland elf…you—you love trees, right?" Jez immediately regretted saying such a ridiculous thing.

"Um, all right." Taenya wrinkled her nose, obviously puzzled.

But there was no time to waste, so Jez squatted, braced her legs, and interlaced her fingers. The elf placed her boot into Jez's hands and the fennex boosted her up.

Above her, Taenya grunted and clawed at the bark to get a hold. "It's not far. Can you get me a little higher?"

The fennex blew out a breath and hoisted her friend up another notch.

"I have it!" Taenya shouted, and as she did, Jez's boot slipped on the snow-covered tree roots.

The two of them tumbled into a heap with Jez flat on her back and Taenya on top of her, face-to-face. The powerful scent of icing sugar permeated the back of Jez's nose.

For what seemed like an age to Jez, they both seemed frozen as Jez gazed into Taenya's emerald eyes. She had a fleeting thought of what it might be like to kiss the elf. Would it be nice? Would it taste like icing sugar? The questions wafted through Jez's mind before she pushed them away.

"Oh, stars," Taenya finally said and scrambled to her feet. "Are you hurt? Did I hurt you?"

Jez blinked a couple of times, still trying to ward off the thoughts she'd had about her friend. "Um. Shit." She propped up on an elbow and looked down at herself. "No."

But Taenya bent down, her eyes full of concern as she stuck her hand out. "Let me help you up."

Jez gulped and her gaze fixated on Taenya's red gloved hand. "I'm okay." Without taking the elf's grasp she managed to stand. She quickly checked her tail for injuries, but it was the same as it always was. The envelope lay in the snow with their team number scrawled on the front. To avoid saying anything else, the fennex snatched it up and ripped open the seal.

This final clue will bring you back
But hurry now to beat the pack.
Bring each token to prove your worth
And swiftly move across the earth.

Jez's heart sped up. "We need to get back."

Taenya patted her pocket. "I have all the envelopes in here. Let's go!" She grabbed Jez's hand, and they raced out of the forest and onto the road back to town.

Excitement buzzed in Jez's veins, and before long the finish line was in sight. The crowd cheered as they sprinted down the path.

"The Bakers!" someone shouted, and Jez almost wanted to slow down to see who it was. They had a fan!

But up ahead she saw that at least some teams had already returned, including Doli and Sarson and the orcs… and Ronan and his brother. "Are we too late?" Jez panted. Disappointment pressed on her chest.

The cheers picked up again. "Team twelve!" another voice yelled.

Jez looked back. Arleta and Theo were right behind them. "Move it!" Jez yelled. She loved her friends, but that damn sure didn't mean she didn't want to beat them.

Taenya glanced back at Arleta and Theo and growled.

Jez hadn't seen her like that before…and she kind of liked it. New energy burst into her legs and she took the lead, pulling the elf along. "Get the clues ready!"

The two women slid across the finish line and thrust the envelopes at Mr. Figlet. The audience erupted when team twelve came in right on their tails, panting for breath.

Mr. Figlet flipped through the envelopes, then handed them two long-stemmed roses.

"What are these for?" Jez asked.

"All the winners get them from the florist's shop," the marsupial said and waved their envelopes in the air. "Team one is the last team to advance to the second round of competition!"

The crowd went wild. "Bakers!"

Jez's chest tightened at the fact that Theo and Arleta had been disqualified. She'd wanted to beat them *and* still have them in the running.

Arleta groaned behind them, disappointed. "Aww, Tae."

The elf turned and gave Arleta a quick hug.

Theo patted his Fated on the shoulder and then handed Mr. Figlet their envelopes.

Arleta smiled. "But I'm glad it was you two and not someone else. Congratulations!" Theo took her hand and led her away from the stage.

Taenya turned to Jez and leaned in close to her. "Now's the time to show off."

The fennex's eyes widened when Taenya raised up and planted a kiss on her cheek, then threw her rose in the air.

As the crowd whistled and hooted, Jez melted inside.

Just a little more.

14

If Jez had thought that Doli's Yule decorations had looked like fairies gone wild, she hadn't seen anything until she arrived at the Night Yule Market.

The fennex's eyes widened at the hullabaloo, and she stopped at the outskirts to take it all in. The square was so bright with twinkling fairy lights that the stars were blocked from vision. Dancers and jugglers in bright costumes wove through the crowd while the people oohed and aahed.

Scents of the market, spicy, savory, some stinky, came at Jez from all directions, and her head spun. She tucked her gloved hands over her chest and quickly clamped down her scent magic.

"Pies on a stick!" one vendor shouted.

Another called out, "Hot chocolate! Finest in the Northern Lands!"

Jez scanned over their offerings, half wanting to spin on her heel and get the stars out of that place, and half wishing she could let herself smell the food and drink. From the sign over the cart, the pie seller had nearly every flavor she could imagine tasting good—peach, raspberry, apple, and several others. And a hot chocolate didn't sound half bad either… minus all the people.

Even suppressing her sense of smell, she still caught a whiff of the nutty, roasted aroma of the sweet chocolate and, if she wasn't mistaken, a hint of spice.

The fennex sighed. Her feet frozen in place, she looked around for Taenya or any of her other friends.

"Mulled wine?" A dark-haired human bundled in a warm yellow coat thrust out a mug of the drink with a floating orange slice and a pod of star anise floating on top, forcing Jez to step back.

"On the house for the Yule Games contestants," the short woman said, while baring her toothy grin.

"Um…" Jez wanted the liquid courage for the evening but also knew that drinking any alcohol before the Games were over, particularly one containing brandy, was a terrible idea. She stared at the mug, then at the others balanced on a wooden tray in the woman's other hand.

She shoved the mug toward Jez again, wafting a ghost of the spicy cinnamon and cloves into her nose. "It's free."

In normal circumstances, when Jez didn't want

something, she had no difficulty saying no. She might even have something snappy to say. But that evening absolutely nothing came to mind except Taenya's voice reminding her to be nice to garner fans. So instead she took the mug and nodded her thanks.

"You know." The woman leaned in with her tray. "I really like your team…you and that other baker. You're cute together. I was glad you made it in at the end today."

Jez stepped back and bit the side of her bottom lip. "Um. Thank you."

The mulled wine vendor patted her on the arm and waddled off with her tray while Jez stared into the red liquid in her mug.

"Isn't it amazing?" Doli said.

The fennex nearly screamed and almost dropped her steaming wine onto the ground. "You scared me!" Jez gazed down at the dwarf, her heart pounding.

"I'm sorry! I didn't mean to startle you." Doli held out her hand, and pink magic sparkled in her palm. "Do you mind?" She raised her brow in question.

"No. I don't mind," Jez said.

Doli had recently discovered that her magic could provide a sense of safety and comfort. She almost never used it on anyone else without asking permission first.

The dwarf blew on her hand and the magic settled over Jez with a light fizzing like sparkling wine. Her nerves immediately calmed.

"Better?" Doli asked in a cheery tone. "You don't seem like yourself lately."

"Yes." Jez held out the mulled wine to Doli. "You want this? I've sworn off it for a while."

Doli reached out and clasped the mug.

Jez gazed around. "Where's Sarson?"

"Around," she said and took a drink. "I left him to find you."

"Well, here I am." It came out drier than Jez had intended, but Doli didn't seem to mind.

"You left right after the round today, so I didn't really get to talk to you," Doli said.

Jez kicked at the snow with one foot. "I went back and napped at Taenya's."

"Taenya's? Is that where you were last night too?" Doli grinned up at the fennex.

Blood immediately rushed to Jez's cheeks. "It's quieter there and we…we had team stuff to discuss."

Jez hadn't discussed any team *stuff* with Taenya while at the house. Instead, the elf had offered Jez her bed for a snooze and then prepared them both lunch, including two small pieces of chocolate cake decorated with tiny pink flowers made of the most delicious cherry-flavored frosting Jez had ever tasted. Her mouth watered at the thought of it.

"Mm-hmm," Doli said with another sip of wine. "Sarson and I have a lot of team *stuff* to discuss too."

"Doli!" Jez scolded. "It's not like that."

The dwarf shook her head. "I don't know what you're talking about. Sarson and I came in sixth. If we're going to win this thing, we need to up our game. Makes sense that you place at eighteen, you'd want to do the same." Her lips stretched into an overly innocent grin.

"Congratulations on sixth place," Jez said dryly and rolled her eyes.

"The orcs finished third," Doli said, still smiling.

"Who else?" Jez asked, not exactly wanting the answer.

The dwarf tucked her hands into her pockets and twisted her body back and forth before answering. "The halfling team, they came in second."

That was a surprise to hear, but it was obvious Doli was avoiding her question. "And first?"

"Did you know you and Taenya picked up ten points from the audience?" Doli asked.

Jez's eyes widened. "We did?"

The dwarf took a sip and nodded. "Exciting, right?"

"Very." Jez pinched her lips and asked again, "Who came in first?"

"Your bearded *friend* and his brother." The dwarf's tone was uncharacteristically sarcastic. "Where is Taenya, anyway? Why isn't she with you?"

Jez's thoughts were still trained on the fact that Ronan had come in first place and she and Taenya had been eighteenth, even if they had picked up ten points. But at the same time she was simply grateful to still be in the game. Sort of.

"She wanted to get down here early. I didn't." A pair of fire-breathing centaurs dressed as dragons passed them, and Jez let out a sigh. "How are Arleta and Theo?"

"A little disappointed, but Arleta said it's a good opportunity to enjoy the Games with him since the bakery is closed," the dwarf said. "Like a mini holiday."

Jez pursed her lips. "I'd enjoy a mini holiday."

Doli chuckled and threaded her hand through the crook of Jez's elbow. "How about we get you a hot chocolate, meet up with the others, let you make your appearance, and then you can go home…or back to Taenya's? What do you think about that?"

A small headache worked its way over Jez's eyes, and the hot chocolate didn't sound like a bad idea.

Several minutes later Jez had her steaming drink in hand, and she found herself searching the crowd for her other friends. But mostly Taenya, if she was honest.

The two of them weaved their way through the crowds while Jez sipped her hot chocolate and mildly wished she hadn't given away the mulled wine. Up ahead she spotted Theo, Arleta, the orcs, Sarson, and Taenya, who gave her a short wave.

The fennex's heart bounced at the gesture, but she quickly stamped it down. She and Taenya were faking their relationship, and she had to remember that.

As Doli skipped ahead of her, Ronan appeared and caught Jez's arm.

"Congratulations, fennex," he said in too jolly a tone for Jez's taste. "You and your elf made it to the next round."

Jez narrowed her eyes, suspicious of his pleasant demeanor. Gingerly she loosened the reins on her scent magic. It was a mistake. Instantly smells from all over the market flooded into her nose—her hot chocolate, buttered popcorn, people a week overdue on bath time—but nothing from Ronan other than the ghost of sausage on his breath.

Jez backed away and narrowed her gaze at him. What if he had some sort of magic that masked deceit? That had to be it. Several curses were at the tip of her tongue, and she almost had them out when a tug came at her coat.

"Good game today, Ronan." Taenya's voice was friendlier than Jez thought it should be. "But we're going to catch up to you."

Ronan chuckled and ran one hand over his beard. "Better do that unless you have that twenty silver."

Jez winced as the elf pulled her away toward their friends. "He's cheating," she whispered into Taenya's ear when they were too far away for Ronan to hear.

"Cheating?" Taenya said too loudly.

"Shhh!"

The elf lowered her voice. "How do you know?"

Without thinking, the fennex tucked in closer to her friend. Taenya smelled sweet, and the aroma caught her off guard. "I…I can smell these things. Usually."

Taenya halted and kept her voice low. "And you did? Do you have proof? Is that why they came in first?"

But Jez realized she didn't have any proof other than… She didn't have *any* proof. "I just know they're cheating."

The elf sighed and tipped her head. "Is it possible you're trying to get out of finishing the Games?"

"No." The fennex pulled back as if horribly offended.

Taenya chuckled and patted her on the shoulder. "The silver you bet is kind of a big deal, but you can't go around accusing everyone of cheating."

"I haven't accused everyone of cheating," Jez said. "Plenty

of people are playing fair." She looked off into the distance where Ronan was buying a large bag of sweetened popcorn. "It's just *that* guy."

"*And* his brother?" Taenya waved her hand in front of Jez's face to draw her attention back.

"Obviously," Jez said indignantly. "They're a team. That guy Landon might be in on it too."

Taenya pursed her lips, then said, "If that's true, then I'm sure it will sort itself out in the end."

Jez wasn't so sure about that, but before she could say anything else, two children tugged at the hem of her coat.

"Excuse me," the first child said, holding out a card and pencil to Jez. She recognized her as Rhegea, one of the two faun children she'd seen fangirling over Arleta the day before.

Annoyance buzzed in her chest but quickly dissipated when she realized what was happening. The top of the card read "Team One: Taenya Carralei and Jez," and beneath that was a drawing of the two of them.

Surprisingly Jez's first thought wasn't that it was silly… but that they looked nice next to each other. As the thought registered, she blushed. She must have stared at the offering for too long since Taenya cut in and brought Jez back to reality.

"You'd like our autographs?" she asked.

"Yes, please!" the twins said in unison, bouncing up and down. Their shining eyes darted from Jez to Taenya and back again.

Taenya took the card and wrote her name on it, then handed it to Jez.

"Your story is so romantic," Ronorae said. "We saw you both at the Baking Battle too."

The elf slipped her arm around Jez's waist and pulled her in tight. "You did?"

Jez nearly gasped and her arms suddenly went limp, almost unable to sign the card, but somehow she managed and handed it back to the first faun.

"Your cake at the end was fantastic," Rhegea said.

The second cut in. "But Arleta was our favorite."

If Jez could have managed talking right then, she wouldn't have known what to say.

But Taenya leaned in a smidge toward them with a coy grin on her lips. "I'll let you in on a little secret."

"What?" the twins asked in unison, and Jez couldn't help but wonder too.

"Other than Jez"—she paused and then smacked a kiss right on Jez's cheek—"Arleta is my favorite too. She's a good friend."

The two looked at each other, giggled, and ran off into the crowd.

Taenya gave Jez a little squeeze and then released her. "That was cute."

"Uh, yeah" was the best Jez could do. Before she could process what had just happened, they were off to find their friends.

But she knew one thing. She wanted more than anything to win the Games. Not for herself…not to beat Ronan… but for Taenya. Because at that point Jez was pretty sure her favorite friend…was that elf.

15

The next morning was cold. But every winter morning felt unbearably cold to Jez. So it was nothing out of the ordinary.

"So," Doli said as she and Jez left the bookshop and started walking to the starting line. "Did you enjoy the scavenger hunt yesterday or have the Games been as bad as you expected?"

"Yes," Jez said and jammed her hands into her coat pockets. "I'm exhausted. And all these damn tourists." She left out the part where she spent half the night thinking about Taenya. Her brain had refused to turn off.

The dwarf grinned slyly and shook her head. Her dark, curly hair was drawn up onto the crown of her head and secured with a ribbon. "What if you hadn't stayed out so late with Taenya at the Yule Market last night?"

It was true; Jez had stayed out hours past her normal bedtime. In fact, most of the vendors were long closed when they'd finally parted. Jez bit her lip at the realization that Doli must have noticed when she'd gotten home, even though the light was off in the dwarf's room.

Avoiding a halfling that nearly tripped into her, she said, "I had to." She leaned closer and lowered her voice. "We were working the crowd."

The halfling turned. "Oh, hey! Team one!" He thrust a small bound booklet out to Jez. "Can I get your autograph?"

"Uh, sure?" Jez said and took the pencil he was holding out. She quickly scrawled her name on the open page.

"Thanks," the curly-headed halfling chirped, then turned his attention to Doli. "I guess you can too."

Doli pinched her lips and grabbed the booklet and pencil. She scribbled something on a page, then handed it back to the halfling. He took off down the road without even a thank-you.

Her friend shook her head. "You're a regular celebrity now. How will you manage when it's all done?"

Jez grimaced at the thought. "Sarson has those big wings. You two should play that up more."

Doli looked the way the halfling had gone and planted her fists on her hips. "Apparently they're not *big* enough."

The sudden attitude coupled with the sour face the dwarf was putting on amused Jez slightly. "Let's get out of here."

"And disappoint your fans?" Doli asked sarcastically.

"Fans." Jez scoffed and shook her head as she started walking. Before long they were out of town and could see the setup for the Games in the distance. The bench seating looked almost full, and Jez slowed her pace slightly. She blew out a deliberate breath.

"You never *really* answered me," Doli said, the honeyed tone back in her voice.

"About what?" Jez shivered against the cold. The morning sky was clear, but a little frosty wind whipped through the air.

Doli drew up her furry hood and pulled her coat tight against her frame. "If you enjoyed the scavenger hunt with Taenya yesterday?"

The question made Jez freeze inside. The reality was that she had enjoyed quite a bit of it—not the part where they almost didn't figure out their last riddle, but spending all that time with the elf was fairly enjoyable. What she didn't like was what spending that time with Taenya was doing to her…and not being able to sleep. "Meh," she finally got out. "It was fine."

"Sarson and I had a fantastic time," Doli said. "But I'm a little sad Arleta and Theo came in too late, even if it does mean Arleta gets a holiday."

"They'll have more time for *sledding*." When Jez realized the words had actually come out of her mouth and not stayed in her head where they belonged, brow furrowed. That joke was between her and Taenya.

Doli gave her a quizzical look, but before she could ask what Jez was talking about, Sarson appeared ahead of them.

He waved, and Doli tugged on her coat to straighten out any rumples.

"You look good," Jez said to assure her friend.

"Of course I look good," Doli said with a chuckle. "I'm going to go now. Don't want to be seen fraternizing with the enemy." She gave Jez a little wink and jogged down the path to Sarson.

When Doli reached him, she appeared to show Sarson her coat, and from his interested reaction Jez surmised he liked it a lot. The gargoyle picked the dwarf up and kissed her, then holding hands, they walked toward the starting line.

Jez suddenly felt very alone and looked down at the striped pair of gloves Taenya had loaned her. She needed to find her teammate. As she began walking again, she straightened out her own coat.

Just to make sure there weren't any rumples.

It wasn't long before she entered the area where the Games were being held, and everything was louder than she preferred it again. A band near the stage was playing music, and people chatted up in the stands while vendors called out whatever food or drink they were selling out of baskets or carts. And those ridiculous team banners fluttered in the breeze where the remaining teams were to assemble. The whole thing made her neck tense and ears flatten.

"Hey," a voice called out from Jez's left. "You look a little lost."

Jez turned to see Taenya walking toward her and instantly relaxed. Once again the elf's hair was pulled into two short bunches. When she reached Jez, she produced an orange cranberry muffin from her pocket.

"I thought you might need breakfast," Taenya said, holding out the muffin.

The fennex gulped. She hadn't any appetite for food at the apartment, but when she saw Taenya's offering, her belly rumbled. "Thanks." Jez's lips stretched softly upward, and she took the muffin.

"You sleep okay?" Taenya asked as they walked toward the starting area.

"Uh, great," Jez lied and took a big bite of the muffin. She didn't want Taenya to know she'd tossed and turned most of the night, replaying the day's events and wondering how she could have done things better…not really for herself but for the elf's sake.

Taenya leaned in and whispered, "Our little ruse is working, so I'm going to hold your hand now…for the crowd." She slid her fingers along Jez's lower arm and laced her fingers through the fennex's.

Jez shoved at least half the muffin into her mouth.

"Good luck today, Bakers!" a minotaur woman called to them as she waved.

Jez's mouth was entirely too full to return the sentiment apart from a forced smile.

But Taenya bobbed her head enthusiastically and said, "We're ready to win!" She looked up to Jez. "Aren't we, dear?"

Dear? Jez thought. She worked to swallow and managed, "Mm-hmm."

"Contestants," Mr. Figlet said from the stage, "please take your places."

Off in the distance, Jez spotted Doli and Sarson with

the orcs next to a smoked turkey leg vendor. Verdreth and Ervash had a turkey leg in each hand, but at the announcement they finished them in seconds flat before waving at Jez.

Doli gave her a little wave too and mouthed *good luck*.

Jez tipped her chin to her friend.

"You ready?" Taenya asked as they took their places under their banner.

The fennex gazed down the line of teams, and her eyes settled on Ronan and his brother. The man looked like a ridiculous puffed-up fish as he preened to the crowd, exuding confidence.

At the sight, her heart picked up and she let out a low growl. Partly because she despised the guy, but also because if he did win, it would let Taenya down.

And then she really wouldn't be able to sleep.

"Now I know you're not a morning person, but that's not the way to earn the favor of the crowd," the elf said through her teeth, keeping her grin. She threaded her arm through the crook of Jez's elbow and pulled the fennex in tight.

Jez snapped to attention, nearly forgetting about Ronan. Yes. She needed to focus.

Mr. Figlet stood onstage with a set of judges seated behind him and a team of fairies buzzing around at the sides. "Welcome, welcome! Day two of the Yule Games will be an ice maze!" he announced.

The crowd burst into applause.

The marsupial continued, "And thank you to Oliver Whitflow, who runs Whitflow Blacksmith…"

Blocking out his introductions of the judges, a confused

Jez searched the area for the maze. The field behind them was empty save for the snow. But no sooner had she noticed this than three wizards in long fancy robes walked out from behind the stage, icy magic sparkling over their hands. Squinting, Jez was pretty sure she recognized one of the wizards as the owner of the Spells and Sortilege shop in town.

The three turned, faced the empty field, and raised their hands. Their magic grew and converged, then spread out onto the field, unveiling giant walls of ice that formed a sprawling, roofless square.

"I present to you our ice maze!" Mr. Figlet announced and the applause grew, accompanied by gasps and shouts.

Mr. Figlet continued. "Our guest wizards spent the better part of last night conjuring the maze for our competition."

The structure really did look impressive glistening in the morning sun.

"But as always," the marsupial said to the teams, "personal or purchased magic may not be used by any team to gain an advantage." He leaned forward as if to tell a secret. "And later today, after all the teams have finished, the maze will be an open attraction. So bring all your family and friends!"

Jez shuddered at the idea of being packed into a maze with so many tourists. *In what land would that ever be fun?* she thought.

"Once will be plenty for me," Jez said without looking at Taenya.

The elf snuggled closer. "Yes, dear."

Jez's eyes widened at the realization that Taenya had called her "dear" even when no one else could hear. She barely heard Mr. Figlet's announcement about the fairies flying over the maze to report the goings-on to the audience.

"Take your places! And remember, the magic imbued into the maze means that once you enter through your team's door, you will not encounter any other teams before you exit." That was the last thing she heard clearly before Taenya pulled her across the field and toward the maze.

As the eighteen teams drew closer, the wizards waved their hands again and a series of entrances appeared, a team number etched in the ice over each one. Then the wizards made their way past the teams back toward the stage.

To their right Jez watched as one wizard, whose name she believed was Ibus Ironflame, passed Ronan. He bowed his head slightly.

What was that? Jez thought, her mind nearly on fire. *Do they know each other?*

Before she could dwell on it further, Taenya was yanking her toward their maze entrance.

"You need to focus, Jez," she said. "This is a race, and you need a clear head."

Jez returned her attention to the elf. "I'm fine."

"You were looking at Ronan again," she said, frustration in her tone. "Don't let him get under your skin."

"I was looking at the orcs," Jez lied.

"Mm-hmm," Taenya said as they reached the entrance and turned to face the crowd.

The fairies had flown out over the maze and hovered in the sky above.

Mr. Figlet gestured toward one side of the stage, where a

banner reading FINISH hung. "Once you exit the maze, you must make it to the finish line. Contestants, make ready!" The bell rang, and color shot into the sky above the ice structure.

"Let's go, let's go, let's go!" Taenya said, grabbing Jez's hand and pulling her through the entrance marked *Team One*.

They were immediately confronted by two possible directions, and the two women stopped. Jez saw a fairy zip overhead and then out of sight.

"Which way should we go?" Taenya asked.

With everything going on, the two of them hadn't sat down to talk about maze strategy like they should have. But Jez thought for a moment. She didn't want to just start running through the maze. That would get them trapped for sure.

"This is a pretty big structure to finish in one night, even for three wizards," she said. "Add on all the different entrances and the magic that separates the teams. My guess is the that the maze itself is simpler than it looks. They are giving it the illusion of being complicated. It might not even matter which way we go."

"Not matter?" Taenya said, confused.

"Yeah," Jez said. "It's easier to make a maze like this look impressive from the outside than design it to actually *be* complex. Plus, you heard Mr. Figlet. They're opening it up to everyone. If the maze takes the teams hours to get through or a bunch of us get lost, then they lose out on all that coin for the entrance fee. So more than likely it's a simple maze. It'll be easy to get out of."

Taenya blinked and then looked left to right again. "And you're an expert in mazes how?"

Jez shrugged. "I haven't solved a maze like this one, but I used to play maze games on paper with my siblings. I thought everyone knew about them."

"So how do we get out?" Taenya asked and glanced up at another fairy zipping by.

Jez picked up the elf's right hand and touched it to the wall. "If I'm right and it's a simple maze, then keep your hand there, and we follow it to the exit."

"It's that easy?" Taenya's eyes brightened as a fairy flew over again, and they heard the faint sound of announcements outside.

"*If* it's a simple maze." Jez shrugged. "If not, we're in trouble."

Taenya leaned in and planted a kiss on Jez's cheek. She grinned and jerked her chin toward the sky. "In case they're watching."

Jez's cheek tingled, and she placed her own hand on the ice wall. "Let's go." She started jogging and the elf followed behind, dragging her fingertips lightly on the icy surface.

The maze took them on a series of seemingly endless turns as the two women zoomed through.

"Are you sure we haven't been here before?" Taenya asked from behind Jez, panting.

A fairy paused overhead and waved at them.

"I haven't taken my hand off the wall," Jez called over her shoulder and then pointed at the snow on the ground. "And I haven't seen any footprints." But inside her heart was pounding with doubt. Was she mistaken? Maybe part of the maze magic erased footprints from the snow. Would Taenya be disappointed in her if they lost?

Despite the negative thoughts zipping through Jez's brain, she kept moving forward. Stopping most definitely would not help.

But finally she spotted what she'd been hoping for…the exit.

"I was right!" Jez hollered.

Taenya squealed and sped past the fennex. Jez smiled. They'd done it! And hopefully in record time. Who cared about that bastard Ronan?

But just as Taenya was almost at the exit, she stumbled and landed face-first in the snow. Seconds later, she cried out and grabbed her leg.

Oh, shit reverberated in Jez's mind.

16

Bits of sparkling snow floated down almost in slow motion as Taenya grasped at her ankle. The elf's cheeks, already reddened from the cold, puffed out as if she were holding in the pain, but she seemed to regain some control. Through gritted teeth she said, "It's like that damn tree root popped up out of the ground."

Jez's gaze dropped to the snow-covered ground between her and Taenya where a thick brown root protruded from the earth. She wasn't sure she'd seen it before either. *Could some kind of magic have made it grow?* Her chest tingled at the thought. But there was no time for such speculation, and she hurried to the elf's side.

"Are you okay?" She felt ridiculous asking. The sharp

scent of fear and pain radiated from Taenya's skin, making it incredibly difficult for her to concentrate.

Tears glistened in the corners of Taenya's eyes. "I'm not sure. But I think I can walk." She pushed up a little, putting some weight on the ankle. "Oww, oww!" The elf dropped to the snowy ground again and sucked her teeth.

"No, you can't," Jez insisted.

Taenya shook her head and eyed the exit. "We need to finish this thing."

"I want to finish as much as you do," the fennex insisted. "But right now I'm going to figure out if you're all right." Still having a difficult time focusing clearly, Jez pulled off her gloves, stuffed them in her pockets, and gently pulled the pant leg up from where it had been tucked into the boot. The pale skin was already turning a variety of colors it wasn't intended to be.

"Is it bad?" Taenya asked, her voice strained.

As she said it, the halfling team raced past the exit, not even seeing them.

"Bastards," Jez growled under her breath. To be fair, the halflings probably hadn't seen them, she wasn't sure she'd stop for them either if it meant the difference between winning and losing. "Hopefully it's only a sprain and we can get you to the healer's tent." But Jez wasn't all that sure since the bruising was spreading before her eyes.

"Damn it. I tore my coat too," Taenya said, looking down at a tear in her sleeve.

"Doli can fix that," Jez said matter-of-factly.

Taenya tried to push herself up again but fell back onto the packed snow.

"What are you doing?" Jez sat back on her knees.

"We have to finish," she said, looking back at the tree root. "We can't let something as silly as that make us lose." The lines on Taenya's forehead were pinched.

Jez's chest tightened. Ronan and his brother were human, so they didn't have any of their own magic, but that wouldn't stop them from paying someone to interfere magically with their competitors. "You said that the root appeared out of nowhere?"

"I don't know." Taenya held out her hand toward Jez. "I probably just didn't see it."

"But you'd assume the Games committee would have cleared all hazards like that out of here." Jez's chest burned with anger the more she thought about it.

The elf shook her hand at the fennex to get her attention. "Stop wasting time worrying about what's already happened. Help me up."

Jez frowned. "You can't walk on that ankle. Could make it worse."

"That's why you're going to help me," Taenya insisted. "If we can make it to the finish line in time, we won't miss our shot."

Shaking her head, Jez stood and looked down at Taenya. Guilt swirled in her chest and her tail drooped, touching the snow. If she hadn't been distracted, she probably would have seen the root and been able to warn Taenya. Then she wouldn't have gotten hurt.

"We're wasting time," the elf insisted, hand still extended.

Jez held her breath and stuck out her clawed hand, which

Taenya took. But Jez knew the elf would not be able to walk, so in one swoop she brought her friend to her wobbly feet and took her in her arms.

"What are you doing?" Taenya asked in surprise.

The scent of fear from earlier was gone, and all that remained was her typical icing sugar scent with a tinge of relief. Jez did her best to ignore it, but for some reason she couldn't this time.

She gulped and strengthened her grip on Taenya. "I'm not letting you get hurt worse. What if it's more than a sprain?"

"But—"

"No," Jez said bluntly. "If you want to continue, then this is how we'll be doing it. No arguments."

A wry smile crept up Taenya's lips, bringing a few flutter-bees into Jez's stomach. "Then we'd best get moving."

And Jez did. With Taenya feeling lighter than expected, Jez jogged straight out the exit decorated with a large snowflake-shaped arch. The wind whipped against her face and the audience cheered, but Jez ignored it all. She needed to get Taenya to the healer.

"And it looks like the Bakers made it," Mr. Figlet's voice rang out from the finish line, and several fairies flew out to greet them.

Jez spotted Ronan and his brother as well as the orcs. Both teams had finished before them, but Doli and Sarson weren't there yet.

"Are you hurt?" the first fairy to arrive asked. They had flaming red hair and wore a tiny sparkling blue knit sweater.

"She tripped over a damn tree root," Jez said, still jogging toward the finish line.

Three fairies flew backward and said in high-pitched unison, "A tree root?"

"We personally checked the maze," the middle one said, their wings fluttering. "There should have been nothing of the sort."

The declaration made Jez grit her teeth as she eyed Ronan again. "Damn right." Tree roots didn't pop up in an hour.

"It's only a sprained ankle," Taenya insisted to the fairies while Jez kept her pace. "I just need to see the healer."

Jez growled at them, baring her teeth. "Get out of my way and we'll figure out what happened later."

The three fairies' eyes widened, but they quickly dispersed and flew back to Mr. Figlet. One of them seemed to whisper in his ear.

"It appears that Taenya Carralei has been injured in the maze," the quokkan announced.

There were audible gasps in the audience, and then they began to chant, "Bakers...Bakers...Bakers..." But Jez barely noticed or cared. She just tightened her grip on Taenya and kept her eyes on her destination, which didn't seem to get closer fast enough.

Finally they crossed the finish line and Jez slowed to a stop, but she didn't set Taenya down. The orcs hurried toward the women.

Mr. Figlet turned and raised his furry hand to the audience. "Team one has made it into the next round of the Games!"

The crowd cheered again, and Jez whipped her attention around, scanning over them. She spotted a large pink dragon next to Arleta and Theo… That would be Evvy, Doli's friend whom she raised from a hatchling.

Mr. Figlet approached. "Are you okay?" he asked Taenya, genuine concern in his voice.

"I'm fine," she insisted. "Jez, you can put me down."

But Jez was too busy looking for the healing booth and replaying in her mind how she should have been first. How she should have been the one who'd gotten hurt.

"Jez." Ervash's low voice cut through her mind's chatter.

Her eyes shot up at the massive orc towering over her, Verdreth at his side. "What?"

"Put Taenya down," he said gently.

The fennex's gaze shot to Taenya, who was nodding.

"You can put me down," she said. "We made it. You did it."

Heat burned up the back of Jez's neck when she finally realized how everyone was looking at them. Another team, not Doli and Sarson, had just finished and it seemed like no one had even noticed. She slowly lowered Taenya to the ground.

Across the way Jez spotted Ronan looking at them with his arms crossed. Narrowing her eyes, she couldn't help but wonder what he was thinking…wonder if he'd somehow caused the tree root to appear. But she'd have to prove it.

The elf whispered in her ear as she balanced on one foot. "This is a perfect opportunity to play to the crowd. We can manage an even bigger win out of the situation."

Before Jez could reply, Taenya kissed her on the mouth, then pulled back and shot her hand in the air.

The crowd went wild.

But Jez was left wide-eyed and breathless. Somehow she managed a half grin and a short wave. *It's just fake. It's just fake*, she reminded herself.

"Bakers…Bakers…Bakers…" the audience started up again as Sarson and Doli finally crossed the finish line.

Jez had no idea if they'd made it out in time.

"Let's get you to the healing tent," Verdreth said as he carefully lifted Taenya in his powerful arms.

Jez followed them to the tent in a daze. The air in front of her seemed thick and foggy, and her feet were as heavy as stones. Her lips tingled from the kiss. She watched as Verdreth ducked into the tent and the fabric flap closed behind him and Taenya. For some reason Jez only stood there and stared at it, breathing raggedly.

"That was some ending you had there," Doli's voice came from behind her.

Jez shook her head and turned toward the dwarf. "Ending?"

"You two had the crowd going." Doli winked.

Jez looked around and saw the finish line off in the distance. She barely even remembered walking from there to the tent. "I guess we did." She laughed nervously.

"Taenya is all right?" the dwarf asked, looking around Jez at the closed tent flap.

"Probably a sprain," Jez answered but felt the sudden urge to find out for herself. She turned but then asked, "Did you make it in time for the next round?"

Doli grinned and shook her head. "We were too late. So Sarson and I will be cheering for you and the orcs now. And

Evvy is here, but she can't stay long." Her brown eyes twinkled as she pointed her thumb back to the stands.

"Um. You should do that then," Jez said. "I think we'll be fine here."

Doli bowed her head slightly. "Oh, I almost forgot. We're all planning to meet at the square tonight for the party. I hope to see you and Taenya there."

Jez tipped her head to the tent. "I better get inside. But we're required to go to those things, so I'm sure we'll be there."

Smiling, the dwarf gave her a little wave and before she left said, "Congratulations!"

Jez turned and entered the tent. It was larger and warmer than she'd expected, and she noticed the red warming stones placed around the tent's periphery. Wizards often cast spells on regular stones to warm and cool spaces. Some wizards also had the ability to play with space, which had to be why the tent seemed so much bigger on the inside. In seconds, it was too hot for her coat, so she removed it and hung it on a standing hook by the exit.

Taenya sat on the edge of a higher-than-normal bed with the orcs and a healer wizard in a white robe standing next to her.

On her way to the elf, Jez passed several other patients lying on other beds. One was a small green troll with some sort of pack held to his shoulder. Blue magic lightly popped and fizzed in the air over the pack.

"I'm Drexon, and I'll be treating you today," said the sepia-skinned wizard, whose hair was pulled back into a low ponytail. He gently but efficiently removed Taenya's boot and then poked, prodded, and manipulated the joint. Setting her foot back down on the bed, he said, "Looks like a sprain. It's a simple spell to fix, but the healing process will take about an hour once I apply it."

"Good to hear," Taenya said. "And I'll be able to compete tomorrow?" She glanced at Jez.

"When you leave, you should be as good as new. I'll begin the preparation immediately. Shouldn't take more than a few minutes." Drexon patted Taenya's shoulder and left.

"Hear that?" Taenya said. "Good as new."

Her coat lay beside her, and Jez spotted the abrasion on Taenya's arm. She winced and sat on the other side of the bed, then reached out and touched the skin beside the wound.

"I'm sure they'll get that too," Taenya assured her. When Jez didn't reply, she gave her a quizzical look before turning her attention to the sweaty orcs. "Thanks for getting me here. Jez and I have got it."

Ervash wiped the sweat from his forehead and said, "Are you sure?"

Taenya nodded. "Completely. Go see the others and have a good time."

"Evvy is here," Jez said. "And Doli said she can't stay long."

Verdreth's eyes brightened at the mention of the dragon. "We haven't seen her in a while."

"Say hi to her from us." Taenya gave Jez a quick glance.

"We'll see you two later then," Verdreth said and patted

Taenya on the shoulder. The two orcs ducked out of the tent, conversing in low tones.

Jez eyed the wizard while he worked to conjure something for Taenya's ankle. He had clear jars and bottles of ingredients lined up at his workstation. Not being a wizard herself, Jez had no clue what any of them were. As he placed bits and bobs of various ingredients into a bowl and waved his hands over the mixture, magic poofed up into the air. The entire process was mesmerizing, and Jez's lids drooped.

"I'm sorry I did that back there on such short notice," Taenya said, breaking Jez from her near trance. "The kiss."

Suddenly Jez's lips tingled again, and she bit the bottom one with her fang. "Uh, no big deal." She chuckled nervously. "The audience seemed to like it."

But it was a big deal. Jez shifted her weight as the air between them grew a little too thick for her comfort.

Luckily Drexon made his way back to them with the bowl in hand. "Okay, this should do it."

Jez stared at the potion in the bowl, thinking.

"This will sting a little," the healer said. He gathered several clear drops on his fingers and allowed them to fall on Taenya's ankle.

The elf winced.

Jez's stomach did a flop, and to distract herself she asked, "Do you or any of the other wizards specialize in plants?"

"Plants?" Drexon looked up from his work.

Taenya shot her a puzzled look but said nothing as the healer rubbed the potion into her skin.

Jez flicked her attention to the elf but turned back to the

wizard. "Say I wanted to increase a tree's root system quickly. Could I purchase something like that?"

"Since when are you interested in trees?" Taenya asked.

"I love trees," Jez said.

The healer shrugged. "That's not my forte, but sure, there's a wizard or two around Adenashire who can conjure plant-related potions. Pretty sure Ibus at Spells and Sortilege can do that."

That caught Jez's attention. "He was one of the ice maze creators, right?"

"I wasn't out there." Drexon raised his brow. "But yes. I believe he was." He turned his gaze to Taenya as he placed her ankle down again. "Have a rest here for the next hour so we can keep an eye on the healing process." He smiled and turned, leaving Jez and Taenya alone.

"What was that about?" Taenya leaned in and asked.

"What?" Jez crossed her arms over her chest.

The elf pursed her lips. "You're a plant lover now? Since when?"

Jez lowered her voice. "You're the one who said that root came out of nowhere."

Taenya stuck out her neck in question. "And?"

Jez leaned closer and whispered, "What if…" She paused for a second, contemplating whether to mention Ronan. "What if *someone* bought a spell off Ibus to cheat?"

"Well, first off we can't use magic in the Games," Taenya said. "Are you still on this thing about Ronan and his brother cheating?"

"I didn't say anything about Ronan," Jez said.

"But that's the *someone* you're talking about."

"I'm just wondering," Jez managed.

A soft sigh left Taenya's lips. "How are we supposed to have a good time if you're constantly worried about Ronan—or anyone else in the Games—cheating?" She reached out and touched Jez's upper arm.

Jez wanted to argue, but instead she froze as the light, gentle touch made her skin prickle and sharpened the memory of their kiss. Not knowing where to look, she dropped her gaze to Taenya's ankle. "I'm tired. Do you think if I left you'd be okay?"

Taenya pulled back her hand and sighed. "Of course. You did all that work of carrying me to the finish line."

Jez didn't really want to go, but she nodded and avoided looking at Taenya's lips. "I'll see you later. Doli said something about meeting up in the square later. Some party we're required to attend."

"Yeah, I know about it. There's going to be singing." Taenya's tone was peppered with confusion, maybe even disappointment.

But Jez needed to get out of that tent. "Okay, see you then." She nodded again, then turned on her heel, gathered her coat at the exit, and left. All the way to the bookshop she had no idea what to do with her hands.

Or herself in general.

17

Overwhelm from that kiss sloshed in Jez's mind like an ocean storm. She needed some time to herself or continuing the Games was going to become impossible. Her head pounded from stress, exhaustion, and repressing her magic.

But once she got back to the apartment, Jez couldn't stand being in her room, not even for a nap. So she packed a sandwich and gathered her fishing equipment. She knew that getting out into nature and fishing almost always cleared her head, sometimes even better than sleep, though she probably wouldn't have admitted that out loud. For now, she had to try to regain some sense of normalcy. If it didn't help, she could make an appearance at the event later and go to bed early.

With her pack slung over her shoulder, she made a bee-line out of the apartment to avoid Doli's Yule decorations—including the tree, which she was pretty sure had substantially more ornaments and garland on it since the last time she'd noticed.

Outside, she weaved through the laughing and chatting crowd out on the streets. The cold air felt heavy, but Jez pulled her jacket tight and pushed through the discomfort in her body and mind. All she wanted to do was get out of town as quickly as possible. And one way to help with that was to keep her gaze to the ground and count her steps.

But as she walked, doing her best to count, focus on her boots and not run into anyone, the ghost of Taenya's kiss still hovered over her lips. Confused feelings worked their way around in Jez's stormy mind.

They were only faking their relationship. Taenya had said so in the tent. And Jez had told the elf that it was better for her to stay friends when they'd talked at the bakery.

That's still true, isn't it? she thought.

Jez couldn't imagine losing any of the people in her life, particularly Taenya. And romance did that sort of thing. It was exciting at first, but that could wane and end up with her first steering clear of the bakery and then asking Doli if Taenya was going to be at something or not so they could avoid each other. It would ruin everything. And that was a risk she wasn't willing to take.

So why was she still stuck on the kiss? And then there was the question of Ronan cheating. And had she taken a thousand steps or a thousand and five?

Finally, having completely lost track of how many steps the journey had taken, Jez came to the crossroads outside of Adenashire. Left would lead out to her normal fishing spot, but she couldn't go there. That area had been completely overtaken by tourists and turned into an ice-skating fiasco. At least that's how she pictured it. Not at all the vibe she was hoping for.

Right led to Sarson's. And he had a small lake behind his house that she knew was full of fish.

She stood there for at least five minutes, two of which she was replaying the kiss in her mind, the other three convincing herself it would be okay to go to Sarson's lake.

The thing was, Jez didn't really enjoy going out to Sarson's, particularly on her own. He was nice enough, but she'd misjudged him when they first met. She had apologized, even gave him one of her best bottles of rum. But she couldn't help thinking he still might hold it against her…no matter how many times Doli had told her that wasn't the case.

Jez was definitely one to hold grudges against people who'd wronged her. But in the end, she needed to fish to clear her head, so she'd have to take the chance of running into him.

To get her mind off the kiss, she started counting steps again.

One, two…twenty…or was it twenty-three? Jez thought, trying to get back on track while trudging down the road to Sarson's cottage. Not too far from his house, she finally gave up counting and turned off the well-worn path toward the lake.

Her breath puffed out in front of her as she studied the little bits of brown reeds sticking up from the snow along the path, but it wasn't long before the frozen lake came into view. The surface was like window glass coated with morning frost.

"Thank the stars," she muttered.

There were no crowds peopling up the calm atmosphere. And despite how chilly it was outside, the scene somehow brought Jez back to a state of normalcy.

She completely relaxed her scent magic and took in a deep breath. Almost immediately her headache decreased, and calm overtook her body.

The only thing she liked about the snow and cold was how it dulled the scents, particularly when she was out fishing alone.

It was her and the fish…the fish and her.

All she could smell was a hint of must from the plants buried under the snow. She wondered if this was how her friends experienced the world every day.

And as much as she despised the cold weather, the lake views were beautiful. Peaceful.

Evergreens in the distance supported snow on their branches while the overhead sun reflected on the portions of the lake ice that were free of snow.

Jez stopped at the water's edge and set her pack on the ground. Instead of walking out onto the ice to make a hole, she pulled a plaid blanket out of the bag, spread it on the ground, and sat. After a few moments she retrieved the sandwich from her bag, unwrapped the crinkly paper around it, and took a bite of the turkey and Swiss with garlic spread. The savory flavors danced on her tongue, and she realized that the thought of eating *anything* calmed her even more.

"Oh." A deep voice resonated behind her. "I didn't know you were out here."

"Shit." She nearly dropped her sandwich on her blanket as she twisted around. Sarson stood in the middle of the path.

"I didn't intend to scare you," he said.

Feeling jittery and completely unlike herself, Jez said, "I'll go," and hurried to repack her lunch.

Sarson held a blanket similar to hers as well as a large basket slung over his massive arm. His wings stretched out slightly behind him like those of a giant bat, rustling as he shook his head. "Oh no, please. Feel free to stay here. I can have my lunch back at the house." He gave her a warm smile that Jez was pretty sure she didn't deserve.

In fact, Jez was so off-kilter she didn't even have anything snappy to say to him.

"This is *your* lake." She began to pack her half-covered sandwich in the bag.

Sarson chuckled. "It simply happens to be near my house. Not as if I own it." He gestured to the frozen lake and said, "You were here first, so enjoy yourself," then turned to leave.

Jez stared down at the poorly wrapped sandwich still in her hand, not relishing the idea of eating it on the walk home. So she opened her mouth and said something that surprised even her. "How about we share the space? We don't have to talk."

The gargoyle stopped and turned back around. "You sure you don't mind?"

For some reason, in that moment Jez didn't mind. She leaned over and patted the ground beside her blanket. "Have a seat."

Lunching with Sarson couldn't be worse than the day she'd already had.

The blue-skinned gargoyle was bundled in a warm coat that appeared custom designed to make space for his wings. Jez wondered if Doli had sewn it for him or if he'd brought it from the Ridgelands.

While she unwrapped her sandwich once more, Sarson spread out his blanket and set his covered basket on it. Jez eyed him as he kneeled and brought out a regular feast: several sandwiches, what looked like a potato salad, cut fruit and vegetables, and a box of scones with toasted almonds on top.

"You expecting someone?" Slightly jealous, she returned to her hastily made sandwich. The savory flavors were good, but the array of options in front of Sarson made her lunch pale in comparison.

"No one in particular." Last, Sarson drew out several utensils and two wooden plates, which Jez found curious. Without a word he sat down and handed Jez a plate and fork.

Confused, she took it, and he gestured toward the spread.

"Are you sure?" Jez asked, her mouth dry.

"Of course."

The fact that he'd brought out the extra plate and a

distinctly large amount of food made fresh guilt swirl in Jez's middle. "I really am sorry about how I misjudged you."

Sarson shook his head and chuckled as he picked several options from the array and set them on his plate. "I don't know what you're talking about."

The fennex narrowed her gaze slightly at him. "Did Doli send you out here?"

"Why would she do that?" he asked and took a bite of his first sandwich.

Fiddling with her own lunch, Jez gazed back toward his cottage as if she might see the dwarf standing out there. But they were completely alone, save for a few birds in the trees.

"We're not always together," Sarson said. He reached for the cut fruit and offered the dish to Jez.

She speared a few apple slices before he placed it back on the blanket. "Could have fooled me."

Sarson chuckled and reached into the basket. "We both need a measure of alone time. To be with our thoughts." He gazed around. "Speaking of alone time, Taenya's not with you. Is she okay? Doli said she injured her ankle."

Jez nodded. "A sprain. The healer took care of it." She suddenly really wished she'd stayed with Taenya to make sure everything was all right…but there was still the problem of the kiss.

"The crowd awarded your team extra points again," Sarson said and took another bite of his sandwich.

Something made Jez want to spill her entire list of problems to Sarson, from the kiss all the way to her suspicions that Ronan was cheating, but she quickly decided against it. "That's nice" was all that came out.

Without another word about the topic, he pulled out a book with a beautifully illustrated cover. All sorts of animals were pictured, and the title read *Fables of the Northern Lands*.

"What's that?" Jez felt compelled to ask. She had almost completely forgotten about fishing.

The gargoyle cracked open the book to a bookmarked page. "Something I've been wanting to get around to for a long time. But I've been too busy."

"With Doli?" Jez joked.

The gargoyle only grinned.

Sarson had recently retired from the job of Head Librarian of the Ridgelands. It was an important job because gargoyles were the historians of the Northern Lands. But Sarson had found the politics of the position quite demanding and turned it over to a trusted colleague before he moved to Adenashire. Jez had thought him worthy of suspicion at first for reasons she shouldn't have.

He held the book up to show Jez the story he was on. One about a lion and a mouse.

Jez knew the story. A mouse begged for his life while trapped under a lion's paw. The mouse had the audacity to declare that if the lion released him and didn't eat him, one day the mouse would repay the favor. The lion was amused… and how big of a lunch would the mouse make, anyway? So he laughed, picked up his paw, and let the mouse escape. But he never thought the mouse could help him in any way.

Sometime later the lion found himself trapped in a rope.

The mouse came across him and without a word gnawed through the rope to release the lion. The moral of the story was not to underestimate people…and that it's better to be kind when one has the opportunity.

"Fables are for children, right?" Jez said, munching on one of the apple slices and wondering why Sarson would be interested in kids' stories. "Simple life lessons? I had books like that around when I was a kit."

Sarson shrugged. "I guess so, but I've found that simplicity doesn't necessarily equal childishness. I like to be reminded that kindness, patience, and friendship are the things that make this life enjoyable. They are what sometimes save us." He looked out toward a cawing crow flapping its wings on a tree branch. "Everything else is mostly noise." The gargoyle brought his attention back to Jez and smiled.

Guilt forced her to look away. She really didn't know how she'd ever misjudged him. In many ways, the two of them seemed more alike than different. A smidge secretive and sometimes in need of a little quiet time. "Can't argue with you there."

Sarson offered Jez the container filled with almond scones. The toasted nutty scent was comforting, and they looked delicious with lightly browned edges, the sliced almonds on the top, and a sprinkling of powdered sugar.

She took one, nodded a thanks to Sarson, and bit into the flaky, slightly crispy scone. The sweetness was perfectly complemented by the almonds.

After she finished it, she sat with her arms wrapped around her knees and gazed out at the lake, while Sarson finished his lunch and read his book. Jez found she didn't need to fish; it was enough simply to *be* for a while alongside a friend.

Everything else was just noise.

18

Despite her better-than-expected afternoon, Jez wrung her hands as she walked from the bookshop to the town center. Part of it was the cold. Clouds had rolled in, looking ready for a snowstorm later that night. But the other part was that she hadn't seen Taenya or any of her friends other than Sarson since she'd left the healer's tent. And the kiss was still niggling at her mind…that and the possibility that Ronan's team might have been cheating at the Games.

Yet, Taenya didn't see the possibility of cheating. The fairies *were* checking the events and likely would have spotted any prohibited magic. Jez should listen to the elf. Maybe worrying about something she had no proof of *was* keeping her from having a good time. Noise.

The logic of it all hurt her brain.

Trying to keep focused on the present, she followed the crowds to the square while keeping a safe distance from strangers. A large stage had been set up, and on it stood Mr. Figlet singing a bad rendition of "Last Yule."

What is this? Jez wondered, but she did remember Taenya mentioned something about singing. "If you can call that singing," she muttered. Just hearing his off-tune screeching about unrequited love made her reconsider her drinking reprieve until the Games were over.

Particularly with an ale seller no more than twenty steps to her left.

The marsupial hit an especially off-key note on the chorus, and Jez's ears went flat. She gritted her teeth, and her attention lingered a bit too long on a centaur carrying two foamy mugs of ale past her.

"Shit." Jez shook her head and forced her attention back to the stage. She blew on her gloved hands to keep warm.

Behind Mr. Figlet were four musicians she'd seen a few months before, each with a different instrument: a drum, a lute, a viol, and a flute. Unlike Mr. Figlet, they were actually quite talented, and they were rumored to have a repertoire of hundreds of songs from all over the Northern Lands which they could play on cue.

But the large audience didn't seem to care about Mr. Figlet's lack of talent as he slid into his big finish, held out the note way too long, and immediately collapsed into a low bow at the end of the song.

Half the crowd, including his wife and joeys, were on

their feet in applause while Mr. Figlet straightened back up and gestured to the band.

Jez let out a sigh of relief that the singing portion of the night seemed to be over. The thought of the next hour filled with one terrible singer after another wasn't her idea of a pleasant evening.

"Well," Taenya's voice came from behind Jez. "*That* was something."

Her breath hitched and puffed out like a little storm cloud in front of her. "Yes, *something*," Jez managed and glanced at the elf. The kiss entered her mind again, and she wondered which was worse, Mr. Figlet's singing voice or her own obsessive thoughts.

Taenya was dressed in a long green coat with gold detailing along the cuffs, collar, and hem. Very elvish. Peeking from around her neck was white fleece. Everything about the coat looked cozy, and Jez crossed her arms over her chest to pull her own coat in tighter.

"Your ankle." Jez's eyes dropped to the ground. "It's better?"

The elf grinned. "Good as new. Like the healer said."

"Let's hear it again for Bard's Honor!" Mr. Figlet shouted. The musicians stood and bowed slightly as the crowd applauded and cheered.

Mr. Figlet continued clapping as the band exited the stage. "We'll be back in twenty minutes for the second half of our Yule singing extravaganza."

Jez gave a nervous chortle. "Damn. I thought luck was on my side and I'd missed all but the tail end."

"You're not a fan of singing?" Taenya asked.

Feeling suddenly even more off-kilter, Jez took a step back, nearly bumping into someone behind her. "Um. I don't know?" When the elf didn't say anything, Jez's thoughts reached for something snappier. She leaned closer to Taenya and shrugged. "Mr. Figlet might want to invest in a few lessons before next year. But that's just me."

Taenya giggled. "You might be right. You can be the one to tell him."

Jez shook her head vigorously.

"Events like this are more about fun than anything else." Taenya looked out at the crowd, some of whom had broken into an impromptu chorus of "The Yule Song." "See? They're just having a good time." Her eyes sparkled. "Like we should be having." With no warning, the elf slipped her hand into Jez's. "You should try it sometimes instead of being so serious." She pulled Jez toward the audience.

Taken by surprise, Jez didn't protest or have any time to contemplate the accusation that she might not be any fun, and she simply followed the elf's lead.

Shortly, Taenya had led them to Doli and Sarson in the front row, mugs in hand. Jez caught a whiff of the steaming tea inside each one.

"Jez, Taenya!" Doli's eyes lit up as if it had been an age since they'd last seen each other and not half a day.

Sarson nodded to them with a friendly expression as he sipped his drink.

"I was worried you weren't going to make it." The dwarf

motioned to the open seats next to her covered in a blanket. There were two similar spots on the other side of Sarson. "We saved you a place."

"Where's Arleta and Theo?" Taenya asked.

Doli glanced back. "Off getting snacks. They shouldn't be long."

Jez pulled off the blanket and sat by her friend. Suddenly chilled, she draped the blanket over her lap but turned to Taenya and held out one end. "You want to share?"

The elf waved it off with a smile. "I'm warm enough." She leaned forward to address Doli. "But I will take a tea if you have an extra cup."

The dwarf's lips curled up warmly. "Of course." She bent down to the same basket Sarson had used at the lake and pulled out two cups. "I'm assuming you'd both like one?"

The fur on Jez's ears stood on end as it suddenly felt like the temperature had dropped a little more. With her teeth on the verge of chattering, Jez pulled the blanket up higher and bowed her head. "Yyy…ess."

"Something light for me, with lemon if you can," Taenya said.

"Of course. I have something perfect I've been working on." Doli hooked her fingers through the handles with one hand and waved her other over the mugs. A few sparkles of magic glistened, and immediately citrusy steam rose from the openings.

"As you like it." Doli presented the mugs to the women. "Might be a tad hot."

Jez was simply grateful to have any warm object in her hands while the heat permeated her gloves. She leaned into the cup and drew in a big whiff of the tea. The earthy, bitter scent of the black tea with cream and just the right amount of sweetness settled her nerves slightly. Jez blew on the hot liquid and took a sip.

"This is delicious, Doli!" Taenya exclaimed with delight. "It would pair perfectly with the cherry scones at the bakery."

Doli beamed. "Right? That's one of the things I was going for."

"I *am* sorry you were eliminated today," Taenya said, taking a sip.

Two of the band members made their way back onto the stage and began fiddling with their instruments.

"We didn't mind," Doli said. "It would have been fun if all of us were in the final, but Sarson and I honestly like the idea of watching you two. I had a chance to make up a Team One sign today and everything."

Jez wondered if she'd be so gracious if the situation was reversed but sighed and took another sip of her steaming tea. Doli was an infinitely better person than she was. Sarson too. Those were simply facts.

"Thank you," Taenya said with a lilt in her tone, though it suddenly seemed peppered with a dose of nerves. "I can't wait to see it."

With Taenya's nervous scent growing stronger, Jez forgot about herself for a moment and turned to the elf. But before she could speak, Arleta and Theo appeared with several large bags of sweetened popcorn. Nervousness was replaced by nutty sweetness.

"We got you each a bag," Theo said, holding out the treats.

Jez took one. "Thanks." She immediately popped a piece into her mouth to get her mind off the cold and the question of why Taenya was anxious. It didn't work. *Is it about me?* The thought poked repeatedly at her mind. She absolutely hated the feelings that came with insecurity. Jez had come to Adenashire to get away from that feeling…the feeling that she wasn't good enough. And now she'd been thrust right back into it.

Taenya held out her hand and said, "I'll have one, but I'm going to save it for later." She grabbed the brown bag, folded the top, and placed it under her seat. Then she leaned back and gripped her mug tightly.

"Did you hear the crowd awarded us bonus points for your injury?" Jez asked. She took a sip of her tea and then rammed a handful of popcorn in her mouth to help block Taenya's scent.

"What? Really?" Taenya said.

Jez nodded, the elf's nerves intensifying her own. "They apparently liked how I carried you across the finish line." She didn't mention the kiss.

"It was the best way for us to finish quickly." The elf swallowed hard.

Jez stared at her, wishing she knew what her friend was thinking. She lowered her voice. "Guess the whole *relationship* thing is working."

"I knew it would." Taenya glanced at the stage briefly as the rest of Bard's Honor took their places. An uneasy smile stretched over her lips and she leaned in close to Jez. "We've just got to keep it up."

Jez gulped. *Is she going to kiss me?*

But instead Tanya said, "I'll be back in a minute." She placed her mug under her seat and fiddled with a button on her coat.

"Where are you going?" Jez asked but the elf was already walking away.

Heaviness sank from Jez's chest to her feet. She felt ridiculous.

"Where's Taenya going?" Doli asked, snapping Jez from her thoughts.

"I don't know," Jez said and pulled the blanket up higher to her chin. "She didn't say."

Mr. Figlet walked onstage, and the crowd applauded. But Jez was still looking around to see where Taenya had gone.

"Is she coming back?" the dwarf asked, her attention half on Jez and half on the stage.

A growl rumbled in the back of Jez's throat. "I told you. I don't know." The answer came out as a snap and Jez immediately regretted it.

The band started to play, and Mr. Figlet announced, "Next, I'm excited to announce a last-minute entry. One of our very own Yule Games contestants—"

Jez looked up at the stage, fully expecting Ronan, who'd of course have some stars-awful version of a cheesy Yule song to pump up the audience for his cheater team.

Jez's attitude had gone completely sour, and she was about to get up and leave…until she saw who was onstage. Not Ronan. It was Taenya.

Doli jumped to her feet and nearly spilled her own tea as she clapped.

Jez's jaw dropped and she stared. Taenya stood there in a sparkling white floor-length gown she must have been wearing underneath her coat all along.

"Taenya Carralei," Mr. Figlet announced, "from team one!"

The crowd's cheers sounded slow and muffled to Jez's ears as everything in the land fell away.

The quokkan left the stage, leaving Taenya alone with the band.

The elf announced, "This is an old elven song called 'Winter's Lost Lover.'" Bard's Honor started to play. Taenya's gaze landed on Jez, and she opened her mouth to sing.

The most beautiful sound Jez had ever heard came from her lips. The song was a tale of love and loss, but also the hope that love could be found again. In Jez's mind it was as if magic had overtaken the stage, blocked everything out, and they were the only two people in the world…

Until Doli elbowed her excitedly and snapped her back to reality. "Did you know Taenya could sing like that?"

Jez looked at the audience, who seemed just as enamored with the performance as she was. "No."

Sarson, Arleta, and Theo were on their feet and swaying to the beautiful tune.

Doli leaned close. "Well, between carrying her across the

finish line and this, you two have gotten really good at playing the Games."

Jez sank in her chair and reminded herself, *We're only playing a game… We're only playing a game…*

But this was going to make life infinitely more difficult for her after the Games were over.

19

The morning was hazy. Fog blanketed the competition area, and everyone was extra bundled. Jez gazed around at the crowd waiting for the competition to start. Some sipped warm drinks with steam coming off the cups.

She couldn't get what over what Doli had said to her the night before—that she and Taenya had gotten really good at playing the Games.

And they had. After Taenya's song, people from the crowd had rushed the elf asking if it had been dedicated to Jez, wanting her autograph and basically not leaving her alone. So that morning Jez put her head down, hoping to reach the starting line without being noticed.

But no such luck.

"Hey, Baker," came a deep voice from behind her.

It was Ronan. She knew it was Ronan.

A shiver ran down her spine and all the way down her tail, causing the hair to stand on end. She could pretend she hadn't heard the man. She wanted to quit worrying about whether he was cheating.

"Let it go," the fennex whispered to herself and kept walking, her eyes on the spot beneath the team one banner.

But heavy boot steps followed her. "Jez?"

She gritted her teeth, knowing there was little chance of avoiding him. With a breath she spun around and crossed her arms over her chest. "Do you bother the other contestants like this?"

The ginger man grinned smugly as he held on to his coat lapels with both hands. "Only the ones I have bets for twenty silver with."

Cautiously Jez allowed her scent magic loose and gave the air a good whiff. She caught the sourness of pomposity, but not cheating. Frustration at herself buzzed in her chest, but she quickly tossed that aside and glared at him.

"And do you have wagers going with all the teams?" she asked, studying his face for any signs of dishonesty. She couldn't tell if it was just his smug nature or something more.

"Nay." He grinned even wider. "Just you."

"Lucky me," Jez said with a caustic edge.

Ronan puffed himself up. "Nice song last night. You're fortunate I wasn't prepared with anything."

Mr. Figlet stepped onto the stage while Jez caught sight of Taenya waiting under the banner and looking over at her.

"I'm sure." Anxiety buzzed in her chest and sarcastic words came from her mouth. "Well, good talking to you. But I've gotta get going."

He bobbed his head up and down but didn't take his eyes from her. "Good luck to you and yours." Before she had a chance to get away, Ronan stuck out his elbow and tapped Jez in the upper arm like everything was a joke.

"What in the stars?" she grumbled as she speed-walked to Taenya. She took one look back at the annoying human. He'd already made his way over in front of the bleachers and was laughing with spectators in the front row. He turned slightly and pointed his thumb her way.

Jez quickly turned away. *Is he talking about me to those people?* She could feel the unpleasantness weighing down her expression as she reached the elf.

"What was—" Taenya started.

"He's trying to throw us off our game," Jez half growled, once more feeling out of place in her skin.

The elf's eyes widened. "Did he say something? What did he say?"

The halflings on team two looked their way and leaned in as if trying to hear.

Jez straightened her back and gave them a forced smirk. "Nothing to see here."

They gasped and quickly turned, then whispered something between themselves.

Jez flicked her attention back down the row of teams to the orcs, again munching turkey legs under their own banner.

"What did he say?" the elf asked again, concern in her voice.

Jez ran the conversation through her mind again, and she couldn't come up with anything specific. "I think it's just mental tactics."

Just then Mr. Figlet announced from the stage, "Good morning! Happy Yule Games!"

The crowd cheered and Ronan strutted over to the spot next to his brother. Jez watched him the entire way.

"Listen," Taenya said, pointing to Mr. Figlet.

Jez turned her attention to the marsupial as he gave the audience a big grin. "It's day three of the Yule Games, and today we have a very exciting event." He gestured to his side, and a man with a large wooden sled climbed the steps onto the stage.

"Today is sledding?" Jez grumbled under her breath. She wasn't emotionally prepared for sledding.

"The *sledding* competition!" Mr. Figlet announced.

Feeling extra grouchy, Jez groaned and turned toward the stands. She found Doli and Sarson, then Arleta and Theo waving flags in the audience. "Too bad. They're really missing out," she muttered.

But Taenya must have heard since she snickered and elbowed her teammate. "Jez? Have you never participated in sledding before?"

Jez stared at her a blink too long for comfort. She wanted to say something snappy, confident, but instead, "What? No! I've...*sledded*," tripped off her tongue. Was "sledded" a real word? It sounded strange...and for that matter, were she and Taenya even having the same conversation?

But if they were actually talking about sledding, then over a month before, Doli had dragged her out of bed at the crack of dawn after the first snow and convinced Jez to go sledding.

If they weren't... Jez tended to be a private person concerning her own affairs. She suddenly regretted the allusion she'd made to sledding at the bakery before the Games.

She coughed. "Yes."

The elf's eyes crinkled as she giggled, then lightly bumped the fennex with her hip in jest. "Good. Now channel that energy. We've only got one more competition after this, so we need to do well."

Jez gulped. Maybe Taenya *was* talking about actual sledding.

"The first leg of this race will be a relay." Mr. Figlet pointed to the hill behind them, where volunteers with team numbers on their coats waited with sleds. "One team member will climb to the top and sled down, then the second team member follows suit. Once a team completes the relay, they will immediately proceed to the obstacle course."

Adjacent to the relay area were two side-by-side courses, each with numerous wooden cones painted red to weave the sled through. Then a ramp led to ten pins arranged at the bottom of the hill in a triangle shape.

"Each team will make their way through the cones, over the ramp, and then finally through the pins, where they'll need to knock down as many as possible on the first pass." He held up one finger. "Winning will depend on how quickly each team makes it down the hill and how well they navigate the obstacles. If one obstacle is missed, the team must start that leg again." The marsupial gave a big smile. "And don't forget—showmanship will be rewarded by the crowd at the end of the round. So it's anyone's game!"

"You going to be okay with all that?" Taenya asked quietly. "Climbing that hill twice is going to take a lot of energy."

The hill was fairly steep. But eyeing it, Jez said, "I think so." In the past, she might have taken offense at the question. Not from Taenya, though. Particularly when genuine concern was written all over her face. "I'll just need to rest after."

"Good," Taenya said, rubbing her hands together. "Since we have the ball tonight, I don't want you too tired." Without waiting for a response, she turned her attention back to Mr. Figlet.

The ball? Jez thought. She'd completely forgotten about the ball, but she had no time to dwell on it. Mr. Figlet had just rung the bell. Taenya grabbed her hand and they raced toward the hill.

Once they arrived, Taenya asked, "You first or me?"

"Me," Jez said quickly and took the sled from the gnomish volunteer. She knew it would give her some time to rest before she had to climb the hill again for the obstacle course.

"Thanks," Taenya said to the gnome.

They bobbed their head. "Good luck! I'll be right here to help if you need it."

The elf gave Jez a quick kiss on the cheek. "I'll be waiting!"

Dragging the sled, Jez took off up the hill, fueled with sudden energy. Farther along the slope, Ronan, Ervash, and

Verdreth had also chosen the first slide and were climbing. Determined to beat them, Jez picked up the pace, forcing her boots through the snow and ignoring any of her typical discomforts that might otherwise slow her down.

Behind her the audience cheered, but she was too focused on getting up that hill. She and Taenya had made it this far in the competition, and she would not let Taenya down.

At the top Jez did her best to ignore the other teams. The only thing that mattered was getting back to Taenya at the bottom in one piece. She pulled her sled to where the human volunteer with "Team One" on his coat was waiting.

"Right here," he said and pointed to the spot.

She did as he said. But motion to her left caught her eye, and she saw Ronan already sliding down the hill. "Damn it," Jez growled, and the thought about cheating popped into her mind again, though she had to admit the man was bigger and stronger than she was. Verdreth and the other contestants, including the halfling team, arranged themselves on their sleds.

"Ready?" the volunteer asked, snapping Jez back to what she needed to do.

She plopped onto the sled, and before the human was even able to get out another word, Jez was sliding.

"Shiiiit!" Jez called out. She hadn't been ready. As quick as she could, she grabbed the sides of the sled and did her best to stay in the middle and avoid toppling head over heels. Freezing wind accosted her face and whipped through her loose white hair. But before she knew it, she was sliding through the finish line at the bottom of the hill and Taenya was pulling the sled out from underneath her.

"I lived!" Jez gasped, barely realizing what was happening.

"I'm so glad." The elf gave Jez a quick peck and was gone.

Jez, in a nearly stunned state at her accomplishment, glued her attention to Taenya as she climbed the hill. "Whoo-hoo!" The cheer came out of her unexpectedly, but in that moment she didn't care. "Go, go, go!"

Taenya was nearly at the top, and within seconds she was speeding back down to Jez.

Like a pro, Taenya slid to a stop at the bottom of the hill, stood up, and grasped Jez's hand.

The orcs were already on their way to the next leg of the race, their long muscular legs taking them up the hill quickly.

Exhilaration flooded the fennex, and she followed her friend, not even caring as her boots sank deeply into the snow. She glanced back and spotted Ronan's team directly behind them.

"We need to move," Jez insisted, her breath puffing out in front of her.

"Yes, ma'am!" Taenya picked up the pace, and with a good push forward they finally made it to the top. Another volunteer helped them with their sled and led them to one of the two starting places.

The orcs caught Jez's eye again. They were already halfway down the hill and headed for the ramp.

"They're going to do it," Jez said, her eyes widening and holding her breath.

The two slid onto the ramp and pitched up into the air.

But they didn't leave the end of the ramp cleanly. In a blink their sled tumbled to the left and into a snowbank.

"Oh shit!" Taenya and Jez said in unison.

But the orcs raised their green arms from the snow indicating they were fine and then headed back up the hill to restart their turn. Several volunteers ran down to escort them out of the way for the next team.

The elven volunteer at the first station pointed below to all the different obstacles. "Weave the cones, jump the ramp, and take out as many pins at the bottom of the hill as you can."

Jez's heart pounded after seeing how fast a team could crash and have to start over.

Taenya nodded while Jez did her best not to look over at Ronan and Brady queuing up at the starting line next to them. Without need to discuss it, Taenya took the front spot and Jez sat behind her.

"Hang on!" Taenya yelled back at her.

They pushed off, and it felt like Jez had left her stomach behind. She whipped her arms around Taenya's waist and held on for dear life as the elf maneuvered them down the hill toward the cones. On the second course, Ronan and his brother had already taken the lead.

A growl came from Taenya that sounded more like Jez, and she yelled back to the fennex. "Lean forward! We need to get as flat as possible. Then when I tell you, pull to the right or left!"

Jez tightened in and brought her head down. In front of her Taenya did the same.

"Left!" the elf called.

Jez leaned that way, then to the right as her teammate instructed.

They zigzagged through the cones and then headed straight for the ramp.

Jez's eyes widened and she tucked close to Taenya's back while snow fountained up around them. "You sure you don't want to skip that?" she called, the question muffled by the back of Taenya's coat.

"Stars, no!" Taenya laughed. "Brace yourself!"

Seconds later they launched upward and stayed there for what seemed like an age as Jez's head spun. Then they landed with a hard thump and careened down the hill toward the pins.

"Take them all out!" Jez screamed.

"What do you think I'm doing?" Taenya yelled as she adjusted their course. They plowed into the pins, knocking them into the air.

Skidding across the snow with one runner up in the air, the sled came to an abrupt stop against a tree stump and thumped down. The two women sat panting for a moment, then looked back to see all ten pins on the ground. Ronan's team sailed in a hair behind them and only knocked over eight pins.

But Jez didn't have time to care. The crowd went wild as Taenya and Jez threw their arms around each other and squealed with delight over their accomplishment.

The judges held up signs showing a perfect score.

So yes, Ronan had made it to the last round…but so had they.

And they'd done it really well.

20

The way back was its regular chaos, but Jez managed to keep her head down all the way to It's About Tome and made it through the back entrance without attracting a lick of attention. In fact, she barely remembered the trip.

She was excited, but also exhausted. Taenya had told her to go get a nap in.

One more day and the Games would be over.

Her boots shuffled against the wooden floor, and she briefly closed her eyes, reveling in the silence. If she avoided looking at the front window display, she could almost pretend everything was normal. But of course it wasn't. She glanced at the staircase leading up to her and Doli's apartment. The thought of stairs after climbing that big hill twice did not appeal, and then there was her roommate's Yule wonderland to contend with.

So instead, she peeled off her coat and started a fire in the fireplace, then flopped herself into the nearest armchair, which was quite roomy as it was ogre-sized. Everything around her was quiet, and she allowed her scent ability to return to normal. She thoroughly enjoyed the aromas of the shop, particularly when it was closed. The slightly acrid tinge of burnt candles and the must of old books smelled friendly to her. She threw her legs across the overstuffed chair's arm and nestled back into the worn cushions. Her eyes drooped, and she quickly drifted into the nicest dream.

Thrump.

The sound shot her eyes open to find Arleta standing in front of her and an enormous book on the floor, whose title she couldn't make out through her sleep-deprived eyes. All she knew was that her neck was pinched.

"Sorry," Arleta said through gritted teeth. "I didn't mean to wake you like that, but I accidentally bumped into that table." She bent to pick up the book and carefully returned it to Doli's Yule Games display.

Jez blinked sleepily. "What are you doing in here?

"Looking for you." Arleta plopped into the other chair. "You and Tae disappeared, and no one knew where you went." She looked around the bookstore for a second. "So I came here."

"Taenya went home, and I really needed a break from everything." Jez swung her legs off the chair arm and placed her feet on the floor.

"The Goat was packed," the human said. "So I doubt you would have enjoyed it anyway."

"How long was I out?" Jez asked, yawning.

Arleta shrugged. "It took over an hour to get our lunch after we left the sled race, so at least that long."

Jez's foggy mind felt as if she'd slept for more than an hour, but that could have been from the crick in her neck. She rubbed at the pain.

"Your bed probably would have been more comfortable." Arleta eyed the stairs. "And it wasn't *that* much farther."

"Have you seen the apartment?" Jez said dryly.

The human chuckled. "No. But Doli mentioned what she'd done. She said you weren't a fan."

Jez slouched back in the chair. "This is fine. I could sleep here well into the night."

"And miss the ball?" Arleta asked.

"That's tonight?" Jez groaned. It was all coming back to her. "All the more reason to go back to sleep."

Arleta reached out and nudged her on the shoulder. "Yes, the Yule Games Ball is tonight. And don't forget that you attended the one at the Baking Battle and enjoyed yourself. Theo and I are going, Doli and Sarson, my dads...who are already planning to compete in next year's Games after their loss today." She shrugged. "It'll be fun. Plus, you don't want Tae to show up by herself."

An immediate picture came to mind of Taenya standing on the sidelines while everyone else was dancing and having a good time. "I can still get a few more hours of shut-eye before it starts."

Arleta rolled her eyes and planted her hand on her hip. "I understand you need your rest. Maintaining good health is always important. *And* you can achieve balance, Jez. I saw you out there today… You and Tae were having a good time."

It was true. Taenya wasn't a magical cure or anything, but being with her increased Jez's energy. Taenya helped her see life a little differently. A small smile slipped over Jez's mouth.

"You are, aren't you?" Arleta said with a lilt in her tone. "Having a good time."

Jez immediately wiped the expression off her face. "I don't know."

The human pressed her lips into a thin line. "You're talking to a person who did a damn good job at hiding my own feelings…even from myself."

Jez's chest tightened. "What are you talking about?" But she knew exactly what her friend was talking about, and she didn't like the accusation.

Arleta stared at the fennex for what seemed like an abnormally long time. At first Jez's upper arms tingled as she waited for a response from her friend. Then the feeling moved into her chest and the hair on her tail stood on end. The entire experience was like tiny ants crawling all over her.

"What?" Jez finally demanded when she couldn't stand it anymore.

"We haven't been friends forever," Arleta said. "But I've been watching you out there. You're happier…smiling more. And don't try to tell me it's your pretend-relationship

silliness. Not one time since I met you have you been able to fake anything for long."

She was right and Jez knew it. Yes, in the past she'd been able to fake cordiality. That was required of her back home, but actual happiness? She wasn't good at that.

"But since you *are* going tonight and your team is doing so well in the Games, how about we go and get you something new to wear?" Arleta stood.

Jez opened her mouth to protest, but her friend waggled an admonitory finger.

"You and Tae are the ones who insist on showing off your *relationship*." She made air quotes with her fingers. "*So* you need to make a good impression." Arleta pulled her up from the chair. "And you're almost through this thing. Then you can nap all you want."

"But then the bookshop will be open again. So, not *all* I want," Jez half whined.

Arleta scoffed and raised a brow. She obviously knew Jez was not entirely serious. "You love working at the bookstore. And if there are days you really don't feel well, Verdreth or Doli will fill in for you. Just think if you had to get up at the crack of dawn and make five batches of cookies for the bakery."

"But you *love* making cookies," Jez retorted as Arleta retrieved Jez's coat and shoved it into the fennex's hands.

"True. And you can't always miss out due to *naptime*." She made quotes in the air with her fingers again.

"I disagree." But Jez said it with the tiniest of smiles and donned the coat as her friend led the way down the back hall and opened the door. The frigid air wrinkled Jez's nose. She turned to look longingly at the stairs leading to her bed. "I do have clothes I could wear."

But Arleta caught her arm. "Of course you do, but you want to make an impression, remember? Plus, the owner of A Silken Spindle was nice enough to provide the remaining teams with clothes for the ball."

Jez sighed. "Fine."

They made their way out to the street and down the road. Jez realized that she'd begun to grow accustomed to all the new smells in the air, and they weren't bothering her quite so much as they had in the past few days.

A Silken Spindle was the fanciest clothing shop in Adenashire. The storefront was painted black and white, and the sign over the eaves had scripty gold lettering outlined in a thin strip of black. Jez had never set foot in this place. The only new clothes she'd gotten since arriving in town were the ones Doli had made for her. And those were completely adequate.

They climbed the stairs, and Arleta opened the shop door. Immediately Jez caught a whiff of spicy perfume and blinked as the scent burned her eyes and sinuses. Her ears lay back against the top of her head. But she quickly shook the negative feeling off and locked down her sense of smell again to get through the next…however long the exasperating shopping trip was going to take.

The quicker she picked something, the more nap time she could fit in before the ball.

The shop was larger than it had appeared from the outside. Scores of long-sleeve shirts and coats hung on the wall. An overstuffed rack of pants waited to her left, and on the right were dresses and skirts in all colors of the rainbow. Jez gulped at the extensive selection.

Arleta was already thumbing through a selection of dresses when Jez plucked a brown mottled leather vest from its place and held it in the air.

"How about this?" she said, feeling too overwhelmed to step more than a few feet into the shop.

"You already have one like that!" Doli said as she stepped into the shop from the back room.

Jez flinched and nearly dropped the vest.

The umber-skinned dwarf was dressed in a slightly too-long satin dress in robin's egg blue with lace all along the neckline. Jez scratched her neck just thinking how it might feel on her own skin.

"I think she has a black vest," Arleta answered.

Jez straightened her back and held the vest up with confidence. "Yes. This one is *very* different."

Taenya appeared from around the corner with a large cloth bundle in her arms and stopped when she saw Arleta and Jez. Jez nearly dropped the vest again at the sight of her.

"Got my dress for tonight." Taenya lifted the bundle, which Jez surmised was a covering for the dress inside, unless the dress was made of tan cotton.

A woman, tall with long white hair and tattoos on her hands, followed Taenya. She wore a long black dress that Jez thought was made of silk. The fennex didn't know her personally but knew that her name was Loreine Lakewood, a wizard with magic related to cloth. She only knew this because Doli had often spoken of A Silken Spindle and stopped in often to chat with Loreine about the latest fashions in the Northern Lands. Not that Jez cared about those things, but she'd listen to Doli talking about them.

The wizard's eyes were trained on Doli and her too-long dress. She waved her hand in the air and immediately the hem of the dress curled under and ended at exactly the right length for the dwarf.

"Perfect," Loreine said, gazing over the round, dark-rimmed spectacles perched at the end of her long nose.

Doli looked down at the dress and ran her hands over it. "It really is. You do the best work!"

The wizard beamed and then turned to Taenya. "I see your partner is here. Would you like to get matching outfits for the ball?"

Jez gulped at the word "partner." Loreine could simply have meant they were partners in the Games…but everyone in town now thought she and Taenya were dating. She caught eyes with the elf.

Taenya glanced away and gave a shy grin as she patted her bundle. "No, I think I'm going to let it be a surprise."

"Very well then," Loreine said. "I believe you are all set."

"Are you sure there's no charge?" Taenya asked as she walked over to stand next to Jez.

The wizard shook her head. "It's been my plan to provide outfits to the top six teams." Her eyes brightened. "Enjoy your evening."

Taenya flitted her attention to Jez. "I hope to."

The words spun in Jez's mind, and she clutched the vest as the elf left the store.

"You are very lucky." Loreine was somehow at Jez's side and took the vest from her hand.

"What?" Jez said, dazed.

Loreine adjusted her glasses and held the garment up closer to her face. "I have something in the back to go with this that you may like." She turned and strode to the back of the store.

Arleta left the display of dresses and came to Jez's side. "Are you okay?"

Quickly Jez turned to a rack of belts and thumbed through them. "These are nice."

Doli gave Jez a quizzical look. "Are you two not pretending anymore?" She kept her voice down, picked up the hem of her dress, and came to Jez's side.

"I don't know what you're talking about," Jez declared. She grabbed a brown belt with a gold buckle and held it out to Doli.

The dwarf smirked and didn't take it. She exchanged glances with Arleta. "We weren't born yesterday, you know."

"There's nothing going on with Taenya and me," Jez whispered and widened her eyes at her friends. "We're only trying to win."

Before they could interrogate her more, Loreine thankfully came out of the back with no fewer than five pairs of pants and matching shirts. Despite the horror of trying them on, the fennex knew the only way to move on to another subject was to oblige.

"Those look nice," she shot past her friends to the

seamstress, but she felt both Doli's and Arleta's interested eyes on her back.

As Loreine held up the seemingly endless options, Jez only nodded; her mind was unusually stuck on whatever Taenya had in her bundle and how she might look in it that evening.

21

Ronan entertained a large group across the room from the buffet table. Jez did her best to ignore the annoying man as she stood next to the orcs, tugging at her brown leather vest and then the golden button at the top of her shirt. Doli and Arleta had ultimately chosen the uncomfortable ensemble.

"Is it hot in here?" she asked Verdreth.

Verdreth wore a freshly pressed pair of black pants with a tailored blue cotton shirt, while Ervash actually had a shirt on for the occasion. He looked about as uncomfortable as Jez felt.

"It's always hot," Verdreth said and popped several tiny pink cakes decorated with sugar snowflakes onto his plate. "So don't ask me."

Ervash didn't have a plate. He simply selected morsels from the table and placed them directly in his mouth. "He's right."

The buffet was the largest Jez had seen since the Baking Battle. There were desserts, hot and cold appetizers, drinks. Servers even walked around with more overloaded trays of food. But Jez wasn't hungry for any of it. She shook her head and blew out her breath so hard that her cheeks puffed up.

Taenya was late, and worries swirled around in the fennex's mind. *Did she change her mind? Maybe she's not coming.* Jez's tail flicked behind her in irritation.

She left the orcs to their grazing and moved toward the wall where the crowd was thinnest. She took deep breaths while eyeing the musicians and the people out on the dance floor. Arleta and Theo were dancing and smiling like they were having a great time…and they hadn't even gotten new clothes for the event. Arleta had told Jez that she and Theo were trying to save up coins for something, though she didn't say what. Instead, she wore the ruffly yellow dress Doli had made for her during the Baking Battle.

Jez tugged at her collar again while trying to ignore the itchiness of the pants. How she'd let Arleta talk her into the outfit, she still didn't know. But everything about the Yule Ball brought back bad memories and expectations.

"I should go," Jez muttered to herself.

"Sarson and I got you a lemonade." Doli's voice came from behind her. Jez turned just in time for the dwarf to push the glass into her hand.

Jez stared at the drink for a second. It had slices of lemon in it and was slushy, as if the lemonade had been mixed with snow. Then she looked up at Sarson and Doli, who were of course smiling. Doli wore the overly frilly dress she'd bought at the dress shop, but it suited her. The fennex eyed Sarson's giant blue wings tucked as usual behind his back and his tail lightly wrapping Doli's waist. Normally she would have rolled her eyes at the sight of them but decided to keep the sentiment to herself this time.

Sarson held two lemonades in his clawed hands. "I'm going to give these to Verdreth and Ervash," he said to Doli.

"I'll miss you," Doli cooed. He gave her a wink and left.

This time, Jez did roll her eyes while Doli wasn't looking. "Thanks," she muttered when the dwarf turned back to her.

"You were considering leaving, weren't you?" Doli accused.

"No!" Jez shot back.

The dwarf pinched her lips. "You need to stay."

A growl rolled in Jez's throat as a spot on the left side of her waist suddenly became almost unbearably itchy. "What if she's not coming?"

"Is that what you're thinking in that silly head of yours?" Doli sipped her own lemonade.

"My head is not silly," Jez insisted, giving into the need to scratch.

The dwarf shook her head and swayed slightly to the music. "I'm pretty sure—on occasion—the thoughts inside it are."

She wasn't wrong, and Jez knew it.

"Before I went to get ready at Sarson's this afternoon, I

ran into Taenya," Doli said. "She showed me her dress and seemed really excited to wear it tonight. She's coming. No need to worry."

Jez glanced at the clock on the wall across the room. "Then why is she so late?"

Doli's brown eyes moved to the ballroom entrance and lit up. "There she is now."

With a quick twist Jez turned to lay eyes on the most beautiful person she'd ever seen. Taenya stood under the twinkling lights of the entrance. She wore a long, green crushed velvet dress that flared out at the waist. The lights above and behind her cast a halo on top of her head and gleamed on the jewels around her neck.

Jez sucked in a breath.

"She looks so pretty!" Doli squealed and lightly pushed Jez forward. "Don't just stand there."

"Uh, yeah." Jez picked up her feet and walked toward the elf, ignoring everything else in the room as Taenya handed her coat to someone.

The elf saw her and smiled, but Jez's lips stayed frozen. She had no idea what they were actually doing.

"Did you bring me a lemonade?" Taenya said when the fennex finally got to her.

Jez looked down at the drink still in her hand. She'd completely forgotten about it. "Yes?" She held it out to the elf, who took it.

"Thank you," she said and took a gulp. "I'm so thirsty."

The two moved away from the doorway and stood side by side overlooking the dance floor. Jez's hands didn't quite know what to do with themselves, so she crossed her arms over her chest to keep them from dangling.

"You look nice," Jez managed without looking at Taenya.

"Oh, thank you," she said. "The dress has pockets." Taenya shoved her hands into the openings and spun around to show Jez.

The fennex glanced down and then back up at Taenya's face. Her lips were stained red and looked incredibly soft. "P…pockets are good."

"They are!" Taenya set her empty cup down on a tray and looked out at the dance floor again. "We should probably dance and give these people a better show than standing off to the side."

Jez liked standing off to the side, but she knew what Taenya meant, and tomorrow was the last day of the Yule Games. "Maybe one dance."

Taenya took Jez's hand. The touch was warm, but Jez barely had a chance to process it before she'd been pulled into the middle of the dance floor. With a flourish Taenya had one hand around Jez's waist and their other hands clasped up in the air.

"I assume you want me to lead?" Taenya whispered.

Jez had no clue how to dance; she'd always avoided the activity when possible by hugging the walls instead. "That would be good."

Everything started a little shaky, but by the fourth dance Jez was starting to get it. And being out there with Taenya made everything that much easier.

A woman dancing with a tall, hat-wearing gnome swung

in close to Jez and Taenya. "Congratulations on making it to the top six."

Jez actually smiled upon hearing it. She was surprised to realize that she was having fun. The sight of Ronan in his own fancy suit soured her thoughts for a moment. But she was determined to cast the negativity aside and have fun with Taenya.

"*Bready* or not, here we come!" The words slipped out of the fennex's mouth before she could stop them, and she instantly regretted the silliness.

But the woman only laughed and danced away with her partner.

Taenya giggled, her green eyes sparkling under the fairy lights. And for Jez everything else seemed to melt away as they moved to the center of the dance floor and into their own little world. Perhaps being silly sometimes wasn't such a bad thing, and she was going to enjoy the time while she had it. Jez smiled at the elf.

"I like you, Jez," Taenya whispered, her voice slightly shaky.

Jez rolled her eyes and chuckled. "Of course you like me. We're friends." She leaned closer and whispered, "You're doing a great job at this fake relationship thing. People really love us."

The elf lowered her gaze and gulped as if she had something else to say but was having a difficult time saying it. "I don't mean like that. I'm not faking it anymore. I don't know if I ever was."

Shit, shit, shit. The words rotated in Jez's mind. Had

she thought about Taenya in a different way? Yes. But how would they ever make that work? It was simply easier to remain friends. What would happen if they fought…broke up? Then everything would be lost. Panic swelled in Jez's chest and it felt as though she couldn't breathe.

The music suddenly got louder while her thoughts whirled. Taenya couldn't be serious. It had to be a joke… part of showing off their fake relationship.

The fennex stepped back and stared at Taenya. Her mouth became as dry as the Southern Desert and someone bumped into her. Still, she got out, "That's not something you should be saying." She wanted to flee, go anywhere else but here, but her legs felt like they had bricks at the ends where her boots should be.

"Why not?" Taenya said, coming back in to resume the dance. But she sounded unsure, like she'd made a mistake.

Jez's upper half suddenly stiffened, but somehow her heavy feet moved side to side to keep up with Taenya. "Because…because I'm not a good dancer." What a ridiculous thing to say.

"You think I didn't know that?" the elf said into her ear and then spun the fennex in an awkward twirl. "Your dancing ability is not what drew me to you. You're protective and loyal."

"I'm so protective I make poor judgments about people all the time." She glanced over at Doli and Sarson dancing and having a regular old good time being in love. "I nearly ruined Doli's chances with him when they first met."

"And you apologized, and everything is fine between you

all now." The elf pushed the corners of her lips into a hopeful grin, keeping Jez's hand clasped in hers.

The music kept getting louder, and Jez winced. Old feelings swelled inside her…feelings that made her want to dash from the ball and hide under the covers in her bedroom, or even leave Adenashire completely. "It's not that easy, and you know it."

"It can be if you like me back," Taenya said and lowered her eyes. "In *that* way, of course."

Jez pulled away from Taenya. *And what if I don't?* The question gripped onto her tongue and she glanced around, nervousness pricking at her chest. But she didn't say it for two reasons. The first and most important was because it wasn't true. Jez *did* like Taenya like that. She was the kindest, most hardworking person she knew—and that was saying a lot because all of her friends possessed these qualities. She was also heartbreakingly beautiful in her emerald dress and sparkling necklace, with her auburn hair held back on both sides by jeweled combs and curling ever so slightly at the ends.

Jez almost never noticed things like that. But when it was Taenya, it seemed she did.

She didn't want to admit it was true, but it was.

As if the air had magically been sucked from the room, Jez's lungs gasped for breath, and her head became light. "I need some air," she said, then spun on her boot heel and pushed through the crowded dance floor, leaving the elf behind.

A moment later she found herself outside, coatless, with the cold quickly settling into her bones.

"I think you forgot something," teased a faun with curly red hair standing in the entrance, thick laughter in his tone.

"No shit!" Jez snapped, baring her teeth. She immediately felt guilty but didn't change her expression.

The faun flung his hands chest high in surrender, and Jez regretted her words a second time.

"Sorry," she muttered as the faun scurried away. "Sorry," she yelled, then started as she realized that Taenya stood in the doorway with Jez's coat in hand.

The elf held it up, then marched down the stairs. "You left this."

Jez grabbed the coat and threaded her arms into it. With chattering teeth she quickly buttoned it up and retrieved the gloves from the pockets. "Thanks." The word came out tainted with the shame Jez felt for the way she'd acted.

Taenya pulled Jez back inside and into the coatroom, where thankfully the loud music and chatter were muffled by the walls. "You didn't answer me," she said. "If we really are friends, I deserve a different response than running away."

Jez felt compelled to pace like a caged animal, but there was no space for it in this cramped little room.

"Running away is what I do," she said, keeping her voice down and pushing her hands into the striped gloves Taenya had given her on the first day of the Games. "You don't want me as a partner. I'm not good at it." She turned toward the exit.

But Taenya grabbed Jez by the shoulders to keep her from leaving. "Who lied to you and told you that?

A human walked into the room, and her eyes widened upon seeing the pair.

"What do you want?" Jez snapped.

"Um, my coat," the lady said in a small voice.

Jez ripped a random coat off the hook and handed it to her. "Take this one."

"That's not mine," she said, horrified.

"Take it anyway," Jez and Taenya said in unison.

The human woman gripped the fluffy fur-collared coat, which was so big it looked like it had been tailored for a giant. She stood frozen, but neither Taenya nor Jez budged.

"I think I'll stay at the party a little longer," the woman said and slowly placed the coat on the nearest hook.

Taenya patted her on the shoulder. "Good plan. See you tomorrow at the Games." She gave a forced smile.

When the woman finally left, Jez let out the breath she'd been holding, and the elf's icing sugar scent permeated her nose. Her knees went weak, but she quickly locked them to keep upright.

Taenya stepped closer and rested gentle hands on the fennex's shoulders. "Who said you're not a good partner?"

"No one," Jez managed, but it wasn't true. She'd heard it hundreds of times. "I'm just not."

"I know when someone is hiding a part of themselves, Jez." The elf tightened her grip. "I did it for years, and it took Arleta to see through the façade and invite me in." Her voice softened. "You and me…we're not that different. And you deserve to be happy."

Jez looked into Taenya's green eyes. She wanted to tell her

everything…her whole story. But it was stuck at the back of her throat. "I'll see you in the morning." She averted her eyes. "Thank you for my coat. But you should go back to the party."

Taenya glanced around the coatroom. "And leave you here?"

The fennex gulped and nodded.

"Okaayy." Taenya released Jez's shoulders and let out a long, frustrated sigh. "But this conversation isn't over."

Jez stood silently as the elf turned and walked from the closet. When she was completely out of sight, Jez leaned back against the wall beside the giant furry coat she had handed the woman moments before.

"Yeah." Ronan's voice wafted from outside the coatroom, and Jez scrambled to bury herself behind the coat. "We've really got this thing in the bag."

Jez gritted her teeth.

His large boots clunked into the room, and Jez looked down at her own boots sticking out under the coat's hem. As quietly as possible, she slid them back against the wall.

"Oh, you stopped into that shop to get the you-know-what, right?" It was his brother, Brady.

You-know-what? Jez frowned.

"It wasn't ready," Ronan said and grabbed two coats off the wall. "I have to go back to Spells and Sortilege first thing in the morning. But he's going to take care of everything."

They are *cheating!* Jez thought. She released her scent magic but immediately got a whiff of musk from the coat in her face. Her throat closed up and she was barely able to hold back a cough. She shut it down again.

"Well," Brady said, "tomorrow is the last day, so we'd better put it to good use."

With that, they left. Jez waited a few minutes to be sure they were really gone, then came out from her hiding place. She wanted to confront them right then and there but stopped herself. She'd need to follow Ronan to the shop first thing in the morning.

22

The moon and stars were still in the sky. Jez stood under them with chattering teeth and a near-frozen tail as she watched the Spells and Sortilege shop. But she hadn't wanted to miss Ronan if he got there very early.

She was regretting her choices.

Adenashire was mostly deserted at such an early hour, so all she had were her thoughts. And those weren't good company. Mostly they were wrapped up in how cold it was even though she'd donned her coat, her warmest sweater and pants, two pairs of socks inside her boots, and the gloves Taenya had given her. But the layers weren't nearly warm enough to be standing outside when instead she could be tucked into her cozy bed.

Then there was the fact that she'd wanted to forget about

Ronan cheating. She'd wanted to just move on and finish the Games.

"Why did I have to be in that damn coat closet last night?" she grumbled to herself.

Even so, she stood across the street at Floral Fantasies nestled among the Yule trees for sale. They were a perfect hiding place and still provided a good view of the spell shop.

If she didn't fall asleep, that is. Her eyes had drooped closed at least five times since she'd arrived.

Jez's stomach rumbled, and she pulled her arms around it to stop the noise. She had been so wrapped up in thoughts about Ronan and Brady cheating that she hadn't thought to pack something to eat before she left.

After what seemed like hours, the sun cracked over the horizon, painting streaks of watercolor oranges and pinks across the sky. The tones quickly swallowed up the moon and stars and replaced them with a new day.

A day Jez wasn't entirely sure she wanted to start. For one thing, if Ronan was cheating, she'd need proof to show the judges and Mr. Figlet.

She pushed the other reason to the back of her mind, but it rebounded.

Dropping to a squat, Jez closed her eyes for a moment and replayed the conversation with Taenya the night before. They'd been having such a good time…dancing, laughing… and then the elf did what she did. She announced to Jez that she liked her…like, *really* liked her.

And it went and ruined everything.

Jez's stomach clenched. She wasn't sure if it was the

hunger or something else. But before the Games she'd told Taenya that romance could ruin a perfectly good friendship, and it was true.

Didn't the elf see that?

It didn't matter that Jez might return Taenya's interest. What would happen if she reciprocated, and then it didn't work out? Everything would be awkward from that point forward. The bakery would be off-limits…any get-togethers at the orcs' home…even walking on the street might be a problem. How would they be able to sit together and have conversations?

Jez would miss that. Her chest pinched.

"What if I kissed her?" Jez muttered, not meaning to say the words out loud. Embarrassed, she glanced around to see if anyone was there. But the streets were still empty. Of course, there was the fact that during the Games, Taenya *had* kissed Jez. And Jez had liked it. But that was under the guise of pretending to date…to give the spectators a good show.

And that was different.

Then realization heated up Jez's chest. Taenya had said she might have never been faking her interest. So was the kiss after she hurt her ankle real for Taenya?

What did it all mean? Was everything *already* awkward and ruined?

Confusion jumbled Jez's thoughts even further when she caught a whiff of icing sugar, and her eyes shot open to Taenya standing right in front of her.

She sprang up from her crouched position to her full

height and looked around, not quite knowing what to do with herself. "What are you doing here?"

The elf's eyebrows furrowed as she clutched her bag. "I couldn't sleep last night."

Not sleeping didn't explain why she was standing there, but a light flicked on in Spells and Sortilege, drawing Jez's attention briefly. "Yeah, me neither," Jez muttered and looked to the ground, her heart fluttering.

"I feel bad about what I said at the ball," Taenya said, keeping her voice soft.

Jez gulped, and sickness roiled in her middle. What did she mean by that? Was what she'd said untrue? The thought both relieved and terrified Jez at the same time.

"We were just having such a good time," the elf said, still clutching her bag. "I thought the moment was right."

"Well, it wasn't," Jez grumbled and flicked her gaze up to Taenya.

Taenya cleared her throat and reached into her bag. "I know that now. So I brought you a peace offering." She drew a tidily wrapped brown paper package out. The sides were stained with patches of oil. "I was up baking all night."

Jez gave a nervous chuckle while she stared at the package. "You sound like Arleta."

"She's told you she stress-bakes too?" Taenya held the package out closer to Jez. "She and I are a lot alike."

Salivating, Jez took it and opened the paper. Inside was an orange slice of brown-specked pumpkin bread topped off with a white sugary glacé. Jez inhaled the scent. "It looks delicious."

"If you like it I've got four more loaves back at my cottage," Taenya said. "And there's no obligation."

Jez took a bite of the sweet, spicy bread and eyed her friend. She knew Taenya wasn't talking about the bread.

Tentatively, the elf held out her hand and said, "Friends?"

The fennex took in a deep breath, nodded, and clasped her hand. But it felt as if a lightning bolt had traveled up her arm. "Friends," she managed.

After a blink, Taenya looked around and confusion took over her features. "So, friend to friend. What *are* you doing out here?"

Nervousness forced Jez to pop the rest of the bread in her mouth and chew for what seemed like a very long time. A small part of her had almost forgotten why she was out there in the first place while they'd been talking. But what she'd heard in the coatroom, along with the other things she'd suspected of Ronan over the course of the Games, came flooding back to her.

Before she could begin explaining, Ronan appeared at the end of the street.

"Get down," she whispered, grabbing Taenya and lowering them both to a crouch between the spiky Yule trees.

"What's going on?" Taenya whispered, alarmed.

"Shhh," Jez hushed her while she watched Ronan open the shop door.

Taenya turned to see what Jez was looking at. "Is that Ronan? Why are you watching him?"

"Shhh!" Jez said again and pricked her ears to listen.

"Good morning. Last day of the Games!" Ronan said in a jolly tone before he shut the door behind him.

Jez pursed her lips. She needed to get closer to hear anything damning. Her attention flicked to Taenya. She hadn't wanted her there, but if the elf heard the evidence of cheating for herself, then their case to the judges would be that much more solid. "Come on!" She stood and pulled Taenya with her.

"What are we doing?" Taenya demanded in a low voice as Jez jogged across the street and around to a side window.

It was covered in a thin layer of frost, but while the people inside seemed to have their backs turned, Jez reached up and wiped a small portion of it away to get a better view.

"I don't understand what's going on," Taenya whispered.

Quickly Jez filled her in on what she'd heard in the coatroom after Taenya had left. Then she added in all the other suspicious activities she'd seen, like the gambling ring Landon was running. It sounded good coming out of her mouth, but the elf's expression remained flat.

"I thought you'd let this go. You don't have any solid proof, Jez," Taenya said.

"What do you think we're here for?" She peeked inside the window in time to see Brady walk in the front door. Jez ducked. But the trio walked farther from the window and stood with their backs to it.

"What are they doing?" Taenya whispered, suddenly seeming a bit more interested. "It *is* weird that they're here in the shop so early."

Jez whipped her gaze to the elf. "See? I told you!" She

quickly drew her attention back to what was happening inside the shop. "I'm pretty sure they've been buying magic spells and potions to affect the outcome of the Games," Jez whispered.

The wizard fiddled with something Jez couldn't quite see but then turned and held out a small clear glass to Ronan, who took it.

"We really need to hear what they're saying," Taenya said. "Even if it's true, we still don't have any proof to show the judges."

Jez's eyes widened as she kept her focus on what was happening in the shop. "So you believe me now?"

"I can see what you're saying, at least," Taenya admitted. "Can you smell anything?"

Jez inhaled but didn't get anything. The scents associated with cheating were often ones that needed closer proximity. Or it could have been her nearly frozen face…or the fact that Taenya's icing sugar was too strong. "I need to be closer."

"Let's check around the front," the elf said and gestured around the corner of the building.

The two snuck around to the entrance and found the door slightly ajar.

Jez sniffed the air but frustratingly still didn't pick up anything damning. She did get a bit of excitement and anticipation coming from inside the shop.

"Anything?" the elf whispered.

"Maybe," Jez fibbed, but she was still confident they'd get something solid.

They stood to the side of the door and listened.

"I can't believe you were actually able to get this for us," Ronan said, his voice low. "And just in time."

The wizard spoke and gave a little laugh as he said, "The right amount of silver makes everything easier."

A chill ran down the length of Jez's spine and made the hairs on her tail stand on end. Taenya leaned in closer.

"By the stars." Brady chuckled. "Isn't that the truth?"

"And you can guarantee that no one will know it was us?" Ronan asked.

Jez pulled back and looked at Taenya. "I told you," she whispered.

The elf's eyes were as wide as saucers. *She finally believes me*, Jez thought.

"As promised," the wizard said. "This transaction will be just between us three."

"Fantastic," Ronan said. "Because no one can know it was us."

The fennex seethed. This had to be stopped. She moved toward the door, but Taenya grabbed her arm.

"We should get help," she murmured. "What are we going to do once we're in there?"

Anger at the situation buzzed in Jez's chest, and her jaw tensed. "If we try to do that, everyone will be gone by the time we get back. We either do this now or we lose our chance." But she didn't wait for Taenya to answer. Instead, Jez threw her arm against the wooden door and flung it open.

Immediately the men flipped around, forming a wall to hide whatever it was behind them.

Jez stormed into the shop with Taenya behind her. Her eyes burned as if with fire, and she clenched her clawed fists into balls. "You're cheating at the Games, Ronan." She flipped her gaze over to the wizard. "And you have been helping him."

"What?" the wizard said in a panic.

But Jez didn't give him the chance to speak. "Using magic in the Games is against the rules, and you've been helping them hide the fact they've been using it."

"What are you talking about?" Brady asked.

"Don't you play innocent," Jez growled. "You've been a part of this all along too. The tree root from nowhere…how you won the scavenger hunt so easily. Plus I heard you in the coatroom last night."

Ronan's features registered confusion. "I don't know what you think you heard—"

"Don't you try to tell me I didn't hear it," Jez snapped.

"Jez…" Taenya said from behind her.

The shop owner stepped forward and reached his hand out. "This is a serious accusation."

"And what you're doing is wrong," Jez snapped.

"What's wrong is accusing someone falsely of cheating," Ronan said. "You could get Ibus shut down by doing something like that."

The wizard raised his brows in alarm. "Shut down?"

"Jez…" Taenya took her elbow. "I think—"

But Jez pulled away, confused, as the three men stepped aside to reveal a large order of sparkling wine behind them.

"What's this?" she demanded and sniffed the air.

Ronan crossed his arms over his chest. "It was supposed to be a surprise for all the Games contestants. To celebrate the winner"—he eyed Jez—"no matter which team comes in first. Just like the roses from Floral Fantasies."

He bought the roses too? Jez's mind whirled.

"My brother has a vineyard," Ibus said.

Jez backed up, still sniffing the air, but she still didn't get anything that would indicate cheating. It *had* to be there. But it wasn't.

Had it all been in her mind? Had she made it up and woven a conspiracy that wasn't there?

Embarrassment twisted in her chest. She couldn't even look at Taenya. "I should never have agreed to the Games in the first place," she said to the ground. "I'm done with this damn thing."

With that, she turned and ran out of the shop.

23

Crunching bootsteps followed Jez on the snow-packed path outside of town.

"Leave me alone." Tears stung at Jez's eyes, but she refused to release them. Tears were a sign of weakness, and she would not be seen as any weaker than she already appeared.

"I will not," Taenya said. "Please tell me what happened to you."

The fennex halted on the crunchy snow, trembling and biting her lower lip.

"What in the stars do you mean?" Jez said. "I was just wrong. I accused Ronan of doing shit he wasn't actually doing. That's on me. I'm not a good person. I always do this."

Taenya stopped directly behind her and gently placed her hand on Jez's upper arm. "I'm sorry someone hurt you."

Jez closed her eyes and enjoyed the warmth. "We've all been hurt in one way or another," she muttered and threw her hand in the air. "It's nothing new in this world. It's no excuse for me hurting people and making a mess of things all the time."

The elf let go and slowly walked around to face the fennex. Jez's nose twitched as she kept her scent magic blocked as much as possible. She wanted nothing to do with icing sugar at that moment.

"But this is *your* pain, *your* story. And I—not to mention all of your other friends—want to be here to help shoulder it." Taenya glanced away for a second and then back at Jez. "You don't have to go it alone." Her voice was soft and sweet. Genuine.

Jez didn't answer. But she wanted to.

"Take a walk with me." The elf slipped her hand into Jez's and the fennex didn't resist.

Jez rolled her eyes. "I was on a walk. By myself."

"You don't have to be alone." Taenya squeezed Jez's fingers. "I'm here. And no matter what *we* are, I'm not going anywhere. And I want to know your story."

Jez's chest pinched and the two walked along the path for quite some time before she finally spoke. "I grew up in a very important household in the Southern Desert. My father is Mallo Sanddriffter."

"The Baron of Dryward?" Taenya said. "My parents mentioned him from their diplomatic travels."

"I'm sure they did," Jez muttered. "He's fairly well-known."

"Well-known. That's an understatement." Taenya scoffed. "Your family is *really* high ranking in the Southern Desert."

"Tell me about it," Jez groaned. "When I was a small kit, my scent magic developed, and my family was ecstatic. All fennex have strong scent abilities, but magic on top of that made me a great candidate to take my father's seat…eventually. Smelling people's intentions and emotions is apparently an asset in negotiations."

Taenya didn't speak but squeezed Jez's hand.

"And when I was old enough to understand, I wanted to use the magic," Jez said. "I really did. I used it at social events, and then my father would ask me questions about the people who attended them. But every time ended in headaches and overwhelm. And the more I did it, the more severe they became. For a long time I didn't even tell my parents, and they thought I was doing great. But it kept getting worse, and one day I locked myself in my room and didn't come out for a week.

"So after that I simply shut it down whenever I could. But even that didn't work. The more I shut my magic down, the more doing that affected me in negative ways."

"Like the tiredness?" Taenya asked.

"And irritability." Jez crossed her arms over her chest. "It's been like a never-ending cycle. Not using my magic hurts my body…but using it often hurts my state of mind. They brought in several wizards to help, but it's not a problem that heaping on more magic can solve. Then came the tutors. But nothing worked and I felt useless. I was never going to take over for my father if I couldn't come out of my room."

Taenya placed her hand on Jez's forearm. "There's nothing that can help?"

"Leaving the Southern Desert helped," Jez said. "Even if my parents never said it, I know they were disappointed in me. I rarely accomplished more than making cookies and breads at home. I could tolerate using my scent magic for baking. It was the only reprieve I knew."

"And that brought you to the Baking Battle?" Taenya asked.

"Even that was rough for me," Jez said with a shrug. "But I wanted to prove to myself I could do *something*."

The elf grinned. "And you did that." She held her hand out and gestured at the distance. "And look how far you've come."

"To a freezing pasture where I've been forced to compete in the Yule Games?" Jez said dryly.

Taenya giggled. "No silly. You've proven that you can do what you want to do with yourself. That taking your father's seat wasn't your only option in life."

"I guess," Jez said. "But it doesn't make me a good person. I feel like I'm barely hanging on most of the time even if I pretend otherwise."

Taenya stared at Jez as if trying to work out something in her mind. Finally she said, "So it's *you* who's been lying to yourself."

Jez scoffed. "It's not a lie. I'm not a good friend. There's way too much going on here." She waggled her hand over her chest.

The elf stopped walking and turned Jez to face her. "I'm

not going to tell you what to do. Only you know what's right for you. But none of us are out here being perfect. We all have faults and shortcomings that people we love get used to. But your ability to control or not control your magic isn't one of those shortcomings."

"No one wants to get used to this." Jez gulped and ignored the part about her magic. "You saw how I behaved when I roped us into the Games."

Taenya pursed her lips for a beat. "Could you stand to lay off the rum sometimes? Yes. But in the end what I saw was a friend stepping up for her friend. You did that without hesitation. And when I got hurt in the maze you immediately took action. You took care of me."

"That's the shit friends do for each other." Jez looked away, but flutterbees buzzed around inside her at having the elf so close and speaking well of her. It simply wasn't something she had allowed in her life for a long time.

The elf gently turned Jez's face back to her. "And it's what good *life partners* do too. You have to know that."

Jez averted her eyes.

"You shouldn't be ashamed of what has happened to you with your magic…how it changed you," Taenya said. "You might need to get better at communicating what you need sometimes. Pretty sure all of us, including me, would be willing to work on listening."

For a blink Jez relaxed her control on her magic and took in Taenya's icing sugar scent. The smell was familiar…and soothing if she admitted it to herself. She nodded and said, "Thank you. But I've got to go fix what I've done."

"Yeah. You do." Taenya tipped her head and softened her gaze. "Looking behind yourself all the time made you too suspicious." She paused as if in thought, then narrowed her lids. "Your family does know where you are, right?"

"I left a note before I came to Adenashire," Jez said. "So they know."

"Did they respond?" Taenya asked.

Jez placed her clawed hand over her heart and remained silent for a moment. Vulnerable. "I have the letter here."

"And what did it say?" The elf's eyes were wide with interest.

Jez let out a nervous chuckle. "I haven't opened it."

"What?" Taenya asked and stepped closer. "Why not? You mean to tell me you've made yourself suffer all this time?"

For a moment Jez didn't speak, just studied Taenya, who nearly made her forget all about the cold. Then honesty poured from her mouth. "I was afraid." The words surprised Jez. But they were true. She'd often been afraid. Afraid of rejection because she couldn't live up to other's expectations. Or the expectations she had for herself. It had been easier to keep people out before they might admit she was a disappointment to them.

"Don't be afraid," Taenya said. "Whatever it says can't be worse than your mind made it out to be."

Jez considered this, then pulled off a glove and pocketed it. With her shaky hand, she reached into her inside coat pocket next to her empty flask and pulled out the letter. The parchment was thick, expensive, as were most things from her family. The fold was sealed in red wax with her family crest, a fox.

She slid her finger under the seal and popped it open, heart racing. Slowly she unfolded the paper to reveal the fancy lettering inside. It was her mother's handwriting.

Dearest Jezlyn,

Seeing her full first name made her wince a little. It wasn't that she didn't like her name; she did. But Jez had never admitted to a name other than "just Jez" to any of her friends.

I'm so glad to find you are doing well in Adenashire. The family misses you very much and understands your need to find your own way outside of Dryward. It sounds like you have found the perfect place to do so. I know you have struggled with your magic, and your father and I only wish for your peace. We all love you and look forward to a time when we can be together again.

The letter went on with news of her siblings and various goings-on in the Southern Desert, then ended with,

Your loving mother,
Etha Sanddriffter, Baroness of Dryward

When Jez had finished, she handed it to Taenya, who pulled off her gloves and seemed to read it through with great interest. "And you plan to see them again?" she finally said. "They sound lovely."

The reality was her family *was* lovely…considerably more outgoing than Jez was, but lovely nonetheless. Their differences had sometimes meant their communication left something to be desired. But her parents and siblings did love her.

"Yeah, I think it might be time for a quick trip back." The idea of the over-the-top celebration they would likely throw gave Jez a headache at her temples, but going back for a visit was probably still the right thing to do.

Taenya folded the letter and held it out to her. Jez took it gently, noting that the elf hadn't mentioned the fennex's full name or said anything remotely like "I told you so." She repocketed it safely inside her coat.

"Thank you," Jez said under her breath, but she meant it with her whole heart.

The elf took Jez's hand and squeezed it. "It's never a bad thing to know people love us…even if we don't always see eye to eye."

Jez wanted to take Taenya in her arms, tell her that she liked her beyond friendship too. But before the words unstuck from the back of her throat, Taenya asked, "So what do you want to do about the Games?"

Jez sighed; she'd almost forgotten about them. "I need to drop out…and apologize to Ronan."

"If that's what you need to do, I'll support you," Taenya said. Her voice sounded sad but not disappointed.

Jez swallowed hard and paused. "And I didn't apologize to you for what I did. You were right."

"I know I was," Taenya said, raising a brow. "But what do you think I was right about?"

There were many things the elf was right about, but there was only one Jez was willing to go into for the moment.

"When you said I was focusing on Ronan's supposed cheating because I didn't want to have any fun. I'm sorry for that," Jez admitted.

"Mm-hmm," Taenya said. "And?"

Jez stared at her. The morning sun outlined her hair and shoulders, and the snow's reflection made her green eyes sparkle. *Stars, she's gorgeous and smart.* The thoughts tingled at Jez's mind. Yes. There were other things Taenya was right about. It was not the time to talk about them.

And there was the fact that Jez might still feel a little cowardly.

"One step at a time," Jez muttered.

Taenya squinted in confusion.

"I need to work on being true to myself," Jez got out. "Instead of focusing on other people's faults or what I perceive as faults." She dropped her gaze to the ground. "I've spent too much time assuming the worst of people before I got acquainted with them. It's allowed me to stay in my shell and never let people truly know me. Almost no one before the Baking Battle, but since then it's still really difficult." The truth was painful to admit.

Taenya reached out and grasped Jez's arm. "We were lucky when Doli and Arleta crossed our paths, weren't we?"

A slight wind picked up and Jez nodded, gratitude stirring in her. "Almost like the stars aligned or something."

The elf shrugged. "We all needed something the others had." She grinned. "And I want you to know that, whatever you and I have, I'm grateful you're in my life too."

Jez blushed. "Even if all I could think about in the Battle was kicking your ass?"

"Believe me," Taenya said, "I was all about kicking ass too." She paused for a second. "And I did."

The two of them broke out into laughter and then stood there for what seemed like a very long time. Jez wished she could make time stand still to enjoy the moment a little longer, but alas that was not the magic she possessed.

The elf gave her a soft smile and pulled her along. "We need to take care of some things."

Jez clicked her tongue, not at all ready to head back to the Games. "You mean *I* need to take care of some things?"

"We're a team, Jez," Taenya declared. "We'll deal with it together."

24

Taenya led Jez back toward town through the snow. The hair on her arm standing high told her she was nervous, but her thoughts focused on Taenya's touch. The elf's skin was incredibly soft, but her grasp was strong. Taenya didn't doubt herself, at least not the way Jez had.

Jez couldn't help but think about Taenya's life and how she'd finally had the strength to break free from the life she'd always known, one she didn't want. She'd woken up after the Baking Battle, taken the gold she'd won, and left Langheim.

But it wasn't just about leaving. She'd taken the time to change…blossom, even, and become a person she wanted to be. One that was lighter and freer than she'd ever been in her life.

Jez had thought she'd done that since she packed her bags and moved on from the Southern Desert. But all she'd done was continue to stuff her past down.

As she'd always done. For too long she'd suppressed her emotions, her magic. Jez had never taken the time to explore who she really was and what she wanted her existence to look like. And that fact had made her angrier than she wanted to be. Suspicious of others' motives.

The letter in her pocket suddenly felt weighty, and her own history replayed in her mind. Her family wasn't perfect. They hadn't understood her. She knew that for a fact.

They had thought magic would heal Jez, make her more like them and fix everything. But magic wasn't the solution to everything…if Jez's differences even needed to be solved in the first place.

From her mother's letter it sounded like they wanted to make amends and try to understand her. Perhaps her leaving home helped them finally to understand. It was okay if she was different than they were. It was okay if her life path took her on a different journey than they—or even she—had expected. The hope of that possibility began to melt her heart, even begin to accept that it was okay.

The main thing that Jez needed to solve was accepting that how she experienced her magic was how she experienced it. When she doubted herself and didn't listen to what her body and mind were telling her, it made her angry, tired, and even suspicious.

Her eyes drew to the head of auburn hair in front of her. Not to mention afraid of revealing herself to anyone for fear they wouldn't accept her…even the people she trusted and regarded as genuine friends.

She didn't like that part of herself, even if it had protected her when she needed it. To move on, Jez would need to take a risk. A big one. She'd never have the life she wanted without it.

The moral of her personal fable was that she needed to free a part of herself that she'd buried a long time ago.

Tears stung at the corners of Jez's eyes, and she drew her hand over the spot where the letter rested in her coat pocket. It wouldn't be easy, but she wanted to see her family again. Risk opening her heart to them and seeing what happened.

Taenya turned her head back and smiled, making Jez's stomach do a flop.

Then there was the matter of the elf.

But before could consider that line of thought, Taenya stopped. They were far enough from the Games field that no other people were around, but they still had a good view of the activity. Brightly colored banners decorated the grounds, and the place was completely packed with spectators. It seemed that everyone in the vicinity of Adenashire had come out to watch the final round.

And without a doubt a good portion of them were there to support her and Taenya.

The thought punched at her, knowing that her terrible choice would let them down. Jez's heart picked up like the Bard's Honor drum pounding in her ears. If it were only her, she'd turn and walk away. Take the escape route. Jez scoffed at the thought. *Stars, if it was only me I never would have been in the damn Games in the first place.*

"We did really well," Jez said. "We can always take that with us."

The spot between Taenya's brows pinched with skepticism. "You'd better be saying that as an encouragement to me and not as an excuse to turn around right now." She crossed her arms over her chest. It was like the elf had read her mind.

But Taenya was pretty when she was mad.

"Um," Jez got out. "The first one." Eventually she drew her attention toward the crowd in the distance and said, "Let's get this over with." She took Taenya's hand and led her toward the judges' station, fully intending to admit what she'd done and tell them team one would be dropping out of the competition.

As they got closer Jez spotted signs with their names on them and guilt roiled in her belly, but she kept walking, gripping Taenya's hand tightly. It was the right thing to do. If nothing else, Jez was honest, except of course when it came down to her feelings.

That was another issue entirely.

She winced at the realization but kept going. It wasn't like a person could change themselves all at once.

Could they? The thought passed over the front of her mind and she pushed it way to the back into a safe spot. Despite the cold, sweat dripped down the back of her neck, but Jez kept her focus on the banner over the judges.

"Hurry up," she said mostly to herself and pulled Taenya

along a little faster, but as they approached the outskirts of the Gaming area, Ronan seemed to appear out of thin air.

"Oh, shit," Jez muttered.

"We need to talk," he said and planted himself directly in her way.

Jez glanced back at Taenya and her heart picked up speed. "I'll handle this."

"You *sure*?" the elf said as if she knew something Jez didn't.

"I'll be fine." Jez veered off the path and led Taenya around the man. As she passed, she said, "I'm speaking to the judges about dropping out."

"Before you do that," Ronan called from behind.

Jez gritted her teeth. She'd hoped he'd just let her pass and do what she needed to do. But this was Ronan. She looked at the crowd ahead and didn't want to have this conversation—or worse, another yelling match—in quite so public a setting. So she turned, letting go of Taenya's hand.

"Look, I messed up. You're not cheating. I'm aware of that. Messing up is what got me into the Games, and apparently that's what I do." She gulped, realizing what she was saying might be creating even more of a mess.

Nothing about the time she'd spent with Taenya had been a regret. Yes, she'd been sloppy about it. But that was her fault and not anything the elf had done. Jez avoided looking at Taenya and resolutely kept her scent blocked. "Don't worry. You'll get your twenty silver too."

Ronan, apparently letting her get it all out, simply stood there, ginger eyebrow raised and arms crossed until Jez stopped talking. When she did the man asked, "Are you finished?"

Jez pursed her lips, still avoiding looking at Taenya. "I guess. What else is there to say, unless you've already spoken to the judges about what I did back at the spell shop?"

The man sucked his teeth. "I only came over here to let you two know that's not necessary."

"I accused you of something in public before I had any evidence. It's poor sportsmanship and against the spirit of the Games." Jez plunked her hands onto her hips.

"And you think I'm on the way to tell them about it?" Ronan said.

Jez eyed the judges in the distance. "Maybe you already have." They seemed to be going on with normal business, not as if they were about to make an important announcement, like a team was dropping out or an investigation conducted.

"Did you?" Taenya piped up. "Tell them? Because we're ready to take care of it."

Ronan let out a long sigh and regarded Jez. "It's obvious you're a passionate person."

Jez's eyes enlarged. She'd never thought of herself that way.

"And a damn good competitor," Ronan continued and chuckled. "I could see it in you from the first time we all met. It's why I made the bet with you."

"What are you getting at?" Jez asked as her tail flicked back and forth.

"What I'm getting at is, there's no harm done," he said. "So you came into Spells and Sortilege and thought I was doing something nefarious. It shows you're a person of character. You want things done fairly. I respect that."

"And what do Brady and Ibus think about it?" Jez said, confused. "They were there too."

Ronan waved his hand in the air dismissively. "My brother doesn't care, and neither does Ibus. I calmed him down, and he only really wanted payment for the sparkling wine. Which he got."

Jez's first inclination was to be suspicious of Ronan's intentions, but she gritted her teeth and freed her scent magic. It searched the air and came back to her. And there was nothing. Nothing out of the ordinary, at least. The only thing she could smell was sincerity. Ronan meant what he'd said. She wasn't sure why she hadn't believed it before.

"So you're saying you want to compete with us?" Jez asked. "Like nothing ever happened."

Ronan nodded. "That's exactly what I'm saying. What good is it to compete in something like this if you don't have a worthy opponent? No need for us all"—he gestured with his head toward the crowd—"to lose out over a misunderstanding."

Jez studied the man for a second, then said with a sly grin, "I *would* hate for you to know you only won on a technicality."

Ronan chortled. "Now *there's* the spirit I was counting on. I'm looking forward to your congratulations." With that he turned and marched off toward the starting line.

Taenya slipped her arm around Jez's waist and whispered, "Let's go kick his ass."

Jez couldn't help but smile.

25

The remaining six teams stood under their banners, waiting anxiously for the final event to begin. A line of forms, each covered by large pieces of burlap cloth, waited on the field behind them.

Jez gulped and gazed out on what seemed like a sea of bundled-up spectators in the stands holding signs and consuming snacks and hot drinks. Seeing how many of them favored their team, including Theo, Arleta, Doli, Sarson, and the orcs, she thought about the points she and Taenya had accrued over the course of the competition. And while they had done well in each event, many of their points were due to their "fake" relationship.

She glanced at Taenya, and heat spread across her chest.

For the elf it had never actually been fake. Even knowing Jez's negative feelings about romance, she'd still been willing to take the risk at the ball to open up.

Jez wanted to do that too. What if their friendship *was* the key to a real relationship, as Taenya had said? What if it *was* okay to have faults, and a person—no, *Taenya*—could love her anyway? What if it was even written in the stars? Her furry ears twitched at the possibility.

"We have finally arrived at the closing round of this year's Yule Games!" Mr. Figlet announced.

A sliver of her was relieved for the distraction.

The crowd cheered, and when Taenya took Jez's hand and held it in the air, the cheers grew louder. The fennex managed what she thought was a convincing smile, but her tail flicked behind her nervously.

Taenya leaned in. "We can do this," she said.

Even though Jez had her sense of smell repressed, icing sugar cut through her defenses. Right along with a sharp tinge of anticipation. "You really think we have a chance?" Jez asked. But she wasn't talking about winning the Games.

"I do." The elf grinned.

Ronan and his brother shouted to the crowd, egging them on to yell louder while the other teams waved and played to their fans.

Mr. Figlet stepped forward and raised his fuzzy hands in the air to quiet the crowd. When they'd finally settled he said, "I'll bet you're all ready for today's competition..." He paused and let them rile themselves up again for a moment. But then, apparently enjoying the power he held, he quickly raised his hands again and the fairies flew out behind him, dragging sparkling colors high into the air.

The crowd gasped as the colors spun and twisted behind the fairies. The judges applauded enthusiastically as if it were their first time seeing the show too.

Jez tipped her head to get a look behind the quokkan, but she still couldn't see where the fairies had hidden any better than she had the last time.

The fairies directed the colors, and slowly they formed words high in the air: *Ice Sculpting—Snowflakes*.

Rumbling chatter came from the crowd.

"That's right!" Mr. Figlet announced as the fairies parted, flew off to the sides of the stage, and hovered as if in wait. "Each of our remaining teams will be sculpting a large snowflake out of ice."

As if on cue, the burlap fabric magically flew off the mystery forms, revealing a series of large blocks of sparkling ice with space enough around each for the teams to work. Beside each block was a large basket.

The crowd gasped again.

"As with all the other competitions," Mr. Figlet said, "competitors are forbidden to use any purchased or personal magic to complete the task."

Jez shot a glance down to Ronan, but he wasn't looking her way.

Mr. Figlet continued. "That said, for the ice carving competition, each competitor will be provided with magical dwarven tools specifically designed for large and intricate carving tasks."

A dwarf woman walked out holding several tools and held up a good-sized ice pick for everyone to see.

"Once the bell rings," the marsupial announced, "each team will be allotted two hours to complete their sculpture."

Two hours didn't seem like enough time, but Jez knew from Doli that dwarven tools were imbued with magic that allowed easier cutting away of stone, ice, and dirt, making the task nearly as simple as cutting butter.

"Have you ever used any tools like that?" Jez quietly asked Taenya.

The elf shook her head as she stared off toward the blocks of ice. "Not exactly. But I think it's going to be similar to cake decorating and carving fondant. And I've done plenty of that." Taenya winked.

Doli had said that Taenya might be particularly good at working with ice since detail work was one of her strong suits. Jez straightened her back, ready to get over to the ice block and get started.

"Each team should take their places," the marsupial said, gesturing. "We will begin shortly."

Jittery inside but ignoring the other teams, Jez slipped her arm around Taenya's waist and led her to their ice block. It was slightly taller than either of them and nearly as wide across. In their basket waited two sets of dwarven tools.

A fairy with robin egg blue hair and a matching sweater and pants flew up to them. "I'll be assisting you today in choosing a snowflake design," they said in a typical high-pitched voice.

"Oh," said Taenya, obviously pleased. "I thought we'd have to come up with it on our own. What's your name?"

The little fairy's eyes, the color also matching their hair, lit up at the question. "It's Shade. Shade Fancyfleck. And you will have the opportunity to customize the design if you like." White magic sparkled from their hands and an assortment of snowflake designs appeared in the air.

From the corner of her eye, Jez saw the other fairies doing the same for the other teams. She eyed Ronan and his brother for a second but quickly brought her attention back to the task at hand.

Taenya folded her hands together and leaned in close to study the options. "They're amazing, Shade."

"These are all based on real snowflake designs gathered and studied by fairies," Shade said proudly. "We have several new options this year. Choose something you like, and we'll go from there."

For a moment, Jez was distracted by the light of the snowflake designs reflected onto Taenya's face and the excitement in her eyes. From what she could tell, the elf was finding this a new and exciting challenge. Jez found her friend's facial expressions strangely invigorating.

"Do you have one you particularly like?" Taenya asked, breaking Jez's trance.

"Yes?" She didn't mean for her answer to come out like a question.

The elf raised her brows. "Maybe you can share, then?"

Jez panicked and shot her arm out at the first one she saw. "That one's nice."

"Oh," Taenya said, "I like it too." She turned her attention to Shade. "We'll take that one."

"Amazing choice." They cupped their hand beside their face as though confiding a secret. "One of my favorites." They whiffled the other options away and with a spread of their arms enlarged the chosen design. "Now you can make customizations if you wish."

Taenya eyed Jez as if for input.

"I picked," Jez said, wanting Taenya to take charge of this round. "You make any upgrades."

The elf nodded and pointed to the center. "How about a swirly design here, and I'd like the outer points to extend a little further."

"That would be lovely." Shade clapped their hands together. "But it will make the actual work that much more difficult. Are you sure?"

A grin stretched across Taenya's lips, and she slipped her hand into the crook of Jez's elbow. "I think we're up for challenges. No risk, no reward."

"Perfect!" the fairy chirped and waved their hands in the air. Magic flew off their hands and in an instant the snowflake sample morphed into the design Taenya had requested.

"It's really beautiful," Jez said without even thinking.

The elf twisted her way, eyes shining. "You think so?"

Jez bobbed her head up and down, not taking her eyes off Taenya. But she quickly cleared her throat. "Very much so."

Shade flew backward and stopped. "Your snowflake will remain visible until the ending bell rings. You can touch, rotate, and enlarge it by pulling your hands out along the sides to see any detail you wish."

Jez reached out and touched one of the points with her index finger, then turned the snowflake slightly.

"Go ahead and try to enlarge it," the fairy said while flitting back and forth in front of them.

Biting her lip Jez placed her hands on either side and pulled out. The snowflake grew. "That's impressive."

"Thank you," Shade said with a giggle. "Fairy magic always is."

And she wasn't wrong.

"I'll be available if you need any help with it during the round. Just call." Shade gave them a little wink while their wings sped up, and off they flew.

Two other fairies followed back to the judges' station, where Mr. Figlet was nearly done re-announcing the remaining teams to the audience.

"Looks like we're ready to begin?" His attention moved to the six fairies, one of which was Shade.

In unison the group bobbed their assent.

The marsupial cleared his throat and once again flourished his hand into the air. "Each team has two hours to complete their masterpiece. You may now…begin!" A bell rang and the fairies shot up in the air, followed by their signature colors.

Jez and Taenya didn't waste time watching the display or listening to the cheering audience. They immediately dug into the basket and pulled out the tools.

"Okay," Taenya said, taking charge. "We need to figure out exactly what each tool is best for."

The first item Jez held up was a saw. She'd used a small saw many times at the lake to carve a hole in the ice for fishing, though she'd never used any fancy dwarven tools and didn't quite know what kind of performance to expect. "We'll need this to carve out the basic shape."

Jez gripped the tool's wooden handle and laid its metal edge against the top of a small block of practice ice they'd been provided. She pulled the teeth across the ice and began shaping it. Just as she'd heard from Doli, the process was surprisingly easy—not without effort, but simple. The challenge in this contest would be less about brawn than precision.

"You try," she said to Taenya. "It's not bad at all."

The elf quickly plucked the second saw from the basket and ran the teeth against the opposite side of the practice ice. She made speedy work of it.

The pair quickly tested all the tools, including two sizes of chisels, tongs, a jig, a chipper, and a compass. They each studied the sample snowflake design and carved out similar portions in the sample ice block using the smaller chisel.

When they were done they stepped back to admire their work. The snowflake wasn't perfect yet but only because it needed considerable detail work.

"I say we go for it," Taenya said, her arms crossed as she studied the small block of ice, then looked up to the main one. "No use wasting more time on the small one when it doesn't count. I think we understand the process. Just take it slow and don't rush things… That's what always gets me to the finish line with my cakes."

Over to their right the other teams had already begun work. Ronan and his brother had a large portion of snowflake already carved.

Jez suddenly felt very behind the others. A light growl rumbled in her throat and she snatched her saw. "You take the right and I'll take the left."

Taenya threw out her hand to stop Jez. "Before we do that I'm going to sketch it out." And before Jez could even ask what she meant, the elf was already using her finger to draw in the frost covering the ice block.

Jez cursed herself. She didn't know why she hadn't thought of it since she often sketched out her bakes and any design they might have for the finished product. She eyed the sample design and took to the other side, and before long they had the basic sketch completed.

"Don't want a lopsided snowflake." Taenya laughed and picked up her saw.

With gusto, the two set to work with the saws and chippers. They started at the top, each working down one side of the block. It went much faster than Jez had expected, and soon the block was transformed with six long points jutting out from the middle.

She stepped back to admire it. "I love it!"

"Me too." Taenya leaned into Jez and gave her a peck on the cheek. Immediately several "awws" could be heard coming from the audience.

Jez's hands hurt from the sawing, but she wasn't that tired, and she suddenly realized that she hadn't been suppressing her sense of smell. Instead she'd simply been enjoying creating alongside Taenya.

With the basic shape completed, they broke out the larger chisels and worked on perfecting the edges. The whole thing was coming along beautifully.

"One hour left," Mr. Figlet announced, and the fairies made a pass over the tops of the sculptures. The crowd applauded and cheered.

"Oh, shit!" someone from one of the other teams shouted. It was one of the halflings from team two. Jez did feel a bit of empathy as she stared at their fourth point jutting from the snow beside their sculpture.

"Well, that's a real shame," Taenya said under her breath with a hint of sarcasm as she continued working.

Jez broke out into a soft chuckle. "Now that's not a very sporting attitude."

"I'm here to win." Taenya gave the fennex the eye and both of their mouths pinched out to stifle their giggles.

Jez looked back at the halflings' snowflake and caught sight of Ronan's entry. Her breath picked up. It was massive and from a distance looked nearly done.

"Damn it." Any levity dissipated as she looked back to their snowflake and compared it to the sample floating in the air next to them.

"Okay," Taenya said. "Take a breath. We only have an hour, but we can do this. By the stars, I won the one hundredth Baking Battle!"

"Yes, you did!" Jez kissed her briefly on the lips.

The elf pulled back and stared at Jez with eyes nearly as large as saucers.

Jez tipped her head back to the audience. "You know, for the show."

Nodding, Taenya smiled and said, "Of course."

After that the two dug into the job, and bit by bit, their snowflake grew more refined and beautiful. Just as Taenya put the finishing touches on the swirl design in the center and Jez cleared away the frost with a brush, the final bell rang.

"Tools down!" Mr. Figlet announced, and the sample snowflake vanished from the air.

26

As the bell continued to ring, Taenya and Jez threw their hands into the air and backed away from their sculpture. Jez scanned over the finished product and the dramatic points the two of them had chiseled into the snowflake. Taenya's detail work on the inside was exquisite and very much like the elaborate style she produced on cakes with her magic. Even without magic, she had an innate sense of style and flair.

The sunlight sparkled on the ice, and Jez squinted in its glory.

It was beautiful, gorgeous, spectacular…but Jez didn't want to get her hopes up. She was all too aware that she might be biased toward their own work.

Taking the pomp even further, fairies flew out to the six

sculptures and each hovered behind one, lighting them up with different colors.

Shade cast a twinkly blue on their creation.

The audience behind them oohed and aahed and broke into applause. Jez had been so focused on the project that she hadn't even looked at the other entries for quite some time.

Each snowflake was entirely different, and with the fairy colors they were all quite beautiful, even the halflings' snow-flake, which was partially broken.

"You did a fantastic job with ours," Jez said to Taenya.

"Me?" she looked from the fennex back to the sculpture. "You did your fair share too."

Against her own sensibilities Jez blushed at the compli-ment. Hopefully the elf would only think her face was pink from the cold.

Jez's gaze wandered over to Ronan's entry. It was larger than theirs and had more points. From this distance, some-thing about it seemed more impressive, but without a closer look she couldn't be sure of the details.

"If I could have all the contestants make way," Mr. Figlet said, gesturing for each team to move away from the sculp-tures and congregate in a designated spot.

Taenya and Jez gave each other quick, nervous glances and did as they were told. Jez somehow ended up directly next to Ronan.

The judges paraded out while Mr. Figlet introduced each one again. Since they'd all made significant contributions to the Games, they had to get their last chance at advertising to the audience.

"You ready to pay up that twenty silver fair and square?" the bearded man asked with a tinge of humor in his tone.

Jez gulped, but then looked up at his goofy smirk. "Fair and square? What do you mean by that?" She kept her voice down while trying to focus on the judges.

"I couldn't have your team booted over something so silly," he said, eyes twinkling. "What would have been the fun in that?"

"That's why you told me not to drop out?" Jez furrowed her brow. "For fun?"

He waved his meaty hand in the air dismissively. "I enjoy setting up a little friendly rivalry for these sorts of things. Make the events more interesting." Ronan leaned in close and looked out at the audience. "For everyone. And we both know those halflings were never going to win."

Jez shook her head. The halflings had actually done a lot better than she'd expected. She still didn't understand Ronan at all but decided to get into the spirit of the thing. She straightened her posture and said, "You might have a nice bauble over there, but Taenya and I have this in the bag." She grinned, and she was surprised to find that she didn't have to force it one bit.

"We'll see. We'll see," Ronan said.

Taenya slipped her hand through the crook of Jez's elbow and leaned out to address Ronan. "Oh, we're totally winning this thing."

Ronan's eyes snapped to attention. "Yes, ma'am!" He gave a hearty laugh, then returned his attention to where the judges walked around each snowflake and made notations on clipboards.

"You think so?" Jez said quietly to Taenya as she eyed their entry again.

The elf pulled her close for an affectionate side hug. "Yeah. Whatever place we get, I'm pretty sure we won here."

Jez's tail flicked behind her nervously, but she took in a deep breath, held it for a few heartbeats, and let it out again. The week prior she couldn't have cared less about the Games. She would much rather have been snug in her room drinking tea…or a shot of rum. And while all that still sounded like a good idea, and she might need to sleep for a week to make up for all the energy she'd spent, she didn't regret what had happened.

In fact, she *had* enjoyed the Games. That is, if she took out all the parts where she'd thought Ronan was a cheater.

"Ooh," Taenya said, shaking Jez back to reality. "I believe it's time."

Snow fluttered toward the earth from a smattering of clouds as one of the judges handed Mr. Figlet a paper. He thanked them with a nod, turned toward the audience, and said, "Ladies and gentlemen, I now have the final results."

Ronan and Brady stood next to them preening for the onlookers as Jez gripped Taenya's hand. She knew now that his behavior was mostly an act, not so different from the one she and Taenya had put on to play to the crowd. Ronan seemed more comfortable with it than Jez ever could be.

Pulse racing, she gazed over the crowd, which was a sea of signs with words like BAKERS or TEAM ONE, some crude, some skilled renditions of their faces, and Jez felt a pool of gratitude in her stomach.

She spotted all their friends—the orcs, Theo and Arleta, Doli and Sarson—in the front row, looking as if they were on the edge of their seats. Gratitude swelled in her chest for each of them, along with a twinge of disappointment that her family hadn't known about the Games in time to be there. But she'd tell them all about it when she visited… which she silently resolved to do soon to get out of the wintery weather.

Taenya leaned in and whispered to Jez, "No matter what happens, I'm glad we did this together."

Jez tightened her grip on Taenya's hand and gazed at her profile while her waiting eyes returned to the quokkan. Her auburn hair was slightly messy from working on the sculpture. A strand had fallen into the middle of her forehead, and she quickly swept it away with her free hand. The elf's reddened cheeks were the same color as a crisp summer apple.

Mr. Figlet raised the paper and paused for dramatic effect. "And the winners of this year's Yule Games are…Team One, Taenya Carralei and Jez!" In unison the fairies set off a display of colorful fireworks in the sky.

The crowd went absolutely wild, and Arleta led them in the chant "Bakers! Bakers! Bakers!" The chant grew until it seemed every single spectator was shouting it.

"And the clear audience favorite!" he added with a grin. "To celebrate, Spells and Sortilege has provided sparkling wine for all those who competed in this year's Games! All twenty-four teams, please join us."

Jez's eyes widened as she looked out over the audience

and then back at Taenya, whose green eyes danced with excitement.

"Can you believe it?" the elf asked, her voice breathy and full of joy.

"No, I can't," Jez admitted. Out of the corner of her eye she caught Ibus from Spells and Sortilege and what must have been two of his employees popping corks and pouring the sparkling wine into cups.

Taenya's lips curled into a wry smile. "I can. There was no doubt in my mind that we'd make a good team."

The corners of Jez's eyes stung with impending tears. She had rarely ever allowed herself the privilege of such strong emotion. There were things she needed to say to Taenya. Important things, both for her to say and for the elf to hear. But when she opened her mouth she was interrupted.

"Congratulations!" Ronan boomed as he offered Jez and Taenya two cups of sparkling wine.

Jez stared at the cup for a second but took it. Taenya accepted the other.

"I'll have you that twenty silver soon," he said, looking at their sculpture. "Mighty fine work you did." Ronan reached out his right hand to Jez, and without hesitation she shook it. "Sorry I might have come on a bit strong. My brother and I are a mite too competitive sometimes."

"You had a good showing," Taenya said, taking a sip of her wine.

Ronan winked at the two of them and let go of Jez's hand. "We did. And we expect a rematch next year."

"Oh, shit no," Jez said without thinking about it. "I'm on the sidelines next year."

Taenya and Ronan laughed, and Taenya linked arms with the fennex. "I'll be wherever she is."

Jez lifted the sparkling wine to her lips and took a big drink.

"Then I'll definitely be back to take it all," Ronan cackled and exited the stage.

"Bakers! Bakers! Bakers!" came from the crowd, making Jez's head hurt, but she pushed through it to focus on the present.

Turning to Taenya Jez asked, "Did you mean that?"

"Mean what?" The elf gave a sweet smile, eyes crinkling.

The fennex gulped. "That if I don't compete you won't either?"

"I don't think I could find a better partner in the Games," Taenya said, not missing a beat. "So yes."

With her heart in her throat Jez locked onto Taenya's gaze and stepped in close, hardly believing what she was going to ask. She released her scent magic, determined to take in the moment fully, no matter how difficult. Aromas from all over came at her, but only one mattered. Icing sugar. "Do you mind if I kiss you?"

Taenya cast her gaze to the ground. "The Games are over, so you don't have to. No need to pretend anymore."

Trying hard to take her next breath, Jez bit her bottom lip as she worked up the courage to say what she had in her heart. "At first it was true…what I told you in the bakery. That romance would spoil a good friendship. I really thought being friends was the right thing for me. So when I started feeling differently I had to push those feelings away…and pretend we could only ever be friends." Jez sucked in a nervous breath. "But I don't want to anymore." Despite the snow coming down harder, at that point Jez felt so hot she barely needed her coat. "In fact, I'm pretty sure I'm in love with you, Taenya Carralei."

The admission was raw, vulnerable, uncomfortable. But for the first time in her life Jez didn't mind the feeling. She wanted it all…the aromas of the excited crowd, the brightly colored magical fireworks still exploding over their heads, which somehow smelled of overripe fruit, the smoke of vendor foods, the snow sprinkling down on their heads. But mostly she wanted Taenya's sweetness, which grew more intense by the second and somehow made everything better.

The elf closed the gap between them and placed her hand on the side of Jez's face. She looked up and gently stroked one of the fennex's furry ears.

And Jez struggled to not allow her knees to go weak from the soft touch.

Taenya continued with a shy giggle. "I've been in love with you for months, so thanks for catching up."

With that, everything else melted away, and Jez kissed Taenya full on the mouth. Nothing in the realm had ever felt or tasted as sweet, as *right*.

When they parted, Jez realized again that they were not alone, but she regretted nothing. She and Taenya held their cups high in the air, which only brought more thunderous cheers. Arleta, Theo, Doli, Sarson, Verdreth, and Ervash all stood below the stage and raised their own cups to the winners in a toast.

Taenya leaned close to Jez and said, "You know, after we get out of here I wouldn't mind a nap. Care to join?"

Jez grinned as she continued to take everything in. "I thought you'd never ask."

Epilogue

Theo

While standing over the oven in his and Arleta's snug little home, Theo was nervous. So nervous that a few tiny sparks of yellow and green magic hovered over his hands. Flutterbees darted around in his belly as he put the final touches on the dish he'd prepared for the dinner celebrating the first day of spring. The roasted chicken resting in front of him was a perfect shade of golden brown and smelled delicious.

But he had a surprise for Arleta and the rest of their friends, and he'd been keeping it under wraps all week for the occasion. But waiting until the dinner party had been difficult. He'd swept the floors twice, dusted each and every knickknack he and Arleta owned, darned three pairs of socks, repaired one of the tablecloths he took to the outdoor market each week to sell pastries for Arleta's shop, A Little Dash of Magic Bake Shop…as well as trussed and prepared the chicken and vegetables for dinner.

And that was all before 5:00.

The elf chopped the fragrant fresh herb garnish with shaky hands, and instead of sweeping it into his palm, he cleared half the pile from the counter directly onto the floor.

"Oh stars," Theo cursed under his breath as he watched the green pieces float to the earth.

"Why are you so jittery today?" Faylin asked, sniffing the air from his fluffy bed nearby. The forest lynx's dark tail flicked lazily across the worn maple floor.

"You know exactly why." The elf bent to clean up the wayward herbs and then deposited them in the trash. Before he rose, he reached out and ran his hand over the cat's soft head, then his left horn.

Besides Arleta, Faylin was Theo's closest confidant. He told the lynx almost everything since they'd been together for years, ever since the lynx was no more than a kit.

"I don't worry about these kinds of things so much. Everyone is going to love the idea," Faylin said while purring and obviously enjoying the pets. "But just a little to the right."

Theo obliged and ended with a chin scratch before he stood.

"Them loving it doesn't make me less nervous," Theo said. "It's a big decision for Arleta and me."

The cat opened his mouth into a giant yawn, revealing all the pointed teeth inside. "But you and Arleta have been planning this for over a year now."

"And she doesn't know yet that I've saved up enough silver to make it happen. Plus, Taenya doesn't know, and she's Arleta's business partner." He sprinkled the sparse remaining herbs over the chicken surrounded with roasted carrots, potatoes, and parsnips. The elf had made sure to prepare some of the vegetables with a thickened sweet vinegar glaze separate from the main dish since Sarson, their gargoyle friend, never ate meat.

"Well, you'd best hurry up before you drop anything else." Faylin lowered his head on the pillow and closed his eyes. "I'll be out for my dinner after a quick nap."

Theo knew this nap was likely the tenth for the day. But that was completely ordinary for the lynx. Without another word he picked up the platter of chicken and the extra side of roasted vegetables and made his way out the back door into the garden.

It was Theo's favorite time of day. The sun was falling below the horizon, leaving pink and blue swirling above it in the sky. The garden plants were reveling in the cool spring air, casting a profusion of vines and leaves every which way. He loved the peace of working and communing with the vegetation, aided by his magic.

He took in a big breath to settle his nerves, but the magic sparks didn't completely dissipate from his hands. He knew if Arleta saw them, it would tip her off that something was up. Even so, Theo made his way over to Ervash and Verdreth's side of the garden via a small gate. The orcs' cottage was nearly identical to his and Arleta's, and they shared the enormous garden. There had also been enough room for

Theo to build a stable and small pasture area for his horse, Nimbus. Theo smiled as the horse shook his long, glossy mane at him.

Everyone had already arrived and gathered around the long wooden table the orcs had permanently set up in their portion of the yard. Taenya, Jez, Doli, and Sarson sat in a row on one side of the table. The four of them seemed deep in conversation, and Theo couldn't help but notice Jez's hand laced with Taenya's on the tabletop. He was glad for them.

Even though Taenya was an elf like him, she'd never discovered a Fated in her dreams. But it seemed the stars had brought her to Adenashire and someone to share a lifetime of love with after all.

He grinned at the happiness each of his friends had found and his privilege to share in it.

The table was almost overflowing with food already, and as Theo got closer, he scanned over it to find a place for his chicken and roasted vegetables. In the middle of the feast, an impressive three-layer chocolate cake sat decorated with sliced oranges and green leaves. Since dessert had been assigned to Taenya, Theo was nearly certain the decorations were made of frosting, candy, and other edible ingredients even though everything looked real.

"Let me help you with that." Sarson stood, leaving Doli chatting with Jez, and came over to Theo. He took the dish of veggies from him and placed it in an open spot near the end of the table.

"Thank you," Theo said to the blue-skinned gargoyle. He was dressed in a gauzy white shirt with beautiful iridescent shell buttons. Just like Doli, Sarson had quite the fashion sense.

"They look incredible." Sarson stared down at the dish and then back at Theo.

The elf shrugged. "I tried something new this time with a glaze."

"Well, I can't wait to sample it." Sarson bowed his head in thanks and took his seat beside Doli again.

Theo set down his roasted chicken next to a platter of rice with toasted almonds on top. Then his eyes moved to Arleta, who was visiting with Verdreth and Ervash. Her long chestnut hair cascaded down her back, and something about her looked even more radiant than ever.

His heart warmed simply by looking at her. Even after nearly a year he couldn't believe he'd found his Fated. She was everything he'd ever dreamed her to be…both perfect and imperfect at the same time, and that was entirely fine by him.

She was his and he was hers. That's all that mattered.

With a quick deliberate breath in and out, he made his way over to her and kissed her soft cheek.

"Oh, Theo," she said and immediately looked down at his telltale hands. "I didn't know you had arrived."

Theo shoved his hands into his pockets. "I brought the chicken," he said, the best he could manage.

Verdreth, towering over both Theo and Arleta, pushed his spectacles up on his nose. "Then we should eat."

The moment he said it, Ervash's stomach rumbled loudly enough for everyone to hear, and he ran his hand over his

orc belly as they all chuckled. "No disagreement from me."
The orc drew Arleta into a side hug and kissed the top of
her head.

"Love you, Dad," Arleta said.

"Back at you," Ervash said. He grabbed a roll from the
basket and popped it into his tusked mouth.

"Why are you nervous?" Arleta whispered to Theo.

"Nervous?" Theo said with surprise in his voice, but he
knew he wasn't fooling her.

She tipped her head as if to confirm what he already knew.

"I have an announcement to make," the elf admitted,
tempted to let her in on the secret before everyone else.

She opened her mouth to speak but didn't get anything
out.

"Hey." Jez's obviously annoyed voice came from behind
them. "We're waiting."

Ervash chuckled and gave a wry half grin. "Not me."
With a flourish, the orc reached over, grabbed the platter
of chicken, and tore off a drumstick. He stuffed it into his
mouth and cleaned the bone.

"Have some manners," Verdreth said, feigning sophisti-
cation, then swiped the other drumstick and plopped it on
his plate. "At least wait until everyone is here."

"Why?" Ervash said with his mouth full.

By that time, Faylin had slunk outside. He made a long,
artful stretch, yawned, and curled up on the ground at the
end of the orcs' bench.

Arleta rolled her eyes and gestured to the table with the
top of her head. "Better fill your plates before it's all gone."

"Yeah," Jez complained. "Save a scrap for the rest of us. I'd like a drumstick occasionally."

"Ya snooze, ya lose," Ervash teased.

Jez growled and snapped her teeth at the orc.

Ervash held up the cleaned drumstick in faux surrender.

But everyone knew Jez wasn't serious.

Taenya pulled the fennex in close and grinned. "There's plenty to eat."

"Would you behave, Dads?" Arleta scolded. The two orcs sat up and stopped messing with the chicken. She laid her hand on Theo's arm, then cleared her throat and said, "Theo…and *I* have announcements."

Theo's head whipped toward her, completely caught off guard that Arleta had news as well. "You have one too?"

"Mm-hmm," she said and squeezed him around the waist. "But you first."

Heat bloomed in the elf's chest. He hadn't expected to make it so soon. But he lowered his shoulders and spoke. "Arleta and I may have mentioned it before, but we've decided to expand the bakery into a café."

Arleta's grip tightened on his arm, and he turned his attention toward her grinning, excited face.

He continued, "We've been saving for quite some time, but I've put away more than we expected. I've spoken to the owner of the building next door, and they are willing to sell."

"What?" Arleta squealed. "I can't believe you were able to pull this off without me knowing!"

Doli stood and clapped. "That's so exciting!"

Several others nodded in agreement.

"I found a few more ways to cut costs—" Theo started, but Arleta squeezed him too hard to finish.

"We've been wanting to add more drinks like juice and coffee," Arleta declared.

"And tea?" Doli asked.

"Of course tea!" The excitement in Arleta's voice was contagious. "And more places to sit so people can stay longer to enjoy their pastries and beverages."

A round of congratulations came, and Theo felt a little silly about his nervousness earlier. "I'm glad you're happy," he whispered into his Fated's ear.

She had tears in her eyes as she hugged him. "I love you so much."

He returned the embrace, then asked, "Didn't you have an announcement?"

She pulled back with the widest smile he'd ever seen on her face and mouthed *I do*. "We have one more announcement." Arleta squeezed Theo's hand before she said, "We're having a baby!"

Everyone shot up from their seats at the table and several of them screamed (Jez may or may not have been one of those people).

Theo's eyes widened and his heart instantly felt as if it grew. "We are?"

Arleta turned and placed her hands on both sides of his face and kissed him squarely on the mouth. When she drew back, she nodded and said, "Mm-hmm."

Having a baby had been a topic of many discussions for

Theo and Arleta. They had both been apprehensive. Arleta's parents had died when she was a teen, and it had scarred her so deeply that before she met Theo, she'd been terrified to allow anyone into her heart—because the danger of losing them seemed too great. Then, of course, Theo's relationship with his mother back in Langheim was still strained, and his father had left them years before. But the love and support Theo and Arleta found in each other and the people around them made the risks seem less daunting. They had both agreed that starting a family was a priority.

Stars willing.

"I can't wait," Theo said with tears streaming down his face.

"Me neither," Arleta got out before all their friends rushed her.

"But maybe we shouldn't go forward with the café?" Theo said, managing to catch her attention.

Arleta shook her head and gazed at their friends. "When we have so many people to support us? Not a chance." She leaned over and kissed him.

Theo stepped back, magic hovering over his hands from her touch, and watched fondly as everyone took turns hugging and congratulating Arleta.

Faylin pushed his nose into the elf's palm. "You know, she told *me* yesterday," he said, sitting and flicking his tufted ear.

"Of course she did." Theo scratched the purring lynx under his chin. "Who can resist a cat's charm?"

"Exactly," Faylin said. "Now, about this café. I have a few ideas."

And this fellowship, which sometimes played games and often believed fables to be true, settled into the meal, the conversation, and the warmth of friendship and family. And of course there were many mentions of Ervash and Verdreth's newfound excitement at becoming granddads.

None of them could wait for their next adventure, whatever their lives had in store.

Bonus Chapter

A "Kneaded" Break

Perched on a small stool, Jez Sanddrifter's small clawed hands plunged deep into the ceramic bowl of sticky dough as she worked to bring the mixture into a ball. Leaning her belly onto the counter, the earthy fragrance of wheat, spicy cardamom, and bright dried citrus clung to the back of her sinuses while the heady concoction tingled her taste buds. Jez's large, furry light-brown ears flicked on the top of her head.

The surrounding kitchen was massive, stocked with everything a cook or baker would ever need. Over the stove hung all sizes of copper pans and pots. Bowls, large and small, sat on thick wooden shelving, and the two pantries were overloaded with every ingredient Jez's eight-year-old self could ever wish for. And if something was missing, all she'd have to do to get it was ask the head cook to order the item. No questions asked.

As the fennex kit worked, she closed her eyes and blocked out every other sensation but the feel of the dough squishing between her fingers and the complex fragrances of the ingredients lighting up her mind. With each knead of the dough, her fox-like tail undulated behind her, almost as if the motions were moving Jez into a trance.

In truth, she couldn't get enough of the feeling and had sneaked down to the kitchen in her family's massive estate every night during the last weeks while everyone else was asleep. Baking was the relief Jez needed and what she turned to when responsibilities became too much.

If she didn't eat what she'd made, Jez would simply stash the bread, cake, or pastry with the ones made by the cooks. No one ever seemed to notice the extra stock.

But that night she planned to devour the bread all by herself. Orange was one of the fennex's favorite flavors, and when she'd seen the jar filled with candied orange peel in the pantry, she knew she'd have to make something with it.

Jez's mouth salivated at the thought of the bread slathered with soft butter, melting in her mouth. But just as she licked her lips, a soft, powdery, floral aroma crept into her solace… along with notes of freshly cut wood.

Jez's eyes shot open, and she whirled her head around to her older sister, who'd only recently taken a liking to overly scented perfumes that completely overpowered her natural aroma—which Jez thought was infinitely more pleasant.

The lanky fennex stood under the arched kitchen

opening, dressed in a sky-blue silk nightgown. Her white hair was combed straight and fell down her back. Her look was in stark contrast to Jez, who'd recently lopped off her own white hair because she hated when it fell into her eyes. That and Drywell, situated in the Southern Desert, was a hot place. Long hair ended up sticky and sweaty in the sun. As of late, Jez had also shunned wearing anything with a skirt if she could get away with it.

But to each their own, Jez reminded herself. Not everyone needed to be alike…and for her sake, that was a good thing. Although the potent scent of her sister's perfume brought back a whisper of the headache she'd been trying to escape from all day.

"Why aren't you in bed, Imogen?" Jez got out before her sister could admonish her first.

Imogen placed her sand-colored hands on her hips while her chestnut tail flicked behind her. "I could ask you the same, Jezlyn. It's *way* past your bedtime."

Jez gritted her sharp teeth. First, she hated being called by her full name, but her family always insisted on doing it. Shortened names weren't proper for the Baron and Baroness of Dryward, they would always say. But Jez didn't care about any of those formalities. Particularly not in private. Second, Imogen was only two years older than Jez and wasn't allowed to stay up at all hours either.

But there they both were.

"I'm making bread," Jez announced to avoid an actual response to her sister.

Imogen stepped further into the kitchen and gazed

around at the emptiness. "Why? You could just ask Cook to make it in the morning."

It was true. Jez could do that. The cooks would make most anything they wanted if they only asked for it. Plus, her parents would be horrified if they knew Jez was doing the kind of work the hired help performed. But Jez found baking so relaxing she didn't want to give it up. So her mind quickly worked on forming what she could say to her sister to ensure she wouldn't give Jez's secret away.

When she found the words, Jez shook her head and gave a wry grin. "Then how would we eat it tonight?" Her sister was a rule follower, but Jez knew that sometimes she could convince her otherwise. Particularly if the rule-breaking made her sister feel grown-up.

And if all that failed, Jez could "threaten" to tell on Imogen for being up past her bedtime too.

As expected, Imogen's delicate features scrunched for a moment. Then she smiled back. "I *am* hungry. What are you making?"

Jez poured the dough out onto the floured counter and kneaded it. "A cardamom orange loaf."

Her sister's green eyes brightened. Jez was well aware orange was one of her favorite flavors too. "Oh." She hurried over to the counter next to Jez.

Being ten, Imogen was taller than Jez and didn't need the stool as she stood at the counter. She gazed down at the dough with sudden intense interest. "How does it work?"

How someone could eat something like bread their entire lives and not have a clue how to make it was beyond Jez.

But she tried to accept that other people had different priorities. Even so, it made no sense to her. Still, Jez knew by the question she had her sister hooked and simply worked on blocking out the lily scent accosting her nose. "Want to give it a try?"

Imogen paused as if in thought before saying. "Sure. Why not?"

Jez stepped from the stool and moved it over to make room for her sister. "Put your hands on the dough."

"Like this?" Imogen barely touched the orange peel-speckled dough with the tips of her fingers.

Jez scoffed and reached to shove her sister's hands into the soft dough. "Now knead it."

Her sister stood there, frozen, but Jez guided her hands forward and back until Imogen continued on her own.

A minute or so in, Imogen giggled. "This is kind of fun."

A smile stretched at Jez's lips. Although she didn't mind being alone in the kitchen one bit…she also *half* liked the company. Even if Imogen was wearing too much lily perfume. "I know. That's why I came down here."

"What now?" Imogen kept her gaze and hands on the dough.

Jez pulled over her prepared loaf pan. "We place it in here and then let it rise."

"How long does that take?" Imogen asked, sounding a tad disappointed.

"A while," Jez said, picking up the dough, forming it, and placing it into the pan. "But it gives us time to eat those oatmeal cookies Cook made this afternoon."

As soon as Jez reminded her of the existence of the cookies, Imogen's eyes brightened again. "Is there milk in the cold box?"

"Yup." Jez had checked for the milk right after confirming the leftover cookies.

So while the bread rose, the two fennex sisters ate too many cookies washed down with milk and spent the evening taking a break from the realm, forming a bond that would wax and wane over the years.

Even at eight, Jez Sanddriffter knew spending even fleeting moments with those closest to her was one of the sweetest parts of life.

RECIPES

Baking can be such a joy if you only put your heart into it. I hope these recipes bring you closer to those you love.

Pumpkin
BREAD

Pumpkin bread is a fall classic. I hope you enjoy this lightly sweet quick bread filled with warm and cozy flavors.

Ingredients

GLAZE:
- 1 cup powdered sugar (120 grams)
- ½ teaspoon vanilla extract (2.1 grams)
- 1–1½ tablespoons half-and-half or milk

BREAD:
- 1 ½ cups all-purpose flour (180 grams)
- 1 teaspoon cinnamon (2.6 grams)

- **2 teaspoons pumpkin pie spice (about 5 grams)**
- **¾ teaspoon baking powder (3 grams)**
- **¼ teaspoon baking soda (1.5 grams)**
- **½ teaspoon salt (3 grams)**
- **2 large eggs**
- **½ cup vegetable oil (112 grams)**
- **¾ cup sugar (150 grams)**
- **1 cup pumpkin puree (250 grams)**
- **1 teaspoon vanilla extract (4.2 grams)**

Instructions

Preheat the oven to 350° F.

Combine the vanilla, sugar, and half-and-half for the glaze in a small bowl and set aside.

Prepare a 4x8-inch loaf pan with parchment paper.

In a medium-sized bowl, sift together the flour, cinnamon, pumpkin pie spice, baking powder, baking soda, and salt. Set aside.

In a separate bowl, mix together the eggs, oil, sugar, pumpkin puree, and vanilla until combined.

Add the dry ingredients to the wet and gently mix, just until combined. Be careful not to overmix.

Pour batter into prepared loaf pan and bake for 50–60 minutes.

Remove from the oven and allow to cool to the touch before turning out and resting on a wire rack.

When completely cool, drizzle with glaze and slice to serve.

Bakery-Style
ORANGE CRANBERRY MUFFINS

These should produce the high domes you expect from bakery-style muffins. They make a perfect snack or sweet breakfast. Pair with your favorite tea or a cup of coffee.

Ingredients

CRUMBLE TOPPING:
- ¼ cup all-purpose flour (30 grams)
- ¼ cup sugar (50 grams)
- 3 tablespoons softened unsalted butter (42–43 grams)
- ⅛ teaspoon salt (.75 grams)

GLAZE:

- 1 tablespoon melted unsalted butter (14 grams)
- 1 cup powdered sugar (120 grams)
- 2 tablespoons milk or half-and-half
- 1 tablespoon orange zest
- ½ teaspoon orange extract

MUFFINS:

- 2 cups all-purpose flour (240 grams) plus
   1 tablespoon to coat cranberries
- 2 teaspoons baking powder (9–10 grams)
- ¼ teaspoon salt (1.5 grams)
- ¼ cup melted unsalted butter (58 grams)
- ¼ cup vegetable oil (48 grams)
- ⅔ cup sugar (130 grams)
- 2 large eggs, room temperature
- 1 tablespoon orange zest
- ¾ teaspoon orange extract
- ½ cup sour cream (123 grams)
- ⅓ cup milk (83–84 grams)
- 1 cup dried sweetened cranberries (120 grams)

Instructions

Prepare a standard muffin tin (fits one dozen) with six regular-sized paper liners, leaving one space open between each.

For topping: Combine the flour, sugar, butter, and salt for crumble topping in a small- to medium-sized bowl. Gently stir with a fork to combine and set aside.

For glaze: Combine the butter, sugar, milk, orange zest, and orange extract for the glaze in a small bowl and set aside.

In a medium-sized bowl sift together the flour, baking powder, and salt. Set aside.

Using a stand mixer with the paddle attachment, beat the butter, oil, sugar, eggs, orange zest, and orange extract for about three minutes on medium speed, scraping the bowl if necessary.

Add the sour cream and milk and continue beating on medium until well combined.

Reduce mixer speed to low and add flour mixture just until combined. Do not overmix.

Combine the cranberries with 1 tablespoon flour and gently stir into muffin batter.

Set aside and allow batter to rest for 15–30 minutes.

During this time, preheat oven to 425° F.

When your batter is fully rested, spoon into your prepared muffin tin and fill each of the six liners fully to the top.

Add about 1 tablespoon crumble mixture to the top of each muffin.

Bake at 425° F for 7 minutes, then reduce to 350° F and bake for 14–17 more minutes.

Remove from the oven and cool for 5 minutes before removing from tin and allowing to cool on a wire rack.

When completely cool, drizzle with glaze and serve.

Almond Scones

I love scones. They have been one of my favorites since I was
a teenager, when my mom and I found a local tea shop. The
pastries always feel incredibly special to me even if they are
a simple bake.

Ingredients

SCONES:
- 3 cups all-purpose flour (375 grams)
- ½ cup granulated sugar (100 grams)
- 1 teaspoon salt (5–6 grams)
- 1 tablespoon baking powder (14 grams)

- 10 tablespoons frozen unsalted butter (140 grams)
- 2 large eggs (room temperature)
- 1 tablespoon almond extract
- ⅔ cup half-and-half (plus a tablespoon extra for brushing scones)
- ¼ cup sliced almonds

GLAZE:
- 1 cup powdered sugar
- ¾ teaspoon almond extract
- 1–1½ tablespoons half-and-half

Instructions

Line a baking sheet with parchment paper. Set aside.

Whisk together the flour, granulated sugar, salt, and baking powder in a large mixing bowl. Set aside.

Use a box grater to grate 10 tablespoons of frozen butter.

Incorporate the butter into the dry mixture, stirring and working it in slightly. The butter should easily incorporate and resemble uneven crumbs.

In a separate medium bowl, combine the eggs, almond extract, and half-and-half by whisking them together.

Combine the wet and dry ingredients and stir gently until the flour is moistened. (Add a tablespoon or two of half-and-half to the mix if it's too dry, until the dough is slightly sticky but not too wet.)

Place the dough onto wax paper that's been floured well and begin shaping it into a rectangle that's approximately 1 to 1.5 inches thick.

Fold the rectangle in half and reshape it into a rectangle that's 1 to 1.5 inches thick. Then repeat this process one more time.

Split the dough into two parts and transfer them to a baking sheet covered in parchment paper.

Take each piece and shape it into a round about 6 inches in diameter, then place them next to each other.

Place the baking sheet with dough rounds into the freezer for 30 minutes.

Preheat the oven to 450° F.

Take the scones out of the freezer after 30 minutes and cut each round into 6 equal wedges using a sharp knife. Remember to clean the knife between cuts if the dough sticks.*

Arrange the pieces on the baking sheet, leaving a 1-inch gap between them.

Brush each scone with half-and-half.

Sprinkle each scone with sliced almonds.

Bake the scones for 14–17 minutes until lightly brown.

Remove from the oven and cool the scones completely on a wire rack.

Prepare the glaze. Combine the powdered sugar, almond extract, and 1 tablespoon of half-and-half. Add one extra teaspoon of half-and-half at a time if the mixture is too dry. It should not be too thick or too thin.

Fill a zip-top bag with the glaze, then cut a small hole in one corner. When the scones are completely cool, drizzle the glaze over each scone.

Scones can be stored for several days at room temperature in a zip-top bag or frozen for up to 3 months.

Note:

* If you intend to keep the uncooked scones in the freezer for more than 30 minutes, I suggest cutting them into

wedges before freezing. Avoid moving the wedges apart on the baking sheet until after freezing as they become easier to handle when frozen or partially frozen.

About the Author

Baking magic into every page, J. Penner crafts cozy fantasy from her sun-kissed San Diego home. With a cat on her lap and a pen in her hand, she invites you into worlds as warm and comforting as a cup of tea.

Website: jpennerauthor.com
Facebook: jpennerauthor
Instagram: @jpennerauthor
TikTok: @jpennerauthor
Bluesky: @jpennerauthor.bsky.social